# SOCIAL INTERCOURSE

# SOCiAL

# iNTERCOURSE

GREG HOWARD

SIMON & SCHUSTER BFYR

NEW YORK  LONDON  TORONTO  SYDNEY  NEW DELHI

An imprint of Simon & Schuster Children's Publishing Division
1230 Avenue of the Americas, New York, New York 10020

For information about special discounts for bulk purchases,
please contact Simon & Schuster Special Sales at 1-866-506-1949 or
business@simonandschuster.com.
The Simon & Schuster Speakers Bureau can bring authors to your live event.
For more information or to book an event, contact
the Simon & Schuster Speakers Bureau at 1-866-248-3049 or
visit our website at www.simonspeakers.com.
Also available in a SIMON & SCHUSTER BFYR hardcover edition
Cover design by Laurent Linn
Interior design by Hilary Zarycky
The text for this book was set in Chaparral Pro.
Manufactured in the United States of America
First SIMON & SCHUSTER BFYR paperback edition June 2019
2  4  6  8  10  9  7  5  3  1

The Library of Congress has cataloged the hardcover edition as follows:
Names: Howard, Greg, author.
Title: Social intercourse / Greg Howard.
Description: First edition. | New York : Simon & Schuster Books for Young
Readers, [2018] | Summary: Told from both viewpoints, Beckett Gaines, an out-
and-proud choir member, and star quarterback Jaxon Parker team up to derail
the budding romance between their parents.
Identifiers: LCCN 2017003287 (print) | ISBN 9781481497817 (hardcover : alk.
paper) | ISBN 9781481497831 (eBook) | ISBN 9781481497824 (pbk)
Subjects: | CYAC: Gays—Fiction. | Toleration—Fiction. | Sexual Orientation—
Fiction. | Dating (Social customs)—Fiction. | High Schools—Fiction. |
Schools—Fiction. | Family life—South Carolina—Florence—Fiction. | Florence
(S.C.)—Fiction. | Humorous stories.
Classification: LCC PZ7.1.H6877 (ebook) | LCC PZ7.1.H6877 Soc 2018 (print)
| DDC [Fic]—dc23
LC record available at https://lccn.loc.gov/2017003287

*For Camden and Violet,*
*my hope for the future*

# CHAPTER ONE

Beckett

If I'd known losing my virginity would be so nerve-racking, I would've stayed home and watched the *Golden Girls* marathon with my dad. That's some quality father-son time I'm missing right there. He even made a cheesecake. Instead, here I am, with my heart racing around in my chest like a horde of drag queens at a Filene's Basement clearance sale.

Easing my death grip on the steering wheel, I lower the window a few inches. Magnolia-scented night air spills into the car accompanied by a sharp, underlying odor that singes my nostril hair. Magnolia-scented dog shit is more like it. But that's what I get for choosing a city park as the setting for my transition from virginal gay ingenue to bossy power bottom.

I take a deep breath to calm my nerves, which only redirects my thoughts back to Dad. Even though we've already seen all 180 episodes at least five times each, he was visibly disappointed when I told him I had an audition for the Florence Community Playhouse production of *Steel Magnolias*. He didn't even blink. I mean, come on. Any serious purveyor of American theater knows there are no male roles in that play. But not Dad. He's a *Rose*—sweet and lovable, but not the sharpest tool in the shed. I, as Dad likes to remind me almost daily, am a *Dorothy*. Cranky, snarky, and a bit bossy. Or to use Dad's word, "bitchy." I prefer "responsible" and "pragmatic." Besides, someone's got to be the Dorothy. She's the glue. And since Mom left us, that's what I am to Dad—the last bit of glue holding his shattered world together.

I could've just told him about my plans tonight. It's not like he would've tried to stop me. He might have pelted me with condoms as I ran serpentine patterns around the living room and out the front door. I can't leave the house these days without him yelling, "Don't forget your raincoat!" That's what he calls them. I guess he assumes I'm a whore just because I'm queer, which is really gaycist of him. He means well. He's just always been a little overenthusiastic when it comes to my gayness. Like he's trying to march in two spots in the Pride parade of my life—his *and* Mom's. However, I seriously doubt he would've approved of my partner-selection methods tonight.

But if I'm ever going to make the leap from exploratory, sexual toe dipping to bona fide slut, I have to spend time with people my own age. Hot, horny guys my own age, to be precise. Honestly, this isn't exactly what I had in mind for my first time either. I've always fantasized about a hayloft on a humid summer afternoon—minus the mosquitoes and the stench of horseshit, of course.

I can visualize the whole thing so clearly. Somehow the

hay is soft like Egyptian cotton and not prickly on my bare ass. My hot, imaginary farm boy lowers me down onto it—sweat glistening on his hairless, muscled chest. But he wouldn't just *screw* me—not my sweet farm boy. No, my future husband, and the father of our adopted Cambodian twins, *makes love* to me slow and gentle in that hayloft. With my ankles locked around his neck, I wrap my arms around his thirty-two-inch waist and hold on for dear life as he expertly brings us to the most mind-blowing simultaneous climax in the history of gay sex. The image is so beautiful, it actually brings a tear to my eye.

But Shelby says I can kiss that fantasy good-bye. She says the first time is going to hurt like a motherfucker. That it'll be awkward and messy, and that I'll probably shoot my load within the first thirty seconds of penetration. According to Shelby, the first time is always a disaster. She convinced me that I need lots of practice before I become solid boyfriend material—a good senior year full of practice—so I can hit the ground running my freshman year of college. Shelby's even the one who installed the Bangr app on my phone. She was more than a little shocked and disappointed that I'd never heard of it.

"It's a hookup app for horny gays," she said, incredulous, like she wanted to revoke my pink card right there on the spot. I don't *think* Shelby has that kind of authority, but you never know with that girl.

"Hooking up with complete strangers?" I asked, clutching the invisible string of pearls around my neck. "How am I supposed to find a boyfriend like that?"

That's what I really want. A boyfriend. I can't help it. I'm an out gay, but a closet romantic. And I'm a little lonely, if I'm being honest. Dad and Shelby are great and all, but I want someone to hold me. To kiss me. To make googly eyes at me and do all that shit they do in the movies. And I *definitely* want that someone to have a penis. I was lucky enough to figure that out ages ago. I swear, I probably came out of my mom's vagina wearing a tiara, swaddled in a rainbow flag, and belting out "It's Raining Men" at the top of my gay baby lungs.

"You don't want a *boyfriend* for your first time," Shelby had scolded me. "Any nameless, faceless dick will do."

Shelby's my best friend and she usually knows about these kinds of things, so here I am. About to meet the nameless, faceless dick I found on Bangr last night. CockyInSC will have the distinct honor of being the first to enter my pearly gates. He seemed like as good a choice as any, but I can't deny that a little hindsight apprehension is kicking in. Probably just nerves.

"Shake it off, girl," I mutter, quoting the Dalai Lama of my generation.

At the end of the road I guide my Prius into the dimly lit parking lot by the duck pond. The gravel crunching under my tires is louder than the engine itself, otherwise I could have made a more ninja-like entrance. My headlights momentarily illuminate a half dozen or so vehicles, and a shiver of excitement runs the length of my body. I didn't think it was possible for my nipples to get any harder, but they're about to slice right through my cotton shirt. At least I'm not the only perv out tonight. There's a small tribe of us and we're all in this together, throwing caution and my virginity to the wind. But the imagined camaraderie does little to settle my nerves, or my nipples, as I ease down the row of cars.

Exhaling all of my Dorothy Zbornak anxiety out through my nostrils in one long, steady stream, I inhale and channel my inner Blanche Devereaux. Well, as much as any gay, seventeen-year-old boy can channel Blanche Devereaux. Which, now that I think about it, is actually quite a lot. The Dorothy side of my stomach is in knots. Like acid-reflux-inducing knots. The Blanche side of my stomach, however, flutters with what must be a swarm of horny-ass butterflies, finger-banging each other with their rock-hard taste receptors, because they haven't settled down since I got into the car.

I scan each rear bumper in search of my mark. All the cars face the duck pond, with just enough space between each to provide adequate privacy. The steam of human sex tints the windows, and the dim glow of the streetlamps overhead enhances the seedy effect of the scene. It's like a Motel 6 campground on the banks of Lake Semen. All that's missing is a serial killer in a hockey mask running around with a machete and a fourteen-inch boner. With my luck that'll be my date. And yes, I define the word "date" quite generously tonight.

Finally, I spot it. The sticker I seek tags the rusted bumper of a late-'80s model Monte Carlo. Purple. Like Barney purple.

*Strike one.*

Understandably, this gives me pause. I mean, do I really want to have my cherry popped in the back of the Barney-mobile? The bumper sticker itself is faded and peeling, but otherwise exactly as described. The garnet and black image of the Carolina Gamecocks mascot, *Cocky*, anchors the left side. Yes, that's the mascot's actual name, and now the guy's Bangr handle makes total sense. The slogan to the right of Cocky is clearly meant to be subtle:

YOU CAN'T LICK OUR COCKS

*Strike two.*

Seeing those words mud splattered and tramp stamped on the Barneymobile's rusted bumper is far less alluring than I'd imagined, and my Dorothy nerves take over again. My palms are slick with sweat and I rub them dry on my jeans. I remind myself that I'm okay with forgoing love and romance (and my hot, imaginary farm boy, Cody) for my first time. Shelby's right. This is bound to be a hot mess. Better to get in a few practice runs. Just pull up the old Bangr app and do a little window-shopping. But dude has only one strike left. That was my promise to myself tonight, a fail-safe of sorts. Three strikes and *no Beckett Gaines nooky for you.*

My *date's* Bangr profile pic looked pleasant enough. Smooth, tanned skin. About seven inches, cut. Nicely manscaped. Manageable girth. No, I couldn't be sure it was a seventeen-year-old penis, but I couldn't really ask, either. The Bangr police would lock me out of the app forever if they discovered I wasn't really eighteen as my profile stated. But CockyInSC assured me we were *close* to the same age. But what seventeen-year-old drives a Barney-purple Monte Carlo with sexually suggestive bumper stickers? Still, I press onward, like my virginity is some kind of sex crazed homing pigeon with OCD.

I pull into an empty space on the opposite side of the lot,

raise the window, and kill the engine with the tentative touch of my finger. I sit there, butt-bumper to butt-bumper with the Barneymobile, only a few car lengths of gravel separating me and my manhood. Looking up into the rearview mirror, I scope out the terrain. Only two vehicles are parked close to CockyInSC's Monte Carlo. One, a black SUV with tinted windows, and the other, a light blue minivan. The SUV is rather nondescript other than the Jesus fish decal tucked in the lower right corner of the back window like an afterthought. The minivan looks the most out of place with all those annoying stick figure, family decals lining the bottom of the back window. Like the whole über-lean family has a front row seat for tonight's X-rated feature.

*From Masturbation to Manhood: The Beckett Gaines Story.*

I'd play myself in the movie, *obviously*. There are bound to be a string of underperforming sequels in the years to come.

I nervously fiddle with the Walgreens bag in the passenger seat, fishing out a small tube of K-Y jelly and a box of raincoats. I wonder if I should take the whole box with me. It might seem a little presumptuous. I don't want the guy to think I'm some kind of perv. Hell, I'd be fine if this was over in time to get home and catch season six, episode fourteen, "Sister of the Bride"—the one where Blanche's *homosexual* brother, Clayton, marries his boyfriend, Doug. Not one of Blanche's finest moments, but a teachable one in the end.

Three raincoats should be enough without coming off as overly eager, I finally decide. I take them out of the box and stuff them into the left front pocket of my jeans. The tube of K-Y I slip into my right. These jeans are way too tight, but they accentuate the perkiness of my ass, so you know, totally worth it. Drawing in a final lungful of Devereaux chutzpah, I get out of the car and lock it behind me. Can't be too careful. No telling how many freaks are out tonight. Other than me, that is.

A heavy blanket of August humidity covers me from head to toe, reminding me of how overdressed I am in skinny jeans, a starched-within-an-inch-of-its-life long-sleeve, button-down oxford, and freshly polished loafers. I wasn't really sure of the dress code for a virginity-sacrificing Bangr date. Sweat seals the shirt to my skin almost immediately, and gravel crunches under my slick soles as I cross the lot with my head down and my hands shoved deep in my pockets. Ghostly moans waft out of the SUV, drawing my gaze. Its tinted windows give away none of the presumed debauchery transpiring inside. The blue minivan sits empty.

I stop in my tracks a few feet away from the Monte Carlo, jarred by a familiar singing voice drifting out its partially downed windows. I wonder for a moment if this should count as strike three. An omen. The singer is Toni Braxton—my dad's favorite. Like I didn't hear that voice blaring through the house enough after Mom left. "Unbreak My Heart," "Another Sad Love Song," "Breathe Again"—I sure hope Ms. Braxton eventually discovered the wonders of antidepressants, like Dad finally did. The music serves only to remind me what a terrible son I am. I lied to Dad and left him alone in his hour of need. Poor Rose. I'll make it up to him tomorrow by suggesting we watch a movie together, one from his vintage DVD collection. He's been wanting me to see one called *The Break-*

*fast Club* for a while now. The way he talks, you'd think it was the *Citizen Kane* of the '80s, but I hate movies about food. I get bloated just watching them.

Satisfied that Toni Braxton doesn't qualify for strike three—on a technicality, CockyInSC couldn't have known he shares my Dad's taste in '90s torch singers—and that I'll eventually redeem myself as a blue ribbon gay son, I grip the lube in my right pocket, the raincoats in the other, and trudge on. As I get closer to the car, I crane my neck to get a better look at my *date* through the passenger side window. I'm only a few steps away, and this is my last chance to bolt if needed. From what I can tell, he's moderately handsome. But like *mustache* handsome. Like a 1970s porn-stache, really. Thank God he doesn't see me yet. He's too busy fussing with his hair in the rearview mirror—*with a comb*!

*Definitely strike three!*

Seventeen, my ass. I'm outta here. Just as I'm about to turn and slip away under the cover of darkness, shame, and the smell of dog shit, the passenger side window of the Barney-mobile lowers the rest of the way down.

"Beckett?" His voice is deep. Like grown man deep. And loud. I mean, like it carries. I curse myself internally.

*Note to self: Never give sexual predators your real name on a gay hookup app.*

He leans across the seat and leers out the window at me. *Jesus.* This guy has to be close to my dad's age. I wouldn't be surprised if any second now he whips out a bag of candy and dangles it out the window at me. Shoving my hands deeper into my pockets—my go-to cloaking device—I spin on my heels and nearly bite it on the gravel. I steady myself and make a beeline for my car, the Barneymobile guy yelling my name louder with every step.

*Jesus, would you please shut the fuck up?* I want to scream. But he doesn't stop. Just keeps calling my name over and over. I ignore him. And then he actually *honks his horn*, trying to get my attention. The commotion seems to have startled the natives, and heads start popping out of windows to see what's going on. Curses are hurled at me and CockyInSC. I. Am. Mortified. Horrified. And now I have to pee.

*Just take me now, Jesus. I don't care how, just make it quick before I piss myself in City Park.*

A door opens behind me, and I look over my shoulder, thinking CockyInSC is chasing me. But it's a very flustered guy with wavy blond hair spilling out of the SUV. He's trying desperately to pull his pants up over his pale, bare ass, nearly biting it on the gravel. He finally finds his footing, stands up straight, and glances over at me with a twisted scowl before disappearing into the driver's side of the minivan.

I look away, my cheeks burning and my heart pounding in my chest. I hustle across the lot and slip back inside my car. I push the ignition button, release the emergency brake, and back out in about three seconds flat. I even spin out a little as I pull away. I have never *spun out* in my life and didn't even know it was possible for a Prius. Even in my rattled state, I am a little impressed with myself. *Baller.*

It takes the whole fifteen minute drive home for my heart to stop trying to bang its way out of my chest. Admittedly, my heart can be *such* a drama queen sometimes, so I'm not overly concerned that I'm about to have a heart attack or anything.

As I pull onto my street, *still a virgin*, but, you know, *still alive* and all, I vow to be more discerning when using Bangr in the future.

*Note to self: Google "10 Signs Your Bangr Date Might Be a Porn-stache Wearing Sex Offender."*

The dark sedan parked on the street in front of our house barely registers in my still racing brain as I pull into the driveway. All I can think about is how bad I need to pee. I mean, my balls are actually starting to cramp up. Once that's taken care of, I can relax in the safety of my home and the genius comedic barbs of four senior gal pals from Miami. *The Girls* always calm me. Dad couldn't have watched more than a couple of episodes while I was gone. God, I hope he didn't eat the whole damn cheesecake. Rose is getting a little thick around the middle.

As I push through the front door, it takes a few seconds for my eyes to adjust to the horror before me.

"Beckett?" my dad says, trying to wriggle himself out from under the thing on top of him.

The thing seems stunned into a petrified state of confusion, staring at me like a topless deer in the headlights—a topless deer with a big mess of tousled blond hair and lots of brightly smeared makeup, that is. Like an idiot, I take a step closer. I don't know why. Maybe I'm in shock or something. But with that fateful step, I get way more of a show than I bargained for. I'm not sure I will ever be able to unsee them. The thing's giant, naked tits with their saucer-sized nipples have scarred my corneas forever. I swear, if I wake up tomorrow blind as a bat, I won't be at all surprised.

"What are you doing here?" Dad says, still pinned under the thing, his face turning the same shade of red as the thing's nipples.

I'm too mortified to look at my dad's face, so I just stare at those ginormous tits. I can't peel my eyes away from them, and the thing they're bolted to isn't in any hurry to cover itself. Here I thought Dad was sad-sacking the night away with Dorothy, Blanche, and Sophia; eating cheesecake and listening to Rose's ludicrous stories of St. Olaf. But instead, he's banging some twenty-dollar whore on our sofa while our gals look on from the TV screen. *Nice, Dad. Real nice.*

Dad keeps trying to get the thing off him, while saying shit like, "I thought you had an audition." And, "You said you'd be gone for hours." And, "I didn't want the cheesecake to go to waste so I invited this twenty-dollar whore over." Or that's what I heard, anyway. The thing finally grabs a throw and covers itself, but it's too late. The permanent damage to my eyes has been done. It's all too much, and I just can't right now. My bladder is about to explode. I shove my hands deep into my pockets, turn, and stalk up the stairs. Closing fingers around the tube of K-Y, I squeeze it so hard that it bursts open in my hand, filling my pocket with its slimy contents. Dad calls after me, but I don't stop. Without thinking, and overwhelmed with the urge to physically erase the image of those giant clay-red nipples, I jam my fingers into my eyes and rub, forever blinding myself with the gooey sting of lube.

And I think I just peed a little bit.

# CHAPTER TWO

# Jaxon

The Crusty Cup Coffeehouse hums with the hustle of a typical Saturday morning, but there's still no sign of JoJo. I look down at my phone, confirming that she's late. Again. Ever since the breakup, she's all over the place. She never used to be like this. She always had her shit together. Hell, she's the one who instilled in me such an obsessive need to be punctual all the time. All the more reason she needs to come home.

I glance up and catch the brunette at the counter checking me out. The shy smile. The quickly downcast gaze and then back up again. She's cute. Long straight hair. Big round eyes. Plump lips. And that body. Damn. She doesn't look familiar, though. I don't think she goes to East Florence—I would remember her. If she goes to high school anywhere in Florence County, she probably knows who I am, though. When she glances over at me again, I smile back and give her that half nod up that says, *Yes—I'm hot, you're hot, and I would normally get your number before you leave, but I have a girlfriend and*

*I'm meeting my mom.* I glance down at my phone so as not to encourage her.

She gets the message, takes her change, and moves toward the door. And just like that I find myself in the crosshairs of a gorgeous set of green eyes that undress me from top to bottom in about two seconds flat. The barista's leer is a hell of a lot more brazen than the brunette's was, practically daring me to look away. And I want to. Look away, that is. But, I can't. That emerald gaze falls, pausing for a second to soak up the results of my six-day-a-week pec pumps, and then drifting down to my crotch. I stiffen instantly at the intense inspection and shift in the overstuffed club chair. That barista ain't playin'. Guys are like that—way more forward than the girls. But I wish they would just leave me the hell alone. I mean, I like the attention, sure. Who doesn't? But most gay guys are just so damn aggressive. They look at me like I'm some kind of fuck toy and not a real person. If just one of them would look at me the way girls do, then, I don't know . . . maybe.

"Hey, sweetie."

The barista finally releases me from his hypnotic gaze, and I look up to find JoJo standing in front of me. "Oh, hey, Ma." I only half get out of the chair to kiss her on her cheek. I need a minute to get Jax Junior under control.

"Sorry I'm late." She drops her keys on the table and glances over at the barista. Planting a hand on her hip, she rolls her eyes at me. "Really, Jaxon? That twink? Come on. You can do better than that."

My cheeks heat instantly. Are we really talking about this? Now? And out loud?

"Don't even try it, son." JoJo waves a hand at me and plops down into the club chair opposite me. "Your mom already told me."

I shake my head, trying to control my rising anger at Mom. "Great."

JoJo tugs at the front of her bright orange Clemson T-shirt and grins ear to ear. Her hair is a little spikier than usual, and there seems to be more salt than pepper these days. She's easily the most imposing person in the coffeehouse and without a doubt the sweetest. But the breakup has been hard on her. I can see it in her eyes. They've lost a bit of their usual sparkle—that magic I always saw in them as she read me bedtime stories when I was a kid.

"Mom promised she wouldn't say anything," I say, shaking my head. "It wasn't a big deal. She just found this app open on my phone. I wasn't trying to hook up or anything. Just looking at the pictures and the profiles. But you know how she gets. Like a dog with a bone. Anyway, you weren't there."

Ouch. Was that last bit really necessary? But I meant it. JoJo should be living at home with Mom and me, not renting some secondhand double-wide in Palmetto Park.

JoJo shoots me that broad, 100 percent genuine smile of hers, assuring me that if I'd intended offense—better luck next time, kid. Jimmy, the manager, appears and sits a mug of hot tea on the coffee table in front of her.

He leans his hip against JoJo's chair and crosses his arms over his impressive chest. "Can I get you guys anything else?"

Only a few years older than me, Jimmy's still in great

shape. We share the legacy of being all-state champ quarter-backs for the East Florence Tigers, which gets me free coffee whenever he's working the counter. Jimmy has the added notoriety of being the first black quarterback to take the tro-phy for East Florence and I was the youngest, so we're both kind of like local celebrities. JoJo thanks him, and Jimmy squeezes her shoulder as he leaves. Everyone who knows JoJo loves JoJo, and Jimmy is no exception.

"I just hope you know you can tell me anything," she says, puckering her lips and blowing over the surface of her tea.

I lean forward and rest my elbows on my knees. "Of course I do. But, like I said, it's really not a big deal. I'm not gay. I was just . . . curious."

JoJo leans forward, mirroring my posture. "You don't have to put a label on it, Jax. Don't put so much pressure on yourself. You do that, you know." She sets her tea on the table and leans back in the chair, pointing her index finger at me. "Overachieving little shit."

I can't contain a chuckle and shake my head at her.

"All-state quarterback, student council president, 4.0 GPA, in the gym six days a week," she says, counting each item off on her fingers and rolling her eyes like my accomplishments are such a drag for her. "Being your mother is exhausting."

I ball up my napkin and throw it at her. She ducks, catch-ing it with one hand and laughing.

"Look at you," I say, impressed with the quick grab. "I'm not the only athlete in the family, after all."

"Played a little softball in my day, like any respectable lesbian," she says, clutching her heaving chest and coughing out a chuckle. She settles, and her mom face returns. "Look, sweetie. I don't care if you're gay, straight, or somewhere in between. I just want you to be happy. You have plenty of time to figure it out."

I narrow my eyes on her. "So it was never your and Mom's evil, lesbionic plan to make me gay all these years?"

JoJo tugs at the hem of her shirt and waves an arm at me. "Oh, honey, I wouldn't wish that on any kid growing up around here."

We gaze out the front window of the coffeehouse, sipping in silence. I get her meaning. The First Baptist church sits just around the corner, and the equally grand Methodist church is only a stone's throw away. But our uneasy silence is reserved for a *house of worship* that can't be seen from here. The Florence Holiness Tabernacle sits just on the edge of town. Their pointed messages of condemnation on their sign out front serve as a constant reminder, not of love and compassion, but of small-town hate and bigotry, all wrapped up in the tidy bow of Christianity.

I raise the cup to my lips and take another sip. "Those Tabernacle assholes are getting as bad as Westboro. I saw them on the news last night protesting a gay soldier's funeral over in Lake City. The *national* news. It's a freaking embarrassment."

JoJo shakes her head and stares out the window. "The old pastor was crazy, but his son has led them from crazy to downright scary in less than a year. People used to leave you alone in this town. At least they would ignore you. But not anymore. It's hard to stay somewhere you're not wanted."

A small volcano of acidic anxiety erupts in my gut. Was

that last bit aimed at the Tabernacle, Florence, or at Mom? "You're not leaving, are you? You said you and Mom just needed to live apart for a while to get some perspective."

JoJo crosses her legs ankle to knee and tugs at the hem of her T-shirt again. "Don't concern yourself with that stuff, son. You start your senior year on Monday. After you graduate you can get the hell out of here and go anywhere you want. Live your life any way you want without people looking at you sideways."

I don't like to hear JoJo talk about the merits of leaving Florence, so I change the subject fast. "Mom joined the local PFLAG chapter."

JoJo grins with a mischievous twinkle in her eye. "Well, first of all, I'm impressed. I didn't know that Florence even had a PFLAG chapter. And second, it sounds like that bothers you a bit."

"Well, sort of, yeah." I can't really explain *why* it bothers me so much. Why should I care? The group's not just for *parents* of gays. I mean the *F* in PFLAG stands for *friends*. Hell, *I'm* a friend to the gays. But still, the implications of Mom joining are so obvious, and *I'm not gay*. If I were, I'd say so. I have two moms, for Christ's sake. It's not like I'd be ashamed of it. But Mom catches me checking out some dick pics on my phone *one time*, and she up and joins PFLAG the next day. So typical.

"If there was a *B* in PFLAG, for "Bi," would you feel a little better about it?" JoJo rests her entwined fingers on her stomach and raises an eyebrow, waiting for me to clarify. I don't take the bait.

"Look, son, everyone knows you love the ladies," she says.

"That's a well documented fact. Hell, you've probably already seen more vagina in three years of high school than I've seen in my entire adult life. But if you're attracted to guys as well, what's the problem? You just doubled your odds of getting laid."

With heat rising to my cheeks, I quickly scan the room to see if anyone is close enough to hear her. Luckily, the crowd is thinning and the tables near us are empty. I narrow my eyes on her. "Can we talk about something else, please? This is not a conversation I want to have in the middle of the Crusty Cup. People know who I am here."

JoJo raises her hands in surrender. "Okay, okay, Mr. Local Football Hero. What do you want to talk about? I have to get to work soon."

I lean forward and look into her eyes, lowering my voice to almost a whisper. "When are you coming home, Ma? For good."

JoJo sighs and shakes her head. "Jax—"

"Mom's a mess," I say, not shy about using guilt if needed. "She'd never want you to know that, of course, but it's true. She's missed work some, and I've heard her crying in her room. And I shouldn't have to meet you at a coffeehouse just to spend some time with you. You should come *home*. I'm sure you guys can work it out."

JoJo sighs, uncrosses her legs, and scoots to the edge of the chair. "I didn't want this separation, son. Your mom did. She said she wasn't happy in our marriage anymore. Said she felt trapped." JoJo stops herself and casts her gaze to the floor. "I shouldn't have told you that. We promised each other we wouldn't drag you into this."

"Well, I'm in it," I say, wringing my hands. "Besides, it's nothing I haven't heard through the walls during your fights."

JoJo looks up, a frown tugging at the corners of her mouth. "I'm sorry, Jax. I didn't know you heard us. After what you went through when you were young, we would never want you to feel unsafe."

I shake my head and pick up my cup. I don't know why, it's empty and I really don't want to go up and ask hot barista boy for a refill.

I shrug. "Parents fight. I'm not that fragile, Ma. And all that other stuff happened so long ago. I was just a little kid. I barely even remember it." A lie. But I look up and smile at her—trying to convince her, wanting her to feel better.

"Besides, you guys saved me from all that." I shoot her a sly grin, trying to cheer her. "My own personal lesbian super-heroes."

JoJo chuckles, raises her fist in the air, and gives it a pump. "Armed with only a lawyer and adoption papers!"

The moment of levity is comforting. It's good to hear her laugh again. But I can't help but ask. "You guys *will* fix this eventually. Right?"

She shakes her head and squints her eyes. "I really don't know. I hope so. I want to come home, believe me. I love your mother. Always have. Always will. I'm willing to work at it, but it takes two to tango. She needs to figure out what she wants."

I shake my head at her, a pesky gurgle forming in the base of my throat. "I just want our family back together."

JoJo glances away, and an awkward silence passes between us. Finally, she breaks it, slapping both hands on her knees.

"Hey, I've got an idea. Why don't you put all those muscles of yours to good use and come help me with a job?"

I groan and let my head fall back on the chair. "I've already been to the gym this morning. Besides, it's Saturday. It's my day off."

She rolls her eyes at me. "Your day off? From what?"

I count off on my fingers like she did. "School, football, and slave labor imposed on me by my mothers."

JoJo wriggles herself out of the chair and gives my foot a light kick. "Come on, it'll be fun. You used to love going to work with me on Saturdays."

I drag myself up. "Yeah, and I used to be ten."

"I have to be honest with you, you were shit help back then. I have to run to the pee pot. I'll meet you out at the truck." She looks back and calls over her shoulder, "And I'm cooking you Sunday dinner at my place tomorrow. Already told your mom."

"Sounds great," I call back. I stand, pocket my phone, and head for the front door. I'm stopped in my tracks by a "Hey" that was definitely lobbed in my direction. Turning, I find myself once again the subject of another intense gaze courtesy of green eyed barista boy.

He pushes a napkin across the counter, and the right side of his mouth curls up. "You forgot this."

I walk over to the counter and pick it up. A phone number is scribbled under the name *Brad*.

When I look back at him, his gaze is locked on my chest, not my eyes. I am so tempted to channel Mom and give him one of her double snaps and—*Hey, buddy, my eyes are up here!*—admonitions, but I don't. He's really cute. Must be a private school kid because I don't recognize him. Toned and tanned. Expertly mussed hair. Nice arms. Plump lips that would feel so nice around my . . .

He looks up as if he can hear my thoughts. His grin widens and heat floods my cheeks. Glancing over my shoulder to make sure no one's watching, I grab the napkin, stuff it in my pocket, and hurry out the door.

# CHAPTER THREE

Beckett

"So are you looking forward to your first day as a senior tomorrow, Beckett?" Big Titties asks as she plops another huge glob of mashed potatoes onto my plate.

Big Titties' real name is Tracee. There's no *y* in Tracee. Don't worry, if you forget that, Tracee will remind you—ad nauseam. I push the mound of potatoes to the side of my plate, hoping the symbolism isn't lost on her. They're too lumpy anyway. Not worth the carbs. I like them creamy, the way Mom made them. And just what the hell is this stranger doing cooking in Mom's kitchen? I'm more than a little pissed at Dad about that. Oh, that and the fact he's been *seeing* this woman behind my back for God knows how long now. But he wanted me to meet his new *friend*, and I'm trying to be civil. I'm nothing if not a classy guy.

"Yeah, I guess so," I say. Civility. *Check*.

Dad seems to really like Big Titties. But when I look at her all I can see are those clay red, saucer-sized nipples staring back at me. Dad and I have yet to discuss *the incident*. I don't think he knows how to broach the subject, and I've been avoiding him like the plague ever since. Tracee doesn't seem the least bit bothered or embarrassed that I saw her in all her glory. I look up and catch her and Dad gazing at each other, sharing a goofy grin. *Ew*. The repeal of Dad's no-devices-at-the-table rule would be sublimely timed right about now. I can't wait to get up to my room so I can check my Bangr profile. Even though my first attempt failed miserably, there's still that unfinished business of my virginity to attend to. I wonder if I've gotten any *ass grabs* or *dick squeezes* today?

"So how did you two meet?" I ask, feigning interest and trying to get my mind off missed Bangr notifications.

"PFLAG!" Dad exclaims like an overly excited contestant on *Family Feud*.

Tracee nods with all of her hair and tits. "I joined about a month ago."

*A month? Really, Rose? Traitor.*

"First thing they do is assign me to the prom committee along with your father," she says. "And if there's one thing I can do, it's plan an awesome party."

Her voice is too loud. It's in my head. And apparently, the do-gooders at PFLAG don't realize that most gay high school kids spend every day trying to be invisible. The last thing they want to do is parade around at a *special* prom created to put them in the spotlight *with their parents*. I can appreciate what the group is trying to do, but they're going to need a bigger draw than virgin cherry punch and a disco ball.

I table my fork and lean back in my chair. "So you have a

gay kid too, Big . . ." I clear my throat. "Tracee?"

"Well," she says, dragging out the word way too long. "The jury is still out, but all the signs point in that direction." She leans in and winks at me. "Fingers crossed. Am I right?"

Too loud again. And what a weird thing to say. I look over at my dad. "You involved in planning this *gay prom* too?"

Dad straightens his spine, proud as a peacock. "Yep. It'll be Florence's first annual PFLAG prom. We're doing it early in the school year so it doesn't conflict with the regular proms in the spring."

Because we're not *regular*. We're the opposite of *regular*. But he didn't mean anything by it. Just Dad being Rose. Speak first, think later.

"We want to get the word out to all the schools in the county," he says. "Your principal is even letting us use the East Florence gym. It's going to be fantastic. Like our own little Pride celebration."

I cock my head at him. "Dad, I don't know if there are enough *out* gay kids in the county to fill a minivan, much less the East Florence gym."

Tracee slaps my arm playfully. It's still a slap, though. It counts. "Oh, come on, it's the twenty-first freaking century, Beckett. Besides, this prom isn't just for the gay kids, it's also for their friends and their parents, oh, and the tranny kids too. It'll be great. Maybe it'll encourage some of the closet cases to come out."

Tranny kids? Closet cases? Is this woman for real? I lean forward and rest my elbows on the table—cool, calm, and apparently the only person here operating in the real world. Why the

25

hell do I always have to be the voice of reason around here?

"First of all, it's just *trans*, not tranny. And I'm not saying it's not a nice gesture, I'm just saying this is still South Carolina and we're talking about high school kids. They can be real dicks sometimes."

Dad puts a hand on Tracee's arm and furrows his brow at her. "Beck was bullied pretty bad in middle school." He glances back at me, one eyebrow raised. "But you said high school's been okay, right?"

I push my plate forward and entwine my fingers in front of me. "*Okay*, sure. But only because I *own* being gay now. Some kids just don't have that kind of commitment, not to mention the wardrobe. Plus I've been *out of the closet*," I air quote for Tracee's sake, "since I was twelve. So I've already gotten all the shit kicked out of me. I literally have no shit inside me left to kick."

Tracee gnaws on a chicken leg about as gracefully as a pit bull would. She dabs her mouth with the corner of a floral print paper towel like it's fine Irish linen and gives the leg a momentary reprieve. "Isn't there a gay-straight alliance club at your school?"

I shrug. "I heard there might be one this year. I guess you could call the choir and drama club our gay-straight alliance right now. I'm in both." I didn't mean to brag, but by the look of her perfectly drawn and arched eyebrows, she's impressed nonetheless.

Dad nudges Tracee's arm with his elbow. "Beck had the lead in *The Music Man* last year. Knocked it out of the park."

Tracee's eyes grow so wide you'd think Dad just told her I shit double chocolate chip ice cream.

I shoot her a forced smile and look back at Dad. "So how many members are there in the Florence PFLAG chapter anyway?"

Dad stares up at the ceiling and counts on the tips of his fingers. "I guess fifteen to twenty."

"So only fifteen to twenty parents in this whole town support their gay kids, and you got the school gym for this event?" I cross my arms over my chest. Case closed. This prom sounds about as sexy as Vacation Bible School.

Dad grins and waves a breast at me. The chicken's. Not Tracee's. "Oh, stop being such a party pooper, Dorothy. Our chapter is less than a year old. We're growing."

I glare at him across the table, pissed that he would so casually use our insider noms de plume in front of Big Titties. It either went right over her head or she really thinks my name is Dorothy, because she doesn't bat a fake eyelash.

*Note to self: Dorothy Beckett would make a fabulous pen name for my erotic zombie novel,* The Hunger Gays.

"I think once we get the word out to all the surrounding towns and high schools, it'll be fine," Tracee says. "You can even bring a date. Anyone you want. Do you have a boyfriend, Beckett?"

Okay. Line crossed. Who the hell does this woman think she is, getting all up in my Kool-Aid like this?

Dad winks at me. "Beck has to beat the boys off with a stick—don't you, son?"

*Normally, I just use my hand, Dad,* I want to say. *A stick would be challenging, to say the least.*

"Can hardly keep it in his pants." He nudges me with his elbow.

I melt into the chair, wishing I were invisible. *Please, Rose.*

*Stop talking. Now. Somebody shove some cheesecake in her mouth.*

Dad touches his finger to his chin and looks up like he's pondering the origin of the universe. "I'll never forget the day he came home from playing over at a friend's house with his shorts on backward. I think you were what, Beck? Eight? Nine?"

I was seven, but that's beside the point. "I don't think Tracee really wants to hear about my prepubescent sexual exploits. Don't you guys have a prom to plan? Gay kids to drag out of the closet?"

"You're absolutely right." Dad claps his hands together, grinning from ear to ear.

I have to admit, he seems happy. I want him to be happy. But why does he have to be happy with Big Titties? I mean, what the hell does he see in this woman?

*Note to self: Check expiration dates on all Dad's medications.*

I push back in the chair and grab all three plates—a table-clearing peace offering. I'm trying here. As I head into the kitchen, I try even a little harder.

"So, Trace," I call over my shoulder. The casual shortening of her name is calculated. "Where does your kid go to school?"

"Yours, actually," she hollers back. And I mean *hollers*. "My son. You might know him."

"Oh yeah? What's his name?" I ask, balancing the plates on one arm like a pro as I head over to the sink.

"Jaxon," she calls out. "Jaxon Parker."

My 180 spin sends the plates right onto the floor with an earsplitting crash.

Oh. Hell. No.

# CHAPTER FOUR

# Jaxon

JoJo doesn't walk me out, but hugs me good-bye at the door. I think it's too painful for her to see Mom. As I slide into the car, Mom subtly cranes her neck to get a glimpse of JoJo. This is so freaking stupid.

She doesn't even wait to pull into traffic before starting the interrogation. "Did you have a good time? How was dinner? What did she make? Was anyone else there?"

I muster all the patience I possibly can. "Mom, why don't you just call her? Talk to her. This separation is ridiculous."

She shakes her head and grips the steering wheel. "It's complicated, Jax."

"Well *that's* not a cliché, is it?" The sarcasm is intended. "I'm practically an adult. I think I can handle it."

She looks over at me and purses her lips like she does every time she's deciding if she should tell me something or not. Ironic, seeing as how she told JoJo about catching me on Bangr.

"Actually, I've been seeing someone." She winces like I'm going to lose my shit or something. It's not an unreasonable assumption on her part.

"What? Who? Wait, is that where you were tonight? You said you were having dinner with a friend."

She straightens her spine and trains her gaze on the road, as if that will stop my interrogation. "I did have dinner with a friend. Someone I like a lot. We haven't been seeing each other for long."

I slump down in the seat and lean against the door. "You didn't waste any time, did you?" I regret it the moment it flies out of my mouth, drenched in piss and vinegar, and the pained look in her eye destroys me. "I'm sorry, Mom. I shouldn't have said that."

She takes a deep breath and gives me a quick nod to let me know that I'm forgiven. "Your mother and I have a lot of issues. Some that I'm not sure we can iron out. We're different people than we were twenty years ago. We want different things now."

"Ma doesn't seem much different. She's not already dating around." What the hell is wrong with me? Diarrhea of the mouth again, that's what. I hang my head. Luckily, she's being really understanding of my reaction to her news and ignores the barb.

"Well, maybe that's the problem. I've changed and she hasn't. I don't know." She glances over at me and grabs my hand. "Honey, I do love your mother. Probably always will, in some way. But more importantly, we both love *you*. We'll always be your moms no matter what happens between us. You know that, right?"

I shrug and nod. But I don't know it. My moms chose me.

I can't imagine where I'd be if it wasn't for them. They saved me. I might not even be alive. I just want everything to go back to normal.

She squeezes my hand and then lets go. "When's your next game?"

"A week from Friday," I say, staring out the window.

"Is JoJo going to be there?"

I look over at her and dare to hope. "Actually, she said she has a job out of town that weekend."

Mom crinkles her face and then nods once. "Then I'd like to bring my new friend to your game, if that's okay with you."

So much for hope. I cock my head at her. This has gone too damn far. "Seriously, Mom?"

She shrugs. "Of course. I'd like the two of you to meet."

"You said you haven't been seeing each other long. Why do I need to meet her so soon?"

A disconcerting smile thins her lips, and she keeps her eyes peeled to the road. Finally, she glances over at me. "Just a quick hello after the game. That's all. Please, honey. It would mean a lot to me."

I stare at her a long time, trying to decide if I want to regress a few years into petulant child mode or not. Or I could regress even further back and not speak at all. But that terrified little boy is gone. Mostly.

"Okay," I say with a bit of a huff. "Fine. You can bring her to the game."

We sit in silence for the rest of the ride home. As we pull into the driveway, I figure I should make an effort so the rest of the evening isn't uncomfortable.

Mom kills the engine, and I shoot her a fake smile as I reach for the door handle. "So what's your *friend's* name?"

Mom opens her door without looking over at me. "Roger. Roger Gaines."

She's out of the car and closes the door before I can respond. Problem is, I'm momentarily unfamiliar with the English language, and my jaw seems to have come unhinged, because I can't close my mouth.

Did she say "Roger"?

# CHAPTER FIVE

# Beckett

Big Titties obviously doesn't know her son very well, because there's no way in hell that *The Great* Jaxon Parker is gay. Even I know that, and I think *everyone's* gay. Jax, however, doesn't ping on my gaydar even a little bit, and his *reputation* around school is legendary.

I stare at him across the cafeteria as he leads several of his primate friends to a table populated by head cheerleader Tiffany Daniels, her bestie Molly Kim (aka Korean Beyoncè), and a smattering of Tiffany's evil minions. Jax carries himself with that natural swagger that comes so easily when you look like a jacked Ken doll. Perfect posture, broad shoulders, a muscled chest, and don't even get me started on that ass. With a perfectly sculpted jawline and perpetually crooked grin, he knows he's sex on a stick, and he obviously loves the attention and station in life that it affords him. Asshole.

Jax squeezes Tiffany's shoulders from behind, and under the table her knees magically part ways. Poor thing probably has a medical condition that causes her legs to spread apart whenever she comes in direct contact with testosterone. I think it's called "whoreacea." Tiffany has a real bad case of it.

*Note to self: Google whoreacea. If it's not a thing, hashtag the hell out of it and make it one.*

Tiffany looks up at Jax and bats her eyelashes. I didn't even know that was a real thing—eyelash batting. But there it is, plain as day. Jax plops down in the chair next to her and takes a bite of her pizza. Look at that smug bastard. He thinks his shit doesn't stink just because he's the star quarterback, the student council president, and he could crack walnuts in his ass cheeks. And now we could be only a few parental orgasms away from being related. *Stepbrothers.* That cannot happen.

"Hey, hooker. Who're you stalking now?"

I look over to my right as Shelby sits. Her straight copper hair is devoid of any styling and her makeup is completely MIA. Don't get me wrong, Shelby Timmons is my best friend in the world and I would kill for her. Well, at least physically harm someone for her. But, *girl.* Curling irons and foundation are your friends. Shelby couldn't care less about impressing anyone at school, though. The effort would be beneath her. I'm still holding out hope that she'll let me give her a makeover. The things I could do for this girl. She's got all the assets, she just needs to let me work my magic, and she would look as boss on the outside as she is on the inside.

I sigh. "Just a hypocritical douche bag, that's all."

Shelby's tray barely hits the table before she stuffs a slice of pizza in her mouth like she's at a food auction on *Survivor.*

"Jax or Tiffany?" she asks, peering across the room.

"Gym bunny quarterback."

"Oh, *that* douche bag." Shelby nods thoughtfully and wipes her mouth with the back of her hand, leaving a small smudge of red sauce stranded on the corner of her mouth.

I pick up her napkin and hand it to her with a dramatic flick of my wrist. Pointing to the side of my mouth, I nod at hers.

"Thanks," she deadpans. "I haven't eaten in like half an hour. I'm starving."

We stare at each other a frozen moment and then both crack the hell up. Shelby buckles over her tray laughing, dotting her boobs with red sauce, which only makes our dry-heave cackling worse. Only Shelby can make me laugh that way. We've learned to make the joke about ourselves before the likes of Jaxon Parker or Tiffany Daniels can. It's the only way big girls and femmy choir boys can survive in high school.

"What did he do now?" Shelby says, dipping her napkin in her water and dabbing at the sauce on her boobs. Luckily, her shirt is burgundy. The two wet spots look like she had leakage from breast-feeding or something.

I lean back in my chair and look over at her. "He didn't do anything *recently*. My worlds are colliding, is all. And why does he get to be so hot? It's fucking annoying. I mean, it takes work to hate someone that good-looking."

When I look back, Carter Treadwell stands across the table, holding a stack of flyers in the crook of his elbow, smiling at me with that puckered smirk of his. I think he means it to be flirty, but it looks like he just sucked a lemon dry.

"Hi, Beckett," he says in a two-note vocal fry.

Shelby elbows me in the side, but I will *not* look at her. I know she's loving this.

"Hey, Carter," I say in an unenthusiastic melody, matching him, note for note.

Carter Treadwell is a junior and the only other *out* gay boy at East Florence High that I know of. Like *really* out. Like march in a parade in your underwear, waving a rainbow flag out. Not these uncommitted amateurs who think being out means talking about all the shows you watch on Bravo.

Carter's also had some kind of misguided crush on me since middle school. I mean, he's cute in a nerdy Frodo kind of way, but he tries way too hard at *everything*—including getting all up in my Kool-Aid. Every day in choir, he jockeys to grab a seat next to me, and he's only a *second* tenor. I'm a *first* tenor. I mean, come on, dude, know your place. He's also the official photographer for the annual club, so there were like nine thousand pictures of me in our last yearbook. I heard the faculty sponsor finally had to put her foot down during production and declare an official no-more-pictures-of-Beckett-Gaines policy. And if that wasn't stalkery enough, he even auditioned to be the understudy for the role of Harold Hill in *The Music Man*, because it was practically a foregone conclusion that I would get the lead. I mean, who auditions to be the *understudy*? I do my best to discourage him, but what can I say? The kid's annoying as hell, but he's got great taste in men.

Now he just stands there smiling at me like I called him over here or something. When Shelby and I give him absolutely nothing to work with, he huffs a little in defeat and slaps one of the flyers down on the table in front of us. Shelby and I lean forward to inspect it with overdramatic caution, like it's a lab specimen of the Zika virus.

Carter sighs and plants a hand on his hip. "It's happening, people. And there's nothing Cassidy Charles can do to stop it."

Carter likes to address any group of two or more as *people*.

"The school's first ever gay-straight alliance! Cassidy and her mom filed a complaint with Principal Healy, but he didn't buckle this time. And guess who's going to be the inaugural president."

Shelby gives him a deadpan stare. "RuPaul."

I have to suck my lips inside my mouth to keep from laughing out loud. Carter rolls his eyes and slings his hair over his shoulder, even though he has short hair and it doesn't move an inch.

"No, Shelby," he says, accenting her name with a jutted jaw. "Me."

"Oh. Wow," I say, feigning interest with everything in my soul. "That's great, Carter. Congratulations. I'm sure you'll do an amazing job."

He smiles more genuinely now, minus the pucker. Shit. I was just trying to be nice, but I wonder if I just gave him some small glimmer of hope.

"Well, thank you, Beckett," he says, and I just know he's dying to do a little half curtsy, but he manages to control himself. "Of course, I would be honored if you guys would consider joining. Our first meeting is next Monday after school in room 150."

"Will there be snacks?" Shelby asks as seriously as asking

her doctor if she has cancer, and again I have to suck my lips inside my mouth. Shelby loves fucking with people and she does it so well that they never know if she's serious or not.

Carter takes a deep breath and stares her down. "I will see what I can do about snacks, Shelby." He looks back over at me and smiles again. "We already have a lot of interest. We might even have a full house."

"Any takers on that side of the room?" I say, nodding over to the south side of the cafeteria where the athletes, cheerleaders, and popular kids congregate.

Carter glances over his shoulder and his smile fades. "I haven't made it over there yet. But Jen and Lexi are coming, and Brent and Kenny, and Chevalier . . ."

He's pointing to people sitting at our table and tables around us like they're thrilled he's acknowledging them in public. It doesn't really sound like a full house yet. He has a semi-closeted interracial lesbian couple, two sweet but straight stoner dudes, and our foreign exchange student from France.

"Chevy will be there?" Shelby says, perking up. She has the hots for Frenchy, but practically curls up into the fetal position whenever he smiles at her. But hell if we can tell if the guy's gay or straight. Europeans really fuck with my gaydar.

I grab the flyer and hold it up, trying to move this along so Carter will be on his way and we can get back to our conversation. Plus, I'll be doing Shelby a solid by creating another opportunity for her to drool over Chevy up close.

"Thanks, Carter. Count us in."

"You'll come?" He seems totally surprised, which annoys

me a little. Like he's *such* a better gay than me.

"Of course," I say, shrugging. "I'm gay, Shelby's a straight ally, and you're bringing snacks. What more could we ask for?"

Carter beams, and I really think he's about to crack his face in half with that grin. "Great. Thanks, Beckett!" And he's off like a puppy with a chew toy, tail wagging.

"You're welcome," Shelby calls after him. She looks over at me. "I swear, no one else exists when that little shit's around you."

I shrug. "Can you blame the kid?"

Shelby rolls her eyes at me.

The Filipino twins, Anya and Asa, sit at the end of our table and wave to us. We like them. They mind their own business and they treat everyone exactly the same. Actually, we can't tell if Asa is a gaysian or not. I'm not picking up anything on the gaydar. It must be like with Europeans—international interference or something. I slide Carter's flyer down to Anya.

"Thanks, Beck," Anya says, looking at it and then showing it to her brother. I watch his face. Just a slight nod to his sister. No expression change. *Foiled again!*

Shelby crosses her arms over her chest and narrows a bushy browed eye on Jax. God, I wish I had my tweezers.

She nods in his direction. "So. Want me to kick pretty boy's ass? Make him disappear? Flick a booger on him? Just say the word. I got you, boo."

I cross my arms over my chest, mimicking Shelby. "No. Don't kill him. Not yet. He's too young and gorgeous now. Wait until he's old and shriveled up, so that's how everyone remembers him." Leaning over to her, I wink and whisper,

"But absolutely flick a booger on him. Aim for his mouth. He's got a purdy mouth."

We share another cackle, but are suddenly silenced by a pointed gaze from across the room. Of all the people in the world, Jaxon Parker stares at us, and he's *not* smiling, not even a little.

"Oh, shit on a tick," Shelby says, wiping her mouth again and shifting in her chair. "Do you think he heard us?"

"It's shit on a *stick*," I say. "And of course he didn't hear us."

But when Jax stands and walks toward our table, I do wonder if he, in fact, *does* have some talent for the dark arts and actually did hear us. And he's not staring at *us*. He's staring at *me*. Just me. Like Shelby isn't even sitting there right beside me. I use the time it takes Jax to reach us to fortify my defenses. I reload my sassy retort rifles and slip on my invisible fuck-you armor, ready for whatever dis or homophobic slur is about to be hurled at me. I'm sure his friends dared him to come over and harass the homo. Hilarious.

Jax stops in front of our table, his stance wide and shoulders squared. This is something that doesn't happen every day. The invisible wall that runs down the middle of the cafeteria has been officially breached. Where's the Night's Watch when you need them? Oddly enough, though, over here alone in no-man's-land, his eyes shift, he rocks back and forth on his heels, and his usual overconfident smirk has all but disappeared. Apparently, he left his cocky swagger at the beautiful peoples' table. It's almost like he's nervous.

He tucks his thumbs in his pockets, and nods up once. "'Sup."

Wow. The first word *The Great* Jaxon Parker has uttered in my direction in almost four years, and it's not even a real word. It's barely even a syllable, for Christ's sake. He doesn't even bother to lift the *s* to denote a question. Translation— he really doesn't understand the general idea behind "'sup." To ask someone—*What is up*? Like *How are you doing*? In his limited vocabulary, it's just a general, one word salutation, I guess. So I roll with it and lower my voice a notch.

"'Sup to you too, bruh."

Shelby coughs a chuckle into her fist. It's like the girl can read every ridiculous thought that runs through my head. If she had a penis, I would marry her. But the penis is nonnegotiable.

Jax squints his eyes at me like *I'm* the crazy one. But I'm not the one who just journeyed through the treacherous terrain of the East Florence High School cafeteria into the barren wasteland that is the *not* beautiful and *not* popular side of the room. It must feel completely foreign to him over here. Where we greet each other in complete sentences. Like—*How are you*? Or—*How was your summer*? But hopefully he won't ask me about my summer. I mean, what would I say?

*It was fine, thanks. You know, the usual. Saw some movies. Read some good books. Saw your mom's freakishly large nipples.*

When Jax glances over at Shelby and nods hello, she swallows. Loudly and with a little gasp of air. I'm not sure if she's afraid of him, disgusted by him, or if she just had a little mini orgasm. My money's on the latter. Standing there with his dirty blond hair hanging ever so casually over the left side of his forehead and dressed in bulge-hugging, dark jeans and one of those homoerotic, peekaboo football jerseys, he's practically eye-fucking us right here in front of everybody, without even trying.

"I said, can I talk to you a minute?" he says to me.

What? Has he been speaking? "Sorry," I say, and inwardly curse myself for the submissive response. I poke my thumb in my chest. "You want to talk to me?" My voice cracks. Shit. *Pull it together, Beck.*

"Yeah," he says, looking over at Shelby again. "In private, if that's okay."

*The Great* Jaxon Parker wants to talk to me. *In private. If that's okay.* Let's see. I wonder what in the world Jaxon Parker could possibly need to discuss with me, *in private.* Probably the fact that his big-tittied mom is boning my dad right off his medication. Let the awkward interaction begin.

Shelby looks over at me with a raised eyebrow, like she's my bodyguard waiting for me to give her the it's-okay slow nod and blink. Which I do. Jesus. We are so much fucking cooler when the pretty people don't acknowledge our existence. Shelby pushes away from the table, and stands. She straightens her spine and glares at Jax. I don't know if she's currently considering the ass kicking or the booger flicking, but one thing is for sure, her unbridled lust is completely under control now. Girl has my back.

She picks up her tray slowly, making quite the menacing ordeal of leaving me alone with the enemy. "I'll be just over there." She nods over her shoulder without breaking eye contact with Jax. "By the ice cream case."

I lower my head and cover my mouth in my palm, about to lose my shit. I barely manage to hold it together. Once Shelby is clear of us, Jax circles the table and sits in her vacant chair. *Right beside me.* He even pulls the chair closer and faces me. He is so close he's practically straddling me. It's really hard not to look down at his crotch. I mean, it's right there. I could rest my elbow on it, for Christ's sake. But my iron will prevails—for the moment.

I turn my chair in his direction, for a couple of reasons. One, to show him that I'm not intimidated by his status, his size, or his off-the-chart hotness. And two, so it's easier to glance down when my iron will breaks into a million shameful little pieces.

"So? What brings you north of the wall?"

Jax scrunches his face and cocks his head at me. "What do you mean? I just wanted to talk to you about something."

I shake my head, letting the *Game of Thrones* reference go without judgment. Well, just a little judgment. "Never mind. What is it?"

It's frustrating that I can see his glistening, plump lips moving, but I can't hear a damn word he's saying. I'm sure it's riveting, whatever it is. But something about those perfectly round, baby blue pebbles he passes off as eyes, have the cerebral wires from my ears to my dick crossed. I just pray I'm not drooling. God, I'm pathetic. Finally, five words compute and jar me back to flaccidity . . . I mean, reality.

". . . my mom and your dad."

"Huh? Oh, that." I make a great show of rolling my eyes as if to say, *Tell me about it, bruh.*

"I know, right?" He leans forward and lightly taps me on the knee, apparently excited that I share his concern.

His breath smells like green apple Jolly Ranchers. My

favorite. I wonder if his lips taste like them too. God, he's such an asshole. I distract myself by picking up a piece of abandoned pizza crust and shoving it in my mouth, imagining I'm chewing on his bottom lip. Pulling a Shelby, I wipe my mouth with the back of my hand. Classy. At least there's no drool.

"I mean, it would never work anyway," he says. "Not with your dad."

A tinge of anger spikes in my gut, but I block it from registering on my face. Did he just emphasize the word "your" or "dad"? I can't be sure, so I assume the worst. Squinting my eyes, I nod at him like a wise old sage. "Must be terrible for your cred around here."

There he goes with the face scrunching again. I'm beginning to think that all subtlety is completely lost on this guy. It's a good thing God made him pretty. I drop the pizza crust on my tray and lean forward.

*I will not look down. I will not look down.*

I point back and forth between us. "You and me. The football star and the nerdy gay kid. Being thrown together by our horny parents. Bad for your rep, I'm sure."

He leans back in his chair, looking genuinely perplexed. "What the hell are you talking about?"

I don't like it any more than he does, but why not let him squirm a little? "Look, my dad has been through a lot the last couple of years, and right now he seems happy. So I'm willing to put the past behind us for the time being, until this little fling of theirs fizzles out."

Jax shakes his head and rolls his eyes. "I think it's more

than a little fling. She wants to bring him to my first game. Wants me to freaking meet the guy."

Something about the way he says it flies all over me. Like my dad is beneath him, or not good enough for his top-heavy mother. I guess I shouldn't be surprised. Suddenly my dad's happiness trumps all of my earlier misgivings about being tied to Jaxon Parker.

"My dad is a great guy," I say, driving a pointed gaze through a sea of baby blue, trying to find his damn eyeballs. "You'd be lucky to know him."

Jax rolls his eyes again and returns a hardened gaze of his own. "Look, I'm sure your dad is awesome. But he's not right for my mom. Trust me on this."

My ears and the back of my neck heat instantly. "*He's* not right for *your mom*?"

"Dude, my mom is *gay*," he says. "I have *two* moms, who are married. To each other."

"Exactly!" Okay. That was a little louder than I intended, and it draws attention from nearly every table in the room. Asa and Anya stop midchew and look over at us. Tiffany Daniels's head pops up, and she looks especially curious. Of course, Jax's face is twisted in confusion.

"Right. That's all I meant about your dad," he says. "He's a guy. And Mom likes women. Besides, I really need for my moms to get back together, and I'm worried that the more things progress with your dad, the less that's likely to happen."

Okay. So he wants his mommies reunited. I get that. But I'm not convinced that the potential lifetime association with me isn't at least part of his problem with this. I shrug and pick up another piece of crust.

"Sorry. But what am I supposed to do about it?"

Jax leans forward and rests his elbows on his knees. "Maybe just discourage your dad a little from pursuing her. I mean, I'm sure you don't want him to get hurt, and I know my mom is way gay enough that she'll start missing the vag pretty soon."

I squint at him and drop the pizza crust on my tray. "Okay, ew. I'm eating here."

"I'm just saying, you wouldn't want your dad to fall for someone that'll eventually leave him anyway, would you?"

Was that a fucking swipe at my mom? Does he know that she walked out on us? Is that information fodder over on the Narnia side of the cafeteria? I look down—at the floor this time. He's right about one thing. I don't want Dad to go through that again. He adored my mom and she crushed him. And me. On the other hand, Dad seems happy now for the first time in a while. And it's not like Mom is ever coming back.

"I don't know," I say, glancing back up at him. "I think he really likes her. And I've only met her once, really, but it seems to be mutual."

He lowers his voice and narrows his eyes on me. "Trust me, Beck. This will end badly for your dad."

I'm rendered speechless by two things. *One*—it's the first time he's said my name in four years. *Two*—was that a fucking threat? I fist my hands at my side. I *won't* be bullied again.

"No," I say definitively. "Sorry, but if Dad's happy, then I'm happy for him." It's a blatant lie. "And he's not an idiot."

Well . . . it *is* Rose we're talking about. "I'm sure he knows all about your mom's diverse sexual history."

The look on his face is one of surprise and confusion. I'm sure *The Great* Jaxon Parker isn't used to hearing the word "no." He stares at me for nearly a full minute as those baby blues harden and those plump lips spread into a thin line. Without another word, he stands, turns, and walks away. I exhale in a one long, steady stream. I hadn't realized how little oxygen I'd taken in during the whole exchange. But I'm also a little exhilarated by the way I stood up to him.

Shelby walks up and stands there staring at Jaxon's retreating, bubbled ass as she licks a scoop of vanilla ice cream like she's tonguing his crack. "So how many times did you look down at his crotch?"

I lace my fingers at the back of my head and lean back in the chair. "Thirteen."

# CHAPTER SIX

# Jaxon

As JoJo describes the intricate challenges of a recent repiping job, all I can think about is my strange conversation earlier with Beckett Gaines.

What's that guy's deal anyway? He acted like I have some kind of problem with him, which I don't. Actually, I always thought he was pretty cool, even though we don't really run in the same circles. The guy is so freaking talented it's ridiculous. His tenor solo at the last choir concert brought the house down, and he kicked ass in *The Music Man*—my favorite musical. Beck's always spouting off some pretty hilarious shit in class too. I don't know if he has any idea how funny he is. And I like that he doesn't try to hide the fact that he's gay at all. Not that he should—I just admire him for that. He doesn't seem to give a shit what anyone thinks of him or says about him behind his back. And he should really smile more, because when he does, he lights up the freaking room.

But I have no idea what crawled up his ass today. Maybe it's the whole my-mom-and-his-dad thing. That I get. And I can understand how protective he is of his dad, especially since his mom walked out on them, from what I hear. That must have really sucked ass. I guess I should cut the guy some slack. Give him some time to think about what I said. Maybe he'll see that I'm right.

"Jax," JoJo says, snapping her fingers in my face.

I look up from my coffee. "Ma'am?"

She crosses her arms over her chest. "Have you heard a damn thing I've been saying?" She leans back on her stool where we sit at a high top table by the front window of the Crusty Cup. JoJo hates sitting here, but it was the only table available. She says it feels like we're in a giant fishbowl drawing the inspection of every passerby on the sidewalk. She's a little sensitive to all those sideways looks thrown her way. Can't blame her.

"Sorry," I say, glancing out the window and back. I don't want her to think I'm worried about her and Mom. We've already been down that road. "Just a lot going on at school, and practice was brutal today. First game's coming up."

Her face sags. "I'm so sorry I won't be there, hon."

"Me too," I lie. The last thing I want is for her to see Mom with someone else, much less a . . . *dude*. "But it's really okay. There'll be plenty of other games this season. Besides, you have to work, right?"

"Yeah," she says, breaking eye contact with me and gazing out the window. "I wanted to talk to you about that."

She pauses. Not good. Ma always pauses before she tells

me something she knows I'm not going to like. I wait. Silently, but not patiently.

"Remember I told you I have that job in Greenville the day of your game?"

I nod.

"Well, I didn't really tell you everything. It's not a *job* so much as it is a job *interview*."

I stare at her, numb all over. "Job interview? You have a good job here."

She leans forward, resting her elbows on the table. "The position in Greenville is with the same company, but it's a step up for me—regional project manager. I can finally quit snaking toilets and actually manage techs on various jobsites. Wouldn't that be great?"

She smiles with her entire face and punches my arm like I should be *so freaking excited* for her. I'm not. But I try to choose my words carefully. On one hand, she's paid her dues and deserves a promotion like that. On the other hand, she *cannot leave Florence*. If she does, the chances of her and Mom getting back together would suck. And when would I even get to see her? We couldn't really meet up at the Crusty Cup whenever we wanted to.

I swallow hard and keep my voice steady. "Greenville's what? Three hours away?"

"Two and a half, tops," she answers quickly, her Christmas morning smile beginning to fade.

I cover my face in my hands even though I know that's the last thing she wants to see right now. Maybe that's why I do it.

She takes my hands in hers and holds them in the center of the table. "Jax, not only is this a great job for me, but like I already told you, it's hard for me here, hon. Your mom seems to be moving on. As much as I hate to say it, maybe it's time for me to move on too."

"It's only been a few weeks," I say. "Maybe she'll come around." And she'll remember that's she's *a lesbian*, I don't say.

JoJo shakes her head and stares out the window, giving my hands a soft pat before releasing them. "That's a nice thought, but I don't think it's realistic."

I wonder if she knows about *Roger*, but I'm too much of a coward to ask.

"I already heard she's dating a man," JoJo says like she can read my mind.

"I don't get it. Mom said she's always been with women. What changed? How can you just switch like that?"

JoJo chuckles. "Well, in my experience, it's not that cut-and-dry with women. Not in every case, mind you. I'm a gold star lesbian and always will be."

I try my best not to give away my thoughts, but it's not cut-and-dry for me, either. There's no doubt that I love girls and I love having sex with them. But I've always been attracted to guys, too.

"So she's bisexual?" I ask with a shrug.

JoJo waves me off. "Don't worry so much about labels. Just love who you love and never be ashamed of it."

That's easy for her to say. She's not an all-state champion quarterback in the Deep South, where people live and breathe high school football. The guys on the team know better than to utter a single disrespectful word about my two moms, but if they knew about *me*, it would be open season. Everything would change.

"Oh, good Lord," JoJo says, staring out the window. "Those crazies are getting fired up again."

I follow her gaze and immediately get her meaning. A couple of Florence Holiness Tabernacle rednecks cross the street, carrying a newly minted batch of FAGS BURN IN HELL signs. My blood comes to an instant boil. They turn the corner, heading our way. One glance in the window of the Crusty Cup and who do they zero in on? JoJo, of course. I mean, she's a walking lesbian stereotype and proud of it. It's a wonder she's not wearing her tool belt.

With just a glance at my sweet, salt of the earth mother, the faces of these supposed *Christians* harden with hate. One of them looks over at me with a furrowed brow, like he's trying to figure me out—whether I'm gay too or just guilty by association. I fist my hands on the table, in plain sight, and meet his gaze. *I dare you, motherfucker.*

"Easy, Jax," JoJo says. "Ignore those ignorant assholes. They're just trying to rile us up."

The larger of the two men presses one of his signs against the window in front of JoJo and glares at her. I come unglued from the inside out.

"Jaxon!"

But it's too late. I'm already off the stool and out the door, with Jimmy right on my heels. I make use of every centimeter of my six foot two inches and stand nose to nose with the big one. When I yank the sign out of his hand and break the wooden handle over my knee, his eyes widen and his face twists into a snarl.

"You little faggot. How dare you!"

Jimmy's glory days on the gridiron are long gone, but he's no shrinking violet. He quickly inserts himself between us and pushes me back.

"Easy, boy," he whispers to me like he's taming a wild animal. He looks over his shoulder at the two men. "Get the hell off my sidewalk and take that trash with you."

The smaller guy scowls at Jimmy and takes a step forward. I brace myself for whatever local variety racial epithet is about to be hurled at Jimmy, but after a quick moment sizing him up, the guy obviously thinks better of it.

He spits on the ground near Jimmy's feet instead. "You don't own this sidewalk."

A menacing female voice silences everyone. "No. *I* do."

I look to the left. JoJo's truck is parked a few feet away on the curb. She stands beside it holding a pipe wrench the size of my forearm. She strolls over to us calmly, but with a dark look in her eyes that I don't think I've ever seen before.

"Back *the fuck* away from my son," she says, the wrench swinging ever so slightly at her side, like a baseball bat.

I can tell the man doesn't know what to make of her and probably doesn't understand what she means calling me her son. His puny little brain probably can't compute such a concept as a lesbian having a child. But if he knew what was good for him, he would do what she says. I stop fighting against Jimmy and allow him to push me back a few steps. JoJo's the one they should be worried about now.

The larger guy stares JoJo down, and I stand ready to go through Jimmy if that creep makes the slightest move in her direction. After an extended, silent standoff, he finally steps back. They walk around us, giving JoJo and her pipe wrench a wide berth. One glares at me and the other at JoJo as they pass.

"Enjoy burning in hell, you ugly bull dyke," the shorter one snarls at JoJo. He spits on the sidewalk in front of her.

I lunge at the guy, but Jimmy blocks my path. The two men laugh as they disappear around the corner.

"I'm so sorry, guys," Jimmy says, patting my shoulder. "That damn church is a blight on this whole town."

I stare at the empty corner, seething. I want so badly to follow them and show them my own special brand of *Christian love*. "Fucking bastards."

JoJo slips her arm around my waist and rests her head on my shoulder.

"Sorry, Ma," I say. "You okay?"

She doesn't reply, but her silent tears are cold as they trickle down my arm.

## CHAPTER SEVEN

# Beckett

High school football in the Deep South is as sacred as guns and sweet tea, and Florence is no exception. Though I'm not a sports fan in the least, I do enjoy other aspects of the games—namely, the people watching and gossiping with Shelby. We usually start with the cheerleading squad, destroying them one by one. Then we move on to the crowd around us in the bleachers. Some of our favorite targets are faculty members, like our chemistry teacher, Mr. Hassel, who always has a sheen of vodka glazing his permanently bloodshot eyes. Shelby delights in tormenting superChristian Cassidy Charles, but she makes herself such an easy target the way she looks down her self-righteous nose at anyone who doesn't walk around school with a Bible in their backpack, that I find her a bore and not worth my time.

Our favorite part of the games is the marching band, and the East Florence Marching Band *rocks*. Shelby and I always plant ourselves in the section adjacent to the band, so we have the best acoustics and view. The members of the marching band and the choir have a mutual respect and appreciation for one another. Like we alone understand how talented we are and how lucky these tone-deaf Neanderthals are to have us entertaining them. Deep down we probably understand that it's our need for acceptance and validation that drives us to devote so many hours a week to our rehearsals, but we would never admit that. We just get off on blowing everyone away with our performances. It's the only time the popular people in school not only notice us, but actually *applaud* us.

My phone vibrates in my pocket, and I pull it out, checking the home screen.

"Will you put that fucking thing away," Shelby says with an eye roll, her hands shoved into the pockets of her red hoodie.

"Sorry," I say, pocketing my phone. "It's just Dad calling." I lean over and lower my voice. "I thought it might be this new guy that's been pinging me on Bangr."

"Pinging you?" she says, serving me resting bitch face. Nobody serves resting bitch face better than Shelby, not even Tiffany Daniels.

I nod. "You know. Virtual *winks*, *ass grabs*, *dick squeezes*, that sort of thing. Like poking on Facebook, but sexier."

Shelby scrunches her face in disgust. "Yeah, a dick squeeze sounds *so* much sexier than a poke."

"Shut up," I say, and nudge her with my shoulder. "His name's Brock. Isn't that sexy as hell? *Brock*. Sounds like a hot, shirtless soap actor. It hasn't gotten much further than a few winks so far, but it's early still. I feel an ass grab coming on soon."

Shelby shakes her head. "Jesus Christ. Queers are so weird. Do you people actually talk to each other before the sex part, or does it just go from winks, ass grabs, and dick squeezes, straight to licky-sucky in City Park?"

"That is a *perfect* example," I say.

A cheer rises around us, and we strain our necks over the tops of heads to see what we missed down below. It was just some cheerleader-on-cheerleader butt-grinding. *Yawn.*

"I chatted with CockyInSC for a week and *still* he turned out to be a freak," I say, wagging a finger in her face. "So talking is *way* overrated."

"A whole week, huh," Shelby says. "Shocking that went so wrong for you. I don't know, hooker. In the interest of you not getting butt-raped and murdered in City Park, might I suggest you focus your efforts within the student body of our school? Or, better yet, one of the other high schools in the area."

She has a point, even though she seems to forget that Bangr was her idea in the first place. The football games are the perfect place to check out possible candidates from other schools. The visitors' side of the field is often well stocked with hotties I wouldn't run into at school after we did the deed. Tonight we play Johnsonville, a nearby town, smaller than Florence, where they grow their farm boys broad and thick, just like the one I always imagined would be my first. If the 10 percent rule applies everywhere—even in Johnson-ville, South Carolina—surely there're one or two farm boys here tonight who might like to drop their overalls, bend me over, and make me see Jesus. One can hope.

The band rips into an ultrafast and punchy medley of

Britney Spears hits. It's an odd combination, but it works for Shelby and me. We spring to our feet and shake our goods like Brit-Brit herself is performing on the field. It doesn't take much to entertain us. When the song ends we whoop, clap, and whistle way louder than anyone else around us. People stare.

"So about the PFLAG prom," I say, sitting.

Shelby sits beside me, shoves her hands back in the pockets of her hoodie, and rolls her eyes. "Ugh."

"Come on," I say. "My dad will be crushed if I don't go, and I think it's going to be so bad it might actually be entertaining."

Shelby serves me another generous helping of resting bitch face.

"We could go shopping, and I can help you find a hot dress."

More resting bitch face.

"I'll even do your makeup."

Shelby sighs and looks back down at the field. "I'll think about it, hooker."

What most of the kids at school don't know about Shelby Timmons is that her wall of sass is a front. Her bitch mom has ragged her about her weight since she was ten years old, and she was bullied as much for being fat as I was for being a sissy, until she grew faster than the boys doing the bullying. It all really fucked with her head. Now she deflects by being abrasive. Other times she just fades into the background like she's trying to disappear altogether. I just want to show her how much *more* fabulous she can be with a smidge of effort.

"You need to let your inner drag queen out, honey," I say,

cocking my head and raising an eyebrow at her.

She looks over at me and grins. "What would your drag name be?" She's diverting the conversation away from the makeover and the prom. Baby steps.

I think about it for a few seconds. It's not like I don't have a running list of about two dozen in my head, but I'm momentarily distracted by Jax stretching his quads on the sidelines.

I lean over to Shelby. "Fussy Bottoms."

She throws her head back, cackling.

"What's yours?"

She puckers her lips to one side of her mouth before a smile spreads across her face. "Connie Lingus."

"Nice!" I say, giving her a high five, which feels unbelievably dorky the moment our palms touch.

Brent and Kenny, the cute stoner boys, shuffle up the steps and wobble into the row in front of us.

"Beckett," Brent says, chuckling and stretching out my name. From the smell of it, I'll bet everything sounds hilarious to him right now.

"Hey, Brent. Kenny," I say with a nod.

Brent is tall and lean with a long torso and broad shoulders. His silky auburn hair usually hangs down over his glazed hazel eyes. I've always thought he was pretty sexy—totally straight though. Kenny's kind of cute too. Also straight. Short with bushy brown hair and eyebrows, and a crooked grin plastered on his face at all times. They're easily the happiest two guys in school. They must get stoned between every period. I swear to God I don't know how they managed to make it to senior year, but they're both really sweet.

"Miss Shelby," Kenny says with a slight bow before he sits and giggles. "I like your hoodie. Sexy."

"Thanks, Kenny," Shelby says, shaking her head and grinning.

Kenny always finds something nice to say to Shelby, which I appreciate, even if it usually doesn't make much sense. Like a sexy hoodie. No such thing. They sit in front of us, and Brent looks over his shoulder at me.

"So who's winning?" he says, flashing his dimples. He must know I think he's sexy, but he obviously isn't the least bit threatened by it, which only fuels my nagging desire to lick him.

"Hasn't started yet, buddy," I say, and pat him on the arm, copping a cheap feel of his rock solid bicep. I'm shameless, but hey, if he's okay with me objectifying him, who am I to argue?

Asa and Anya climb the steps, heading our way. Anya sees me and waves. She thinks I'm hilarious and always likes to sit near me in class. It works out for me, too, though, because she and her brother are easily the smartest kids in school, and I shamefully admit that my eyes have wandered over to Anya's desk for test answers once or twice or three dozen times. Her brother, Asa, is the younger of the two by sixteen minutes. He's quiet and shy whereas Anya is always giggly and bubbly. Even Shelby likes the twins, and that's saying something.

"Hey, guys," Anya says, sliding into the row behind us.

Shelby and I wave. Brent looks back and nods at them with a half-cocked smile.

It strikes me kind of funny that the bleachers at the football games are as segregated as the cafeteria. These are some of the same people who sit around us every day during lunch. The pretty, popular people always sit down closer to the field about two sections over.

As the announcer launches into introductions of the Johnsonville team, our side of the field becomes instantly bored and grows restless through the endless litany of names and positions. I don't know much about football, but it seems like you could trim down the roster a bit by combining some positions. Like, I'm not sure what the difference is between a wide receiver and a tight end, but it sounds redundant to me. But what do I know?

Finally, the introduction of our team begins and the home crowd wakes up. As each player trots out onto the field to rousing cheers and applause, Shelby and I grade their asses on a scale from one to ten. It's kind of our thing. Alejandro "Alex" Cardenas, *seven*. Bobby Jenkins, *two*. Terry Fox, *ten*. Sai Patel, *six*, and so on.

"And in the position of quarterback"—the announcer's voice rises—"your all-state champion, wearing the number eleven, Jaxon Parker."

Of course, *The Great* Jaxon Parker gets the biggest roar from the crowd. Shelby looks over at me and rolls her eyes dramatically. Everyone around us is on their feet, even Brent and Kenny. We begrudgingly join them, but only so we can see.

Shelby leans in and yells over the noise, "And the fucker has the nerve to wear *his* ass score right on his back."

I laugh and look down on the field. Jax runs down the line of players, slapping their hands, waving at the crowd, and as hard as I try, I can't seem to tear my eyes away from him. The prick looks like a football god in those ass-hugging pants, wide padded shoulders, and bulging athletic cup. He carries his helmet at his side, and his sandy blond hair is already matted with sweat. His face glows with boyish exuberance and his jersey billows in the breeze, its hem rising just high enough to expose the tanned ripples of his lower stomach.

Shelby leans in and yells over the cheers, "Close your mouth, whore."

I close my mouth. Yes. It was hanging open. I need to check myself. There are plenty of fish in the sea. No need to get distracted by one that likes vag and probably jacks off looking at himself in the mirror every night. Not to mention the fact that he doesn't think my dad is good enough for his mom. Somewhere deep down in the rational part of my soul, I know that's not exactly what Jax was saying the other day at school, but somehow, that's what I heard. *Not good enough.*

As the Jaxon Parker crowd worship dies down, someone calls my name from down below. It takes me a second to spot the source over the sea of heads, but I finally find them waving their arms like a couple of baboons in heat. Dad and Tracee. I'm too embarrassed to wave back. Mercifully they quickly find seats on the second row and don't climb any closer to us.

"Who's that with your dad?" Shelby asks, scrunching her face at me.

I haven't given Shelby all the gory details yet. "Don't ask." I pull my phone out and quickly thumb a text message to my dad.

*Really, Rose?*

I can just barely see the top of Dad's head over the sea of people. He looks down. Three dots appear on my screen under the message I sent, which soon morph into words.

*Sorry, Dorothy. Promise to lay low. Won't cramp your style, buddy.* 🙂 👍 🏈 👏

Rose loves her some emojis.

Shelby elbows me in the side. "Your dad is hot. You know that, right?"

I cock my head at her. "Okay, ew."

She shrugs. "Oh yeah. Total DILF. And judging by the way Blondie's hanging on to him down there, I'd say she's already tapped that several times. Roger deserves a little happiness too, Beck."

I stare at her dumbfounded and mortified that my best friend wants to bang my dad. "I'm not standing in his way. He can screw whomever he wants. Except you, that is."

I glance down and catch Tracee waving to Jax on the sidelines. He glances up at her but he doesn't smile or wave back. Actually, his face hardens. Probably because he spots my dad sitting beside her.

"Wait," Shelby says, standing up and pointing. "Isn't that one of Jax's moms with your dad?"

I grab her arm and yank her back down. "Would you sit down and lower your voice, please?"

Shelby looks over at me, and a mischievous grin spreads across her face. "Is that what Pretty Boy wanted to talk to you about the other day? Is he going to be your new stepbrother?" Her eyes go wide and her voice rises. "OMG. You want to fuck your stepbrother."

"I do not want to fuck my stepbrother," I say, louder than intended. The rims of my ears heat instantly, and I glance around to survey the damage. It's not as bad as I'd feared. Only a dozen or so people stare at me like I'm the Antichrist. Asa is blushing, and Anya shoots me a confused smile and giggles a little. Brent and Kenny are oblivious.

"He's not my stepbrother and won't ever be," I say, shaking my head, more to our neighbors than to Shelby. A few gazes linger, but finally turn back to the action on the field.

I lean over to Shelby and lower my voice. "They're just dating. Jax isn't happy about it and neither am I."

Shelby shrugs, and the band launches into a raucous version of the new Bruno Mars song, putting a temporary pause on our conversation. During the song Carter Treadwell arrives with his helicopter mom circling him. I duck behind Kenny. Carter doesn't see me, but he must have picked up my scent, because he unknowingly sits directly behind my dad. We won the coin toss, so Jax slips his helmet on and runs out onto the field to another round of obnoxious cheers.

"Don't worry," I say to Shelby. "I won't be forever linked to that guy just because our parents can't keep it in their pants. I've got my eye on her. One wrong move and . . ." With fingers curled in, I run the tip of my extended thumb from one side of my neck to the other.

My phone vibrates in my hand, and I look down at it. My mom's smiling face fills the screen. I stare at the two words flashing above her picture and suddenly forget how to breathe.

*Mom calling.*

My hand shakes.

"Wow," Shelby says, glancing down at the phone. "When's the last time you heard from *her*?"

I don't respond because I don't know the answer. I can't remember the last time Mom called. In a brief moment of weakness, I hold my finger over the flashing green button. It would be so good to hear her voice again after so long. But the odds of her saying anything I actually want to hear are slim to none. Things like *I'm sorry*, or *I made a mistake*, or *I want to come home*. It'll more likely be something to the effect of *I'm moving to another country*, or *I met someone and I'm getting remarried*.

"Well?" Shelby nudges me with her shoulder, nearly knocking me over. "Are you going to answer it or not? Come on. The suspense is killing me *and* every nosy bitch sitting around us."

The robotic shake of my head relays my answer to Shelby and the nosy bitches sitting around us, but it's more directed at my mom's smiling face on the screen of my phone.

I move my finger over to the red button and press decline.

# CHAPTER EIGHT

# Jaxon

I stand in front of my open locker, busying myself with tidying it up, and delaying leaving as long as I can. On the bench next to me Terry ties his shoes. He hasn't said much since the game ended, because he knows me. Knows I need some time to process and beat myself up. Alex and Sai sling their gear bags over their shoulders and slap my ass on their way out.

"Good game, Jax," they both say.

"Thanks, guys. You too."

They're just being kind and supportive. We lost by a field goal because I threw two interceptions. Not my best performance by a long shot. Seeing Mom in the stands hanging all over Beck's dad didn't help my focus. I also couldn't stop worrying about JoJo, alone in Greenville tonight, after what happened at the Crusty Cup with those Bible-thumping hicktards. I know she can take care of herself, but her crying on my shoulder like that really shook me up. The only tears I've ever seen Ma shed were tears of joy, and those were definitely *not* tears of joy. Those bastards got to her, and I hate them for that.

I finally close up my locker and punch in the code to secure it. I can't put this off any longer. I remind myself that Roger is probably a decent guy who doesn't deserve to be the target of my anger at those Tabernacle pricks. Nor was he the reason that my moms broke up in the first place.

"You okay, bruh?" Terry says, standing.

I sling my bag over my shoulder. "Yeah, I'm good. Just a lot on my mind lately. Lost my focus tonight."

He offers his hand. When I accept it, he pulls me in for a shoulder-to-shoulder hug and pat on the back. "It happens. Let it go." He picks up his bag. "And if you ever want to talk about it—"

"Talk about it?" I say with a chuckle. "What are you, Dr. Phil now?"

He punches me in the arm, and we head toward the door. "You know what I mean, asshole." He stops in front of the door and looks back at me. "I'm here for you, bruh."

I nod and smile at him. Drawing in a deep breath, I reach for the door handle. As I pull it open for Terry, one unexpected thought pops into my head, completely catching me off guard. *I hope Beckett is out there.*

He is. Terry waves and walks off toward the parking lot but not before taking note of the odd group waiting for me. His gaze on Beckett lingers. Not in a bad way, just basic curiosity. My mom stands beside Roger with her arm locked in the crook of his elbow. From the high cheekbones, to the wide set jaw, to the twinkle in his eyes, the guy almost looks like a young Robert Redford. His hair, wavy but neat, is dirty blond and graying around the edges. The gray will suit him even more as it progresses. Beckett stands a few feet away from them, with his head down, kicking at the ground like a bored little kid. Finally, he glances up at me but doesn't smile. *Okay, then.* So much for the moral support from the one person here who could possibly understand how I feel. Mom releases her hold on Roger and closes the distance between us in a near trot.

"My boy!" She hugs me. She's wearing her *fancy* perfume. She smells good. She looks good.

I push back, a little from embarrassment. "Pretty dolled up for a football game, aren't you, Mom?"

The hurt in her eyes is instant, and I really didn't mean it as any kind of slam, I don't think. Just my diarrhea of the mouth acting up again.

"I mean you look great," I say, course correcting. "You really do."

Mom recovers quickly, as moms do when their kids say stupid and hurtful things. But I can tell by the fading smile on Roger's face and the firm set of his jaw that he's not so forgiving. Okay, so he's a little overprotective of Mom. On one hand, I like that. On the other, that's my job, so back off, Rent-a-Redford.

"This is Roger," Mom says with a gleam in her eye.

He walks forward and offers his hand. The shake is firm and his smile has returned. "Good to finally meet you, Jax. Great game tonight. Sorry it didn't go your way."

Like Beck, Roger's smile is disarmingly warm, which is annoying because I really want to dislike this guy.

"Win some, lose some, I guess." I shrug, playing off my own disappointment in my performance.

"I guess you know my son," he says, pointing at Beck.

Beck shuffles over, his hands shoved so far down in the pockets of his jeans he could probably give his kneecaps a scratch. "Hey."

I nod and stare at him, trying to read his face, but I can't. His dark eyes bore right through me. It's a bit unnerving. His face is devoid of any trace of human pleasantries.

"I just had the best idea," Mom says, breaking the agonizingly awkward silence. "Why don't we all go for pizza?" She slaps Roger on the arm like this is the best idea since Reese's Peanut Butter Cups. How can she not know that it's actually the worst? I open my mouth to throw out some random excuse as to why I can't go, but Mom gives me that look—that kind of pitiful smile with pleading eyes that she knows I can't deny.

"Sure," I say, fighting off a combination huff and eye roll. "Sounds great."

All eyes shift to Beck.

"Sorry," he says without missing a beat. "I can't." He pulls his phone out of his pocket and looks at his dad. "Remember, I told you I had plans with Shelby after the game."

"Why don't you invite her?" I say, half goading him and half crying out in desperation not to be left alone with these two. At least if Beck went, I would have someone to talk to other than the man that's boning my mom.

His lips slowly curl into what has to be a forced smile. "Sorry. Really wish I could. But Shelby already has a table somewhere and I'm late."

I'm sure the disappointment shows on my face. "It's cool. See you at school, then."

With his hair hanging down over his eyes, he nods at me and then says his good-byes to Roger and my mom. I can tell Mom wants to hug him real bad. Mom is a hugger, and I know that would not go over well with Beck, so imagining it amuses me a great deal.

Robbed of her motherly hug, she tries motherly humor instead and calls after him. "Don't stay out too late."

I wrestle back a smirk. I'm sure the hair on the back of Beck's neck just shot up. She's trying way too hard. But that's my mom. Beck glares at her over his shoulder, and I have to say, when he wants to murder someone with a look, it's pretty freaking hot. He's a little on the lean side of my usual taste— swimmer's build, long legs, and he's rockin' those jeans. Maybe it's his indifference to me that I find alluring as well. I'm not used to that. It doesn't matter, anyway. He's made it perfectly clear that he doesn't like me, though I still can't figure out why.

Mom rattles on to Roger about some play I made in the game. My gaze lingers on Beck as he crosses the parking lot, head down and his hands shoved deep into his pockets. His behavior and body language assure me of one thing. He may not want to stand in the way of his dad's happiness, but he doesn't like the idea of our parents dating any more than I do. But it's going to take more than a glimpse of my abs and the shake of my ass to convince him to help me. I already tried that, and it had absolutely no effect on him.

# CHAPTER NINE

# Beckett

I don't feel bad at all about lying to get out of going for pizza with Big Titties and her Colgate commercial–ready demon spawn. Well, I guess technically she didn't *spawn* him, but that's beside the point. However, imagining *The Great* Jaxon Parker sitting there having to listen to my dad's endless stories of his glory days on the high school football team, the way Rose Nylund would tell stories of her days in St. Olaf, amuses me quite a bit. Dad wasn't the quarterback or anything, but to hear him tell it, he was the shit with whipped cream on top *back in the day*.

My phone buzzes in the passenger seat, and I glance over at the notification displayed on the screen. It's from Brock on Bangr. An ass grab! That saucy little minx is really trying to get my attention. God, I hope he's not really a forty-year-old perv. I'll have to take a closer look at his hot naked torso profile pic again when I get up to my room. I do a quick mental inventory of my personal stash of hand lotion and wet wipes.

I turn onto our street and don't recognize the dark car parked in front of our house. At first I don't think much of it. People visiting our neighbors often park on the street in front of our house. No biggie. But as I pull into our driveway and my headlights illuminate the front porch, my breath catches in my throat. My foot connects with the brake pedal harder than I planned, jerking me forward against the confines of the seat belt. On autopilot, I put the car in park and engage the emergency brake.

She sits there on the top step, hugging her knees, her signature mass of dark curls framing her angular face. She squints her eyes in the flood of the headlights and raises a hand to shield them. I kill the engine and the headlights with robotic detachment. Sitting there in the dark, I grip the steering wheel and stare out the front windshield. I can't decide if I want to get out of the safety of the car or not—to venture *out there*, where I feel everything is about to change, and maybe not the way I want it to. Finally, I take a deep breath and drag myself out of the car.

Moving with tentative steps up the walkway toward her seems surreal. I don't know what to do with my hands, so they go to their happy place—deep inside my front pockets. I stop a couple of feet away from her and rock on my heels. Dumbfounded. She smiles at me, and only then do I really believe it's her and not my hyperactive imagination playing tricks on me.

"Mom."

If I am supposed to say anything else, I have no idea what it is. It's definitely not the scornful diatribe with which I'd always planned to greet her if she ever came back. My voice sounds as small as a five-year-old's. A single tear scurries down her cheek, but she doesn't bother with it. She stands and wraps her arms around me like the maternal stranger that she is. That's the way it feels, too. Like I'm being hugged by a total stranger who smells like someone I knew in a past life.

"What are you doing here?" It seems like the dumbest thing I could possibly say, yet it's the most honest clusterfuck of words I can come up with at the moment.

She pulls away, cradles my face in her palms, and stares at me. Her eyes are glassy with tears, and her smile is so broad that her eyes disappear into slits, just like mine do. For a long moment we are both speechless. Finally, she takes my hand and leads me over to the steps, where we sit on the top one, hip to hip like we used to when we waited for Dad to get home from work. I gaze over at her and catch myself shaking my head. She's still beautiful. Her eyes are deep, dark, and soulful. Her hair is a wild and beautiful mystery all its own. Her porcelain skin perfectly reflects the transient shimmer of the moonlight.

I open my mouth to speak again, unsure of what gibberish might come out this time, but she stops me with a finger to my lips. "Can we just sit here a minute, Beck?"

I nod, and she slips her arm around my waist and rests her head on my shoulder. Her untamed curls tickle my nose with the scent of apples and melon. A lump forms in the base of my throat. I know what that is. It's all the anger that's been bottled up inside me the last couple of years trying to push its way up and out of my mouth. All the hurtful things I've wanted to say to her for the pain she caused Dad and me, but mostly Dad. But I swallow that lump back down. It's stubborn and doesn't go down easy, but I finally manage.

I can't hold my tongue any longer. "Are you home?"

"Maybe," she says, and my heart skips a beat. "Your dad and I have a lot to talk about. A lot has changed in two years."

"He's seeing someone," I say before I can stop myself. I feel five again, tattling to my mom about Dad smoking in the work shed out back.

She just chuckles under her breath. "Well, that is perfectly normal, Beck. I left him, remember?"

Oh yes. I remember. Dad weeping in his room all night. Me spoon-feeding him soup so he would have something in his stomach. Prying him out of that recliner and convincing him that wearing the same pair of sweatpants every day for a month might not be the most hygienic fashion choice. Orchestrating exhausting mini pep rallies every morning just to get him off to work. I remember all too well.

"I've dated my share of people the past couple of years," Mom says. "I can't blame your dad for doing the same."

She's dated *her share* of people? How many is that? Like four, or forty? Because Dad has only dated *one*. Two, if you count both tits.

"Look, I don't expect your dad to just drop everything in his life and take me back. But things are different now. I'm a different person."

"How?" I ask. My protective nature has returned. "What's different?"

Mom squints her eyes at me and pulls her hair back off her crinkled forehead. "It's nice that you look out for him,

Beck. He needs that. And you were always wiser than the both of us put together." She looks down and scrapes the brick with a fingernail. "Look, before I left, there were things that I couldn't deal with. I felt like I was suffocating here. The last thing I wanted to do was to hurt you or your dad, but I didn't want my misery to infect the two of you. And I didn't want you to be the target of my anger at myself."

With my gaze locked on her, I sit there silent, not about to interrupt her. She needs to say this and I need to hear it.

She nods. "I started seeing someone," she says, and then cocks an eyebrow at me. "A therapist, I mean."

"Oh?"

"It was good for me. It helped. I should have done it a long time ago. She started me on some antidepressants and Xanax for my panic attacks."

I cross my arms and rest them on my propped up knees. "You had panic attacks? I don't remember that."

"Never happened in front of you. Sometimes with your dad though. Anyway, the meds and the therapy helped me a lot. I wouldn't say I'm completely transformed now, but I'm a whole lot better. And stronger."

I want to believe her. I really do.

"I'm so sorry I left you, Beck." She touches the back of my head. "I screwed up, in more ways than you know. But if you'll let me back in your life, I won't screw up again. I promise."

I gaze into her eyes, searching for any hint of doubt, but I don't find any. Whether what she says is true or not, she believes it. At least right now. She coughs and clears her throat.

"You want something to drink?"

She nods and coughs again. I hop up and go inside, never even considering inviting her in. That would be too weird. In the kitchen I fill two glasses to the rim with ice and sweet tea. She seems better when I get back out to the porch and accepts the glass with a big smile.

"Beck's sweet tea," she says, tipping her glass at me. "Nothing better."

I flash her a sideways smile. "I might've put too much sugar in this batch."

"No such thing," she says, and drinks half of it down.

We sit quietly, listening to the cicadas and the distant laughter of the neighborhood kids riding their bikes up and down the dark street. A warm breeze carries the scent of jasmine our way, and for that brief moment it's as if she never left. I latch on to a small kernel of hope deep down inside me that it can be this way again. I realize how much I miss her. How much I want her back. How much I want my family back. Dad's recent infatuation with Big Titties has to be just that. A fleeting infatuation. I know, deep down, he still loves Mom. No matter what she did, surely he can forgive her.

She sets her emptied glass on the step and runs fingers through her curls. "Where's your dad?"

"Having pizza with *her* and her son."

Mom cocks an eyebrow at me. "She has a son?"

I nod. "He goes to my school, so that's not awkward at all."

She chuckles and stands. "Well, I was hoping to catch you. You didn't pick up when I called. I just wanted to see you and let you know I'm in town. But I don't think it would be a good idea to still be here when your dad gets home with his new girlfriend."

"His *only* girlfriend," I say with a bit of an edge in my voice as I stand.

"I want him to be happy too, sweetie," she says. "And if this woman makes him happy, I won't get in the way. I just need to know if there is still a chance. For our family."

My emotions are a mixed bag. On one hand I want Dad to be happy with whomever he wants to be with, even if that turns out to be Big Titties, God help me. On the other hand, I want that chance for our family, too. I want Dad to choose Mom. To forgive her. Is that selfish of me? If it is, then so be it. I'm a selfish teenager, after all. It's my God-given right.

A wide beam of headlights momentarily blinds me. Dad's timing couldn't be worse, or better, depending on your agenda. There's no way in hell they already went for pizza, and now I'm busted. He pulls into the driveway and parks behind my Prius. Leaving the car running, he hops out and heads straight for us.

"Forgot my wallet," he calls out to me, and I can tell it hasn't hit him. "I thought you were meeting Shelby." Mom's presence hasn't fully registered with him yet. Maybe it's because seeing the two of us standing there looks so natural to him. But the closer he gets, the slower his pace. With his mouth agape, he stops about five feet away and locks gazes with her.

Mom crosses her arms and glances down, nervously shifting her weight to one side. "Hello, Roger."

Her voice is small. Ashamed of being heard. I hate that

she feels that way. Shit. My loyalties here are swinging back and forth like a leather queen in a sling.

"Lana," Dad says, staring at her.

I glance over at the car. The passenger side window lowers and Tracee sticks her clown painted face out. "Everything okay, Roggie?"

*Roggie? Ew.*

My dad doesn't even look her way. The back window lowers as well, and Jax leans forward. Apparently, he's a bit more intuitive than his mother, because as he takes in the scene, his mouth curls into a smile. The bastard.

"I just came by to let Beck know I was back in town," Mom says, crossing her arms and slipping between Dad and me. "Sorry. Looks like you have company. I'll get out of your hair."

Dad watches her back down the walkway, as eloquent as ever with his silent, gaping mouth. Mom waves at me and blows a kiss. "Call me, sweetie. Okay?"

I nod like a brainless robot. As Mom approaches Dad's car, she lowers her head and nods at Tracee as she passes. It was so submissive I'm embarrassed for her. I want to call out to her, *Don't you bow to that woman, Mom! She is not your equal!*

The scowl that Tracee lobs back at Mom flies all over me. I have a mind to march over there and remove every bit of her clown makeup with my fingernails. From the back seat of the car, Jax meets my gaze, and a silent understanding passes between us. I know that he'll come to me again and try to convince me that we should break up his mom and my dad.

This time he won't have to try so hard.

# CHAPTER TEN

# Jaxon

Beck is ten minutes late.

I wonder if he changed his mind and will blow me off altogether. I doubt it. When I saw the look on his face last night standing there in front of his house between his dad and his mom and looking so torn, I felt kind of sorry for the guy. I knew I had to try again. He was easy enough to find on Quickchat, and he replied to my direct message within a few minutes. I took that as a good sign. Fingers crossed he's come around.

The door squeaks open, and I look up expecting to find him walking in. But it's not Beck. It's that other gay kid, Carter Treadwell. He doesn't look like a Crusty Cup regular like the rest of us Saturday morning slouches. I came straight from the gym, so I'm still in my workout shorts, tank, and kicks. Carter looks like he's on his way to church in his starched plaid shirt, khakis, and bow tie. Geesh. Doesn't that kid ever relax?

He goes over to the counter and asks Jimmy something,

showing him a piece of paper from a stack under his arm. Jimmy inspects it and smiles. He nods, pointing Carter to the front window and also to the back of the room. After Carter tapes a flyer in the front window, he heads straight for me on his way to the bulletin board in the back. His eyes widen a little when he spots me but he quickly shifts his gaze away. At first I think he is going to flat out ignore me. He pauses beside my chair like he's trying to decide something.

"'Sup, Carter," I say, trying to make him feel more comfortable.

His face brightens and he turns in my direction. "Oh. Hey, Jaxon," he says, drawing out my name in one long monotone note. "I didn't see you there."

I shoot him a good-natured smirk and chuckle. "Yes, you did. You looked right at me." Strange kid.

Carter pushes his retro-stylish glasses up the bridge of his nose. "Right. I just mean my head's in a million different places right now. So much to do. So little time."

I nod to the stack of flyers he cradles in his arm. "What's that?"

"Actually," he says as he slides a flyer off the top of the pile and hands it to me, "I wanted to give you this and see if you might come to our first meeting Monday after school. It'd be great if you were there. You know, president of the student council, quarterback, two moms, et cetera, et cetera."

I scan the flyer and a rush of heat floods my cheeks. Jesus. What would the guys on the team think if they found out I joined the gay-straight alliance? *Not going to happen.*

"Thanks, Carter," I say, looking up and smiling at him.

"I think it's really great that we have a GSA club now. But my plate's a little full with football, student council, and my schoolwork."

Carter's hopeful smile fades, his shoulders sag, and I feel like a total turd.

"That's okay," he says, droning and stretching the words out. "Just thought I would ask."

I lay the flyer on the coffee table in front of me. "But I'll give it to my girlfriend and see if she and her friends want to join." I have no intention of doing this. For Carter's sake.

Carter beams again like I just told him Beyoncé would join his gay-straight alliance club. "Tiffany Daniels?" he nearly shrieks. "Oh wow. Thanks, Jaxon. That'd be *a-ma-zing*. Tell her I posted details on Quickchat. My handle's on the flyer."

He bounces off to the bulletin board in the back. Poor guy has no idea Tiff wouldn't be caught dead in any extracurricular club that wasn't stacked with athletes and cheerleaders. How else is she going to hold court? I check the time on my phone, and I'm about to call it when the door opens again. It's Tiffany with her usual shit timing. Flanked by Melissa Dukes and Molly Kim, it's a wonder they don't trip over one another coming through the door, all three with their heads down and eyes glued to their phones. I flip Carter's flyer over and sink down into the club chair, holding my phone up over my face for some semblance of cover.

Jimmy calls my name out from behind the barista counter and holds up a cup with my Sharpie scribbled name on it. Tiffany looks up, and her gaze finds me instantly. *Thanks a lot, Jimmy.*

"Jax," she calls out, her paper-thin voice slicing through the low roar of conversations as she makes a beeline for me. *Perfect.*

At least Melissa and Molly stay in line, mindlessly thumbing and swiping away at their phones. They barely even register my existence. Tiffany swings by the counter, grabs my coffee, and brings it with her. She stands in front of me, and I have to admit, she looks hot as hell in tight, white shorts and a navy halter tank. She knows she looks good too. She flips her hair and plants one hand on her hip. With her weight resting on her right side, she stands at an angle so I don't miss how fantastic her ass looks in those shorts. I don't miss it. I shift slightly in my seat to make room for Jax Junior, who's waking up.

To make matters worse, Carter is coming back this way.

"Hi, Tiffany," he sings, waving like an overexcited puppy. He doesn't stop. *Thank God.* "See you Monday."

Tiff gives Carter the stink eye as he flitters out the front door.

"Hey," I say, drawing her attention away from Carter before she asks any questions. "What's up?"

She looks back at me and down at the bulge in my crotch. Her glossed lips curl into a grin. "You, apparently."

My cheeks heat instantly, and I cross my legs before Jax Junior snakes his way down the leg of my shorts and peeks out to say hello. Tiff flips her hair again and takes a sip of my coffee, tonguing the sip hole of the lid a little too suggestively for so early in the morning.

"We're going to the mall," she says, setting the cup down

on Carter's flyer. "You should come with."

"Oh, that sounds like fun," I say, rolling my eyes at her. "But I think I'll pass. I have to get going anyway."

I don't know why I said it. Like I am afraid to be seen with Beckett or something. Guilt gnaws at the pit of my stomach.

"Whatever," she says, straightening her spine so that her perfect breasts salute me. Jesus, the girl's killing me here.

I squirm in my seat, finally getting things under control. "Text you later?"

"Sure," she says with a shrug. She picks up my coffee cup and takes another sip. When she sets it back down, coffee splashes out all over the flyer.

"Oh. Sorry." She reaches down for it, but I grab her wrist just in the nick of time.

"That's okay," I say, a little too anxiously. "I got it."

Tiff pulls her arm away and furrows her eyebrows at me. "Okay. Whatever. Talk later."

She turns on her heels and runs smack into Beckett Gaines. I didn't even see him come in. *Shit.*

"Oh, sorry," he says, his cheeks flushing rosy red.

If Tiffany could contort her face any more, it would be a medical miracle. She turns the mean girl stink eye on Beck so fast it's chilling. Glancing over her shoulder at me, she raises a questioning eyebrow, to which I shrug like I have no idea what he's doing here either. Jesus, what the hell's wrong with me? Am I really this much of an asshole? Tiff buys my fake-ass confusion, rolls her eyes, and rejoins Melissa and Molly at the counter. I grab a napkin and blot the spilled coffee on the flyer.

"Sorry," Beck says, glancing up at me with those big puppy dog eyes of his. "Didn't mean to interrupt."

"You didn't interrupt anything." I nod for him to sit, and he crosses in front of me in khaki shorts almost as tight as Tiffany's. I can't help myself from checking him out as he passes. Jax Junior twitches back to life. Jesus, what's wrong with me? One minute I'm acting mildly homophobic and the next I can't stand up straight for staring at a dude's ass. Maybe I'm not bisexual; maybe I'm just a teenage sex addict.

I point to my coffee as he sits. "You want something? My treat."

He shakes his head and slings a thick wave of chocolate-colored hair off his forehead. "No. I'm good, thanks."

Sitting forward in the chair, he clasps his hands together and rests his elbows on his knees. A second later, he leans back, crossing his arms over his chest and his legs knee over knee. Then he changes to ankle over knee. Why the hell is he so nervous?

"I'm sorry about last night," I say. "You looked kind of . . . overwhelmed. So your mom's back?"

Beck squares his shoulders and narrows his eyes on me. "I wasn't overwhelmed. Just surprised, is all." There's an edge in his voice.

I nod and wait for him to elaborate, which he doesn't seem all that anxious to do.

I scoot to the edge of my seat. "So? Is she back for good? Do you think your parents will get back together?" I try not to sound so excited, but I can't help myself. That would solve *everything*.

Beck shrugs. "How should I know? She really hurt Dad when she left. And he seems really into Tracee now."

I cock my head at him and turn on the charm. "Didn't you see the way your dad looked at your mom last night? I mean, he was pretty much speechless."

"Well, if you saw the woman who ran out on you for the first time in two years, you'd probably be speechless too, right?"

I lean back and casually separate my knees. I mean, the guy's gay, so why the hell not? If he was a girl and I wanted something from her, I would do the same damn thing.

"And your mom . . . wow. Now I see where you get your smile, your eyes, your—"

Beck clears his throat and gives me the hand. I didn't know that was still a thing.

"Let me stop you right there, Blue Eyes," he says. It's not a compliment. More like he's calling me on my bullshit tactics.

"I know you asked me here because you still want me to help you break up my dad and Tracee. So you can close your legs and stop batting your eyelashes at me."

I stare at him, waiting for him to blink. He doesn't. Closing my legs, I sink back into the chair, feeling like a douche. "I'm sorry, dude. I wasn't trying to work you."

He raises an eyebrow at me.

"Okay, I guess I was." I run a hand over my face and then through my hair. "I'm just kind of freaking out these days."

Beck's face softens a little. Just a little. He cocks his head at me. "Because of your moms?"

I gaze at him, wondering how honest I want to be with this guy. I mean, we've *known* each other since we were kids.

We were even friendly to each other when we were younger. But we sort of went our separate ways sometime around middle school. Different extracurriculars, different friends, different classes. I glance across the room just as Tiff looks away. She's been watching us. She and her friends load their cups down with packets of sweetener and milk. She's taking her time leaving, that's for sure. Finally, she leads the girls out the front door. I scratch the back of my head and refocus on Beck, relaxing a little now that Tiff's gone.

"JoJo, my other mom," I say. "She interviewed for a job in Greenville. If she and Mom don't get back together soon, more than likely she'll be moving there for good."

"Greenville's not *that* far," Beck says with a disinterested shrug.

It stings, and I guess it shows on my face.

"Sorry," he says, recovering quickly and shaking his head. "I didn't mean it like that. Sometimes my mouth moves before my brain computes."

I nod. "I can relate."

We both kind of smile for couple of seconds. Beck stares at me a long time, and I have no idea what he's thinking. His face shifts between soft and hard edges like he might doubt I'm telling the truth about JoJo. Just trying to work him in a different way. I swear I wish I knew what I ever did to this guy to make him distrust me so much. After a few awkward moments of silence he finally scoots to the edge of his seat.

"Okay. I'm in," he says. "But just to be clear, I'm not doing this for you. I'm doing it to get my family back and save my dad from another heartbreak."

I hold my hands up in happy surrender. "Okay, okay. I got it."

Beck nods and glances down at the coffee table. The damp GSA flyer catches his eye. He picks it up and flips it over.

"Carter left that earlier," I say.

He nods and looks up at me. "He told me about it. You going to join?"

"Oh God, no," I say a little too quickly and enthusiastically, because I can see his face change. "I just mean the guys on the team would never let me hear the end of it." Not the explanation I had planned. The one I gave Carter was much better. Should have stuck with that.

Beck shakes his head and huffs a little, letting the flyer drop to the coffee table. "God forbid you should set an example," he mutters under his breath, and glances away.

Heat rises up the back of my neck. I'm sick of taking fire from this guy for no good reason. "Can I ask you something?"

He looks up and shrugs.

"What the hell is your problem with me?" It comes out with more of an edge than I'd planned.

Beck twists his face into all manner of righteous indignation, but he doesn't say anything. Just shakes his head like I clearly should have a clue about something I have no clue about.

"What?" I say, confused and frustrated.

"Just drop it," he says with an eye roll. "Let's just focus on the task at hand."

I let it go for now, but we *will* be revisiting this subject again in the future. I slip my hand into the pocket of my shorts and retrieve the other flyer, sliding it across the table to him like it's some top secret spy shit.

"What's this?" he says, unfolding it.

"Mom gave it to me yesterday. She asked me to put some up around school."

Beck reads the heading out loud. "'First Annual Florence PFLAG Prom.' Wow. They're actually doing it." He looks up at me, raises an eyebrow, and holds up the flyer. "Is this your way of asking me out on a date? Because if it is, you really need to work on your moves."

I can't help myself from grinning. Damn, he can be a snarky bitch. I kind of like it. "No, I'm not even going to it. But Mom is ragging me to volunteer. She says they have too many parents and not enough students on the planning committee. They don't have a clue what they're doing and there's a meeting Wednesday at the public library. She and Roger will both be there, so I figure we should go. Besides, she says if some of us students don't help them out, people will be dancing to Donna Summer and the Bee Gees all night."

A grin creeps up on Beck's face. "Sounds kind of retro fabulous, actually. I mean it *is* a gay prom, after all. But you're right. Queer kids today want Beyoncé and Gaga." He trains his gaze on me. "So why aren't you going to the PFLAG prom?"

I shrug. "Because I'm not gay." Maybe it's not 100 percent true. Maybe 50 percent. Some days, 40. Damn, it'd be nice to have someone my own age to talk to about it. To add—*not totally gay, anyway*—and that'd be okay. But this guy could ruin me at school. And the way he looks down his nose at me—when he's not staring at my ass or my crotch—I wouldn't put it past him.

Beck pushes a wave of hair out of his eyes. "I just thought since, you know, you have two moms, and one of them is on the planning committee, you would rise above your own personal hang-ups and support the event."

I look at him and cock my head. Apparently, he's under the impression that I hate gay people. Maybe that's why he's being a pain in the ass. What a crock of shit.

"Look, obviously I've done something to offend you," I say rather firmly, "though I can't for the life of me figure out what it is. But I've got nothing but love for gay people. Like you said, I have *two moms*, two of the most wonderful women on God's green earth. And I find it more than a little offensive that you think I'm some kind of freaking homophobe."

Beck shakes his head at me *again* and rolls his eyes *again*. His cheeks redden. "You don't even fucking remember, do you? Wow." He slaps his palms on his thighs. "Here I thought you just had elephant-sized balls and didn't care how much of an asshole you were, but you actually don't even remember it—which doesn't make you just an asshole. It makes you a self-absorbed, *heartless* asshole." He stands and plants a hand on his hip. "You know what? You don't need me for your half-assed little plan. I'm just the *skinny faggot* you guys bullied in middle school when I was half your size."

"What the hell?" I say, exasperated.

He takes a couple of steps away but stops. Turns to face me and comes back. "On second thought, I'll make a deal with you." He picks up the gay-straight alliance flyer and shoves it in my face. "You show up for *us* and maybe I'll think about showing up for *you*."

Beck's face is so red I wonder if he's going to burst into flames right there in the middle of the Crusty Cup. He drops the flyer into my lap and is halfway across the room before I can pick my jaw up off the floor and collect my thoughts. *Middle school? Bullied? What the hell is he even talking about?*

"Beckett, wait!" By the time I get to my feet, the door slams closed behind him.

I cross the room in a few strides and push through the door, but he's nowhere in sight. Standing in the middle of the sidewalk, scratching the back of my head, I scan the street up and down, trying to make some sense of what Beck just said. I don't remember bullying *anyone* in middle school, much less Beck. Truth be told he always intrigued me, even back then. He was like some mysterious, exotic gay alien from another planet. But he certainly never gave me the time of day. As I turn and go back inside, my phone vibrates in my front pocket. I pull it out and swipe the screen. Up pops a text from Tiffany.

*What the hell did Beckett Gaines want with you????*

I thumb one word into the virtual keyboard and hit send. *Nothing.*

"Everything okay?"

I look up. Jimmy stands behind the counter, staring at me with a cocky smirk on his face.

I shrug and slip my phone in my pocket. "I have no fucking idea, bro. That guy's got issues."

The place has emptied out a bit so Jimmy has a rare minute to chat. I walk over to the counter. He leans in, rests his elbows on the counter, and cups his hands in front of him.

"Can I give you a piece of advice, Jax?"

"Sure. Why not?" I say, resting my hip on the counter.

"Cut the kid some slack. He's probably into you and doesn't know what to do with that, seeing as how you're the big man on campus, star jock, and confirmed pussy hound." The right side of his mouth curls up. He's making fun of me, but he's serious, too.

I shake my head at him. "Look, bro, I can assure you that even though Beckett Gaines may check me out every now and then, the dude is definitely not *into me*. Not like that. He can barely stand to be around me."

Jimmy nods and arches his eyebrows. "You're sure about that?"

"Yeah, I'm sure," I say, pushing off the counter. "He acts like he freaking hates me most of the time."

Jimmy grabs a damp rag from behind the counter and wipes it down. "Okay, dude, whatever you say." He glances up. "All I know is that I had a girlfriend once who treated me the same way, and she looked at me the same way he looks at you."

"Yeah? How's that?"

Jimmy leans in and lowers his voice. "Like he wants to ride you like a stallion and pummel your face in while he's doing it." He winks. "And trust me, bro. That can be one hell of a hot ride."

Jimmy chuckles, slings the rag over his shoulder, and walks away. I'm glad too. Because the imagery of what he just described—not the pummeling-my-face-in part, but the Beck-riding-me-like-a-stallion part—has Jax Junior on the move again.

# CHAPTER ELEVEN

# Beckett

Mondays always come faster after the school year starts, and then they slam on their brakes the moment the first period bell rings. Admittedly, I'm more ornery than usual today. Jax really pissed me off Saturday at the Crusty Cup, and then I had to spend yet another Sunday night dinner staring at Big Titties across the table. All I could do was wonder where Mom was having Sunday dinner—probably by herself in some cheap motel out by the mall. It's all too tragic to contemplate.

The first three periods pass in one long blur. Eight thirty is too damn early for calculus, nine thirty is downright criminal for Mr. Stoke's stanza-by-stanza interpretation of *Beowulf*, and by the time I got to choir, I was in no mood for Cassidy Charles's subpar and uninspired solo on "What I Did for Love." Still, for some reason, it took three tissues courtesy of Mrs. Norcroft to plug my waterworks. What the hell is wrong with me? By the time the last bell of the day sounds,

I'm ready for the couch, some cheesecake, and my Blanche Devereaux inspired padded-shoulder, satin bathrobe.

*Note to self: Patent the "Deverobe." Commit 5 percent of the profits to the late Rue McClanahan's favorite charity.*

*Note to self: Google the late Rue McClanahan's favorite charity.*

I could so easily skip the gay-straight alliance meeting, but I told Shelby I would meet her there, and she would murder me if I stood her up and left her to deal with Carter and drool over Chevy all by herself. As I turn the corner and stroll into room 150, I have to say I'm surprised by the turnout. There are only a few desks left open. Shelby waves me over to the one she's saved beside her. I make my way across the room, waving hello to the twins and to Brent and Kenny. Brent gives me a high five and giggles a little.

"*Bonjour, mon ami*," Chevy says with a big smile as I pass him and wave. His English is better than 70 percent of the student population of East Florence High but I think he knows how sexy he sounds when he speaks French. Chevy flirts with *everyone*. Another reason he fucks with my gaydar.

"Beckett," Carter squeals over the rumble of conversation as he looks up from behind the teacher's podium. "You came!"

"Hey, Carter," I say, sliding into the desk next to Shelby.

She leans over and whispers, "I bet he just squirted a little bit."

"Shut up, hooker," I say, glancing over my shoulder. "Impressive. Looks like the gang's all here and then some."

"Except for the scissor sisters," she says.

"Speak of the lesbians," I say as Jen and Lexi stroll in *holding hands*. Scandalous.

Shelby looks over at me with a raised eyebrow, and all I can think about is how bad I want to pluck it. Which reminds me . . .

"Hey," I say, lowering my voice as Carter clears his throat, trying in vain to quiet the room. "What are you doing this Saturday?"

"Breaking up with my vibrator," Shelby deadpans in a whisper. "It hasn't been hittin' it right in a while. I think it turned gay. You want it?"

I giggle and wink at her. "It's your birthday, and I have something special planned."

Carter raps his knuckles on the podium. "Okay, people. Settle down. Let's get started. Welcome to the first meeting of the East Florence High Gay-Straight Alliance!"

He claps his hands and bounces up and down a little. I know he wants to squeal so badly, but he manages to contain himself. A smattering of obligatory applause fizzles out pretty quickly, except for Chevy, who looks genuinely excited to be here. He has no idea that Shelby is boring a hole in the back of his head with her lustful gaze.

I scan the room. No Jax. Shocker. Carter clears his throat again, and when I look up he's staring right at me. The grin on his face seems to circle his entire head.

"And to start things off," he announces, "Beckett Gaines has something really exciting to share with us."

"I do?" I look over at Shelby. She just shrugs and looks as confused as I feel.

"Yes, Beckett," Carter says in his chicken-fried voice. "The golden opportunity we have to partner with PFLAG?"

"Golden opportunity?"

"Yes, silly," Carter says, nodding his head. "The PFLAG prom. I just found out that Principal Healy offered our gym as the venue and that you're a student representative on the planning committee."

"I am?" I seriously have no idea what the hell the guy's talking about.

"Well, sure," Carter says, scrunching his face at me. "You and Jaxon Parker."

"Me and—" Holy son of Satan.

Jax strolls into the room, backpack slung over his shoulder, and shoots me the cockiest I-got-you smirk in the history of douchedom.

"Isn't that what you told me at lunch, Jax?" Carter says, beaming at Jax as he plops down into an empty desk close to the door.

"Yes, it is," Jax says, that smirk still twisting his lips. I'd like to bite it . . . I mean *slap it* off.

"Oh," I say, regaining my composure and cutting my eyes at him. "So you're joining the GSA now? What will the guys on the team think?"

The hard edge in my tone isn't lost on anyone in the room. Kenny stifles a chuckle. Everyone else stares at me like I have four heads and then back at Jax like he's the Night King about to pull out his ice sword and relieve me of at least three of them. No one talks to *The Great* Jaxon Parker that way.

"Unfortunately, I can't join," Jax says, still smirking as he returns his attention to Carter. "The meetings conflict with football practice. I can't stay today, either. But as the president of the Student Government Association, I just wanted to *show up* for you guys"—he pauses and shoots me a lingering glare—"at your first meeting and let you know that if there's anything the student council can do to support the gay-straight alliance, just let me know."

I lock eyes with him and decide this would be the ideal moment for Shelby to flick that booger on him.

"Well, thank you, Jaxon, for stopping by to show your support," Carter says-sings.

Jax smiles and stands to leave. "Anytime, Carter."

"Yeah, thanks for your support, Mr. President," I say with more than a little snark as he shoulders his backpack.

He doesn't look back. Just holds a hand up and waves as he swaggers out the door. I try, and fail, to not stare at his ass.

While I sit there stewing about Jax, Carter drones on about the importance of *what we're doing here, people.*

Chevy holds up his hand and asks Carter to explain to him the need for a gay-straight alliance club. Apparently, things are different/easier for the queer kids in France. Asa and Anya take notes on their iPads. They have little wireless keyboards and everything. Brent and Kenny stare at Carter like he's the most fascinating creature they've ever seen. I wonder what color he is in their current state of mind. Most likely pink.

Shelby raises her hand, interrupting Carter's riveting speech about the inequality and injustice in our society. He does not look pleased as he lets out a long sigh and nods at her.

Shelby sits up straight. "Sorry to interrupt. But you said there would be snacks."

He juts his jaw at her and launches right back into his soliloquy without even responding.

Shelby thumbs away on her phone, and a second later a text notification pops up on the screen of mine.

*I don't think there are any snacks. What are we doing Saturday for my b-day?*

I type, *Finding your inner drag queen* and hit send.

The girl's eyes go so wide it looks like they're about to pop out of her head. I can't tell if she's terrified or climaxing. Maybe a little of both.

When I look up, Cassidy Charles is standing in the hallway just outside the door, holding her book bag in front of her and shooting holy daggers at Carter with those perma-judgmental eyes of hers. Cassidy Charles is easily the most *out* Christian at school. She and her family are Assembly of God–flavored Christians. Not quite as bad as the Holiness Tabernacle freaks. More like a distant cousin with more money and makeup. Shelby calls Cassidy "Wanda Witness," because she's always asking you if you've accepted Jesus Christ as your Lord and personal savior. When she asked me, I told her that I was totally down with Jesus, because we had the whole gay thing in common. I mean, the guy never married and spent all his time with twelve bears who hung on his every word. Shelby told Cassidy that she felt a special kinship to Jesus because she didn't know who her real father was either. Cassidy hasn't inquired about our eternal souls since.

Standing out there in the hallway, staring at Carter, she looks like her head is about to do a 360 spin. Carter must feel her holy presence, because he stops speaking and looks over at her.

"Would you like to come in and join the gay-straight alliance, Cassidy?" He says it with a healthy dose of gay stink eye, because he already knows the answer. Gay stink eye is much worse than white girl stink eye. It's actually more akin to black girl neck roll.

Cassidy steps into the room, still clutching that book bag to her chest. Either she's got a Bible in there that she's using as a shield to ward off the evil gay spirits, or she's concerned about Jen and Lexi checking out her communion wafer–sized tits.

"No, I would *not* like to join your disgusting little club, Carter Treadwell," she says, slinging her hair over her shoulder and serving him a mirror image of his own jutted jaw.

"And I will have you know that my mother is on the school board," she says.

Everyone knows this. She reminds us every chance she gets.

"She is the moral compass of that board, and she will not be pleased when I tell her that Principal Healy approved this little *club* of yours. Or about this homosexual prom he plans to allow to take place on school property."

Normally, I'm the first person to jump up and beat back some bigoted bullshit, but Cassidy is so ridiculous, ignorant, and not the least bit believable as a *real* Christian, that everyone pretty much just rolls their eyes and ignores her. Chevy's the only one who seems even mildly interested in what Cassidy has to say, and that's probably for some school term paper he'll write when he gets back to France about how fucked up the American South is. I think he's even taking notes.

"Dang. Chill out, Cass," Brent says with a glazed smile. "You're bumming me out. Love is love, girl."

"It's Cass-i-dy, and shut up, you godless pothead," she snaps back at him.

"Jesus Christ on a cross, Cassidy," Shelby taunts. "We're just trying to have a little intelligent social intercourse here."

Kenny snorts out a chuckle. Carter squints his eyes and cocks his head at Shelby, no doubt perplexed by her word choice.

I thumb a quick text over to my girl. *I think you meant civil discourse, hooker.*

Shelby looks down, reads the text, and giggles from somewhere deep down in her chest.

"Well." Cassidy huffs and slings her bag over her shoulder. "We'll just see what happens when I inform my mother how Satan has infiltrated our school."

Shelby closes her eyes and folds her hands in front of her. She says in a prayerful whisper, "Take her, Jesus."

"Okay, Cass-i-dy. Noted. Is that all?" Carter says with a bored sigh and shrug. She's not rattling this kid one little bit. I'm impressed.

Cassidy takes a deep breath and narrows her eyes on him. "This isn't over, Carter."

She turns and marches out the door. Shelby opens her eyes and looks around in childlike wonder. "I did it."

"Sorry about that, people," Carter says. "Chevy, Asa, Anya, I know you guys aren't used to that kind of thing in your homelands."

"We're from Charleston," Asa says quietly.

"We're going to face some small-minded people around here," Carter continues. "But like I was saying earlier, that's why the GSA and PFLAG are so important in our community."

I look over at Shelby. "We touch lives."

"So, Beckett," Carter says, looking at me. "Will you let the PFLAG chapter know that we want to lend our support to their prom? We'll promote it here at East Florence and through the regional GSA network. We can get the word out to at least a dozen or so other clubs in Florence and the surrounding counties."

I just stare at him.

"You are going to the next PFLAG meeting with Jaxon, right?"

If I say yes, I'll be playing right into Jax's hand. If I say no, Carter will think he's a better gay than me. And, let's face it. He really is.

"Yep," I finally say. "I'll get with Jax on that right away, Carter."

# CHAPTER TWELVE

# Jaxon

It's almost six thirty a.m. when I get to the weight room at school. Terry, Alejandro, Jody, Sai, and some of the other guys are already there and going at it hard in the center of the room. The weight room is pretty big but usually segregated by sport. The lacrosse guys work out in the front of the room near the entrance, the basketball players over by the window, and the baseball guys huddle in the back. The football team usually occupies the center of the room, and then we branch out from there as needed. We're kind of at the top of the athletics program food chain.

"Slackard," Sai calls out to me as I drop my bag on the bench. I flip him the bird and he grins.

Terry looks up and sees me. "Where you been, bro? Come on, I need a spot."

I pull on my lifting gloves and hurry over to him. "Sorry. JoJo was late picking me up again."

"When are they going to get you a car, dude?" Terry says.

I shrug. "Not everyone's dad is a rich dentist, you know?"

Someone to my left grunts and drops a stack on the floor. I look over. It's Bobby Jenkins.

"Jesus, Bobby," I say. "Go easy on those things."

He flexes at me, showing off his guns. "The girls love it," he says, kissing each bicep. Alex and Jody roll their eyes at him.

Bobby's a big motherfucker, I'll give him that—about four inches taller than me and at least twice as wide. I don't like Bobby and he probably knows it. He's a bigot, a homophobe, and a racist. The fact that Terry is all the man that he is and more is probably the only thing stopping Bobby from throwing around the N-word. And he knows better than to direct any of his Muslim-phobic bullshit *jokes* at Sai since he tried it the first day of practice last year and Coach threatened to suspend him from the team.

Bobby and I used to be cool when we were younger, but now we mostly stick to our boys within the team—me with the good guys with half a brain and Bobby with the shitkicking, racist homophobes. Plus his family goes to the Holiness Tabernacle, and everyone is quite clear on their stance on gays. Bobby knows I have two moms, but so far, it's a line he hasn't crossed. Still, he protects me on the field, so our coexistence on the team is a delicate dance, one that we both manage with a surprising amount of finesse.

Terry lies down on the bench, and his shirt rides up. He's already worked up a sweat and it glistens on his skin. Standing over him and gripping the bar above his head, I try not to stare down at his rippled stomach.

"I thought premarital sex was against your religion or

something," I say to Bobby just to distract myself from lusting over my best friend.

He laughs. "Look who's preaching about premarital sex."

"Not preaching. You know me. Live and let live."

Terry pushes out twelve solid reps and rests. His chest looks massive as he heaves oxygen in and out.

Billy Porter, one of Bobby's redneck soul mates, flexes in the mirror nearby. "You guys hear we got a queer club at this school now?"

The hair on the back of my neck springs to life.

"What?" Bobby says, still panting after his last set of dead lifts.

Billy walks over to him. "Yep. And I heard they're planning some kind of fag dance in our gym."

Terry pushes out another twelve reps and sits up. "Could you not use that word, Billy?"

I should have been the one to say it.

"Okay then, *gay*," Billy says with air quotes and an eye roll.

"Gay, queer, fag, lesbian—six of one, half dozen of the other," Bobby says. "Pastor Doug says they're all going to the same hell."

Something deep inside me snaps. I walk over to him and get right in his face. "That's enough, Bobby."

He stares back at me, and I can tell by his shifting eyes that he's trying to decide if he should start something with his quarterback or not. Alex and Sai stroll over and stand behind me. I know they would both love a legitimate excuse to give Bobby's xenophobic ass a beat down. Some of the baseball players stop lifting and stand ready to help break up a fight if needed. A slight grin spreads across Bobby's face as he surveys the vibe in the room. He huffs out a little chuckle, turns, and walks over to Billy. *Smart choice, asshole.* I turn, and Terry is by my side.

"Just say the word, bro, and I will light him up like a Christmas tree," he says. Terry is about as protective of my moms as I am. He knows what it's like to grow up noticing the sideways glances lobbed at your parents for no reason.

I shake my head and nod over to the bench. "Let's just do this. I've got calculus to finish before first period."

The door opens and closes with a bang. I look over and *oh, holy shit.* Beck's coming straight at me, and his skirt's showing a little. I make a quick check of everyone around me, my cheeks heating instantly. The lacrosse guys don't even notice him. A couple of the baseball players look over but don't seem overly concerned. Then there are my guys. Sai does a double take when he looks up and sees Beck. Jody and Alex trade slightly confused glances while Bobby and Billy stand gaping at him with obvious disgust marring their faces. Terry stops loading weights on the bench press bar and looks at Beck like he's an alien. Actually, I get that. It's more than a little odd seeing Beckett Gaines in the weight room. It's like seeing a unicorn at the Kentucky Derby.

"Well, well, well," Bobby says to Beck. "You lost, precious?"

I glare at Bobby and walk toward Beck, trying to head him off before he can open his mouth. I take him by the arm. "Outside."

"Ow," he says, wincing at my grip, which is barely a grip at all.

I lead him out the door and into the empty gym. They haven't turned the lights on yet, so it's dark, and we stop just inside the doorway in the light of the lobby.

"What are you doing?" I say, letting go of his arm.

He squints at me like he doesn't understand, dropping his backpack on the floor.

"Doing *here*." I take a beat and breathe. "School doesn't start for another hour."

His shoulders sag a little, and I can easily read his defeated expression. He thinks I was embarrassed by him in the weight room, which I wasn't. Okay, maybe I was, but that's my shit, not his. It actually has nothing to do with him.

"Tracee told me this is when you work out," he says.

*Great. Thanks, Mom.*

"Look," he says, his eyes cold again. "I don't appreciate what you did in the GSA meeting yesterday."

"What? You said you would help me if I showed up for you guys. Well, I showed up."

"You dropped by," Beck says, crossing his arms over his chest. "You didn't show up. And you told Carter that we're on the planning committee for the PFLAG prom. What the hell?"

"I'm sorry. I saw an opportunity and went for it. Mom was ragging me to volunteer, and I just thought we both should be there. You know, divide and conquer? Two heads are better than one?"

Beck gives me a snarky eye roll. "Present company excluded."

"Look, I did what I could. My mom and your dad were ecstatic that we're both going to help. And I was serious about the student council supporting the GSA. I mean, what more do you want from me?"

Beck pauses and stares at me. I wish I knew what was going on in that head of his. He looks down and shoves his hands in his pockets. When he glances back up, he looks like he's about to cry.

"You okay?" I say, softening my tone. Shit. I wish I knew what I said to make him react this way.

He manages to hold any possible tears at bay, but his eyes are glassy and there's a quick sniffle. I don't have a clue what that's about, but I just want him to be okay—to be snarky, confident, sassy Beckett Gaines again. I have an overwhelming desire to hug the guy. Wouldn't that be a show for Bobby Jenkins? But I'm too much of a coward to actually do it.

"I'm fine," he says, and I can tell he's back in control of his emotions. "Things at home are just all messed up. And, no offense, but a lot of it's your mom's fault."

"And, no offense, but vice versa with your dad."

He nods. "No offense taken. Sounds like we both just want the same thing."

He looks up at me with those huge brown eyes of his, and I am instantly aware of exactly how many inches of space separate us. Not that many.

"I'll go to the PFLAG meeting," he finally says, looking down and picking up his backpack. "I guess I'll see you in calculus."

He walks past me and I turn, watching him leave. I wonder if the sideways glances and snide comments from people like Bobby Jenkins really do get to him, and he just never lets it show.

"Beck?"

He stops, turns, and looks back at me. "Yeah?"

"It's going to be okay," I say, just loud enough for him to hear me.

He doesn't respond—just walks away, fading into the dark void of the gym.

# CHAPTER THIRTEEN

# Beckett

"This is lame as hell."

I couldn't agree more. Though I'm not exactly sure which particular part Shelby's talking about. Is it spending our Wednesday night in the windowless basement meeting room of the Florence County Library? Or that they won't *open* the snack table until after the meeting is over? Shelby and I deal with boredom and stress the same way. Cookies—peanut butter for me, chocolate chip for her. And right now she's bored and I'm stressed the hell out.

For me, the lamest part is watching Tracee in the front row, hanging all over my dad like a stripper trolling for tips. The sight of it turns my stomach. Especially now that Mom's back in play. At least I'm proceeding as if she is. And I can't believe Jax is a no-show after what he pulled at the GSA meeting.

At least Shelby was willing to tag along to the PFLAG meeting and provide color commentary to take my mind off things. We make a good team. We're both, as my grandmother once described us, *a little touched in the head.*

A Vanna White–looking soccer mom with crazy eyes and Trump-colored skin stands down front waving a hand our way. "So, we want to thank Beckett and Shelby in the back there for joining us tonight. Beckett is representing the newly formed gay-straight alliance at East Florence High School. They're going to help with outreach and promotion for the Rainbow Prom and help us get the word out to all the kids in the local schools. So thank you, Beckett. Would you like to say anything?"

Dad turns and claps overhead, a little too enthusiastically for my taste. *Calm down, Rose.*

I stand as Shelby snickers quietly. "No, ma'am. I'm good, thanks."

But everyone in the room looks at me like they expect something more from me.

I look around and address the group with a nod. "Just proud to be queer. I mean *here.*" Shelby snorts. I sit. People stare.

"Well, we hope you help us make the prom all *hip* and every-thing," Orange Vanna says with an uncomfortable giggle.

"I think it's safe to say that there's no chance in hell of that happening," Shelby mutters.

Orange Vanna holds her hand out toward my dad like she's waiting for him to buy a vowel. "Oh, and Beckett belongs to Roger and Tracee, here."

Oh. Hell. No. I grip the edges of my chair and hold my breath waiting for one of them to correct her, but neither of them does. The door in the back of the room squeaks open, but no one turns to see who it is. The meeting is basically over, thank God.

"Sheila made her delicious gluten-free peanut butter cookies," Orange Vanna says, gesturing to the back of the room as people begin to stand. "They're on the snack table by the coffee, so help yourself and thanks for coming."

We stand and I look over at Shelby, rolling my eyes. "Gluten-free. Ugh."

Dad and Tracee chat with their fellow PFLAGers. I can't wait to get out of there, so I turn and head to the back with Shelby in tow. I look up to find Jax standing by the snack table, slowly chewing one of Sheila's *delicious* gluten-free peanut butter cookies. So he finally showed up. Late. Not even late. He actually didn't even make the meeting. Typical.

He nods up at me. "Sorry I'm late. Practice went long." He glances over at Shelby. "You felt the need to bring backup?"

"Shelby wanted to volunteer too," I say, shifting my weight to one side and crossing my arms over my chest. "*True* friend of the gays that she is, and all."

Jax grins. I'm beginning to think he finds my sassiness quite entertaining. Better dial it back a notch. I'm trying to repel him, not amuse him. Gays are unwittingly amusing. We can't help it. It's sometimes a gift and sometimes a curse.

"Just admit that this was a good idea," Jax says, leaning in. He's right, but I won't.

"Jax." Tracee appears out of nowhere and wraps her arms around his neck.

Dad squeezes my shoulder and winks at Shelby. "Thanks for coming, guys."

Tracee guides Jax into our circle. "Yes. I'm so glad you all came." She plants herself between Jax and my dad, locking her arms in theirs like she's about to launch into a square dance with them.

*Swing dem titties round and round, swing dem titties upside down.*

Dad scratches the back of his head and sighs. "And it seems we're going to need your help now more than ever to pull this off."

Shelby cocks her head. "What do you mean 'now more than ever'?" Where two or more are gathered, Shelby's voice is always a decibel too low, which always makes me nervous for her. She's much more assertive one-on-one, or two *against* one. Thankfully, Dad heard her.

He shakes his head. "Some of the parents just told us. The Holiness Tabernacle crowd is all up in arms about the Rainbow Prom."

I guess that's what we're calling it now. I was not consulted.

"They're planning to protest the event, and you know how ugly that could get. I just hope it doesn't scare the kids away."

"We're not going to let those Christian crazies ruin our prom," Tracee says.

"I'm a Christian," Shelby says, so low only I hear her.

I lean over and whisper to her. "But you're the good kind. Not the crazy kind."

She smiles, pleased enough with the distinction.

"Can't you just call the cops on them if they show up?" Jax asks without looking my dad in the eye. He turns his body and shifts his focus to Tracee. "Hey, don't you and JoJo have a friend on the police force? Doris, right? Maybe you could call her and see if she can help."

Tracee fidgets like she has an army of ants crawling down her crack. She wraps her arms around my dad and pulls him close, but doesn't look at him. "We certainly don't need that woman around, and she is not *my* friend, Jax," she says, shooting him a dagger filled glare. "Besides, I should hope that we won't need to get the police involved. This is supposed to be a prom, not a street fight. We'll have enough chaperones around to keep an eye on things."

Jax smiles likes he's satisfied with his mother's rattled response. I don't know what all that's about, but whatever it is, Dad is oblivious to the tension Jax just manufactured out of thin air. I've got to hand it to him. *Well played, asshole. Well played.*

"Mom used to be friends with the new mayor, right, Dad?" I say, manufacturing a little tension of my own. "Maybe she could give him a call to see what he can do about it." I pull out my phone. "I can call her right now and ask."

Dad's face sours and he waves me off with a noticeable glare. "There's nothing that guy can do, Beck. The Tabernacle folks always have a permit for their demonstrations. They just have to stay a hundred feet away from the entrance."

*That woman* and *that guy*. I'd say both Jax and I succeeded in pushing a couple of hot buttons.

"A hundred feet?" Jax says, indignant. "That's nothing. They could throw things from that distance. Our people could get hurt."

Wow. I have to admit, I'm mildly touched that he called the gay kids "our people," but perplexed because he said he wasn't even coming to the prom because *he's not gay* and all.

"Well," I say nonchalantly, pushing my luck. "I'll just call Mom and see if she thinks the mayor could help." I start thumbing her number into my phone, until Dad covers my hand with his.

"Beck," he says with a narrowed gaze. "I said there's nothing the mayor can do."

I cock my head at him, confused by the rare hard edge to his voice. I knew there was a little jealousy there, but Jesus Christ, Dad.

Tracee grins from ear to ear. "You guys just let everyone know that the Rainbow Prom will be perfectly safe. We're not going to let those Jesus-loving freaks bother anyone."

"I love Jesus," Shelby mumbles to no one in particular.

I pat her on the back. *Bless.*

"We still need to figure out the music, though," Dad says, his face softening again. Rose is back from the dark side. "That's one area where we're stumped. I mean, we know of some local wedding bands, and there's that one deejay that does all the Jewish events in town. You guys have any ideas?" He slips his arm around Tracee's shoulders and she nestles up next to him.

Wedding bands and a bar mitzvah deejay. Sweet baby Jesus. It's like watching a big gay train derail. In a moment of sheer inspiration and clarity, I nod over at Jax. "We can help with the music."

"What?" Jax says with a double take. I like catching him

113

off guard the way he did me at the GSA meeting. Suddenly I'm drunk with the power.

"I told you I wasn't even going to the prom," he says with an eye cocked at me and minimal movement of his lips, which seems nearly impossible, given their girth.

Tracee looks over at him with her painted on eyebrows arched up to Jesus. "What's this?"

I casually walk over to Jax and squeeze the back of his neck like we're old pals. Damn, he's thick back there. It's like squeezing a car tire.

"Oh, he's just messing with you, Tracee," I say. "Of course he's going to the prom. Right, bruh?"

Jax looks over at me with a scowl, but doesn't say a word. I love having the upper hand with this guy.

"Well, if you two could take care of the music, that would be fantastic," Dad says.

"No problem at all, Dad," I say, holding Jax's gaze. "Our pleasure. Right, buddy?" I grab another handful of Mt. Jaxon's corded shoulders, which seems a little sexually opportunistic at this point, but what the hell.

Tracee kisses Jax on the cheek. "That would be great, hon. I'll see you back at the house, okay?" She drags Dad away like a puppy on a leash.

Jax turns to me. "What the hell was that?"

I look around as if we're spies behind enemy lines. Too many PFLAGers engaged in muted conversations linger near us. "Later," I say to him. I like keeping him off his usually veneered guard, anyway.

Jax narrows his eyes on me and finally nods in submission. We stand there with Shelby in awkward silence as the room slowly empties out. Tracee and Dad leave with another couple, and both of them wave back at us. Orange Vanna is the only one left in the room. She tidies up the snack table, wrapping up the leftover cookies and, with a shifty glance over her shoulder, stuffs them into her oversized purse.

She spots the three of us staring at her and plasters on a fake-ass smile as she leaves. "Library closes soon, kids. Thanks for coming."

Jax seems to suddenly realize that he hasn't directly acknowledged Shelby's presence. She has that effect on people. She actually prefers it that way. Like a spy hiding in plain sight.

Jax nods at her. "How's it going, Shelby?"

She stares at him like she doesn't know if she wants to punch him or lick him. I know the feeling well. She never verbally responds to him and finally glances over at me. "I'm going home, hooker. See you tomorrow." She looks back at Jax one more time and gives him the I'm-watching-you, two-fingered V-point from her eyes to his and back.

"Bye, Felicia," I say with a chuckle as she strolls away.

"That girl is *so* strange," Jax says, watching Shelby leave. "How the hell did you guys become friends?"

The empty room is eerily quiet and intimate. I relax my shoulders and rest my butt on the back of a chair. "She was the first person to take up for me in middle school when I was bullied for being effeminate. She was a big girl for her age back then. After a few black eyes courtesy of Shelby, the assholes started leaving me alone."

Jax widens his stance and crosses his arms, which only

makes his bulky chest and biceps look bigger. "You said something at the Crusty Cup about me bullying you in middle school, but I swear I don't remember that."

My blood pressure spikes. I shake my head and stand. "Let's just drop it, Jax."

"Wait, if I did something to hurt you or offend you, I want to know, Beck. That's not who I am."

I stare at him long enough to make him shift his weight from one side to the other, but his momentary sincerity is not lost on me. I shake my head at him and sigh with a heavy dose of drama infused. Why do I have a feeling I will regret this?

"Phone," I say, holding out my hand.

After a second or two, looking totally perplexed, he pulls out his phone and unlocks the home screen with the tap of four digits. I take it from him and program my number into his contacts and then send myself a text with only his name so I have his. I hold the phone out to him.

"Saturday night. Ten o'clock. Meet me at the corner of Second Loop Road and South Cashua." It's not a request, and by the incredulous look on Jax's face, he understands as much.

"Are you asking me out?" he says, a stupid grin forming on his lips. "Because if you are, you really need to work on your moves."

I cross my arms so he knows I don't appreciate him throwing my own words back at me. "You're not my type." *Right.* "We're going to get a *real* deejay for the prom of doom. I know a place."

I head for the door and Jax follows me.

"Wait," he says, grabbing my arm from behind. I'd be lying

if I denied the sensation of a thousand invisible needles pricking my skin where he touches me. I turn back to face him.

"You still haven't told me why you're suddenly on board about helping with the prom."

I take a beat and remind myself that I'm dealing with a meathead football player here. I need to break it down for him.

"Did you see the way my dad reacted when I wanted to call my mom about the mayor?"

Jax shrugs and nods.

"And the way your mom tensed up when you mentioned the lady cop?"

"Yeah," he says, taking a step closer to me. "What about it?"

"Well," I say slowly like I'm talking to a six-year-old. "What would happen if your other mom brought a friend to the dance? A friend that Tracee obviously feels threatened by. And what if my mom runs into her old flame the mayor at the dance?"

"What?" Jax says, surprised. "Your mom and the mayor?"

"Yep. They dated in high school or college or something. Dad's always been funny about it. We have a unique opportunity here to get all four of our parents in the same room and stir up some shit. And stirred shit is the best ingredient for heartbreak stew."

Jax cocks his head at me.

"It's not an actual stew . . . never mind," I say. "Look, the bottom line is, we have to make sure this prom goes off without a hitch. Besides, I really do want people like me to have their special school memories too. So we remember more than just hateful names, the harassment, and the ass kickings. And

I'm not about to let Cassidy Charles and a bunch of gay-hating Christian hypocrites ruin that."

A crooked grin curls Jax's plump lips, just as the lights shut off. It was actually a perfectly timed, dramatic close to my speech. *Lights down, scene over.* I couldn't have planned it better if I tried. The theater gods are always with me. Jax and I stand face-to-face in complete darkness. Only the dim red glow of the EXIT sign backlights his frame.

"I guess we'd better get out of here before we get locked in all night," Jax says. His breath tickles my nose. Did he just move closer?

"Right," I say. I try to step around him, but I can't see shit and plow into a row of chairs. Jax grabs me, one hand on my arm, the other on my waist, and holds me upright, pulling me closer to him. His hard body presses against mine, and his cool, Jolly Rancher breath brushes my lips.

"Easy there, tiger," he says in a low and, dare I say, *seductive* voice.

Thank God it's dark enough that he can't see how red my face is, because my cheeks are on fire. We stand there without moving for what feels like forever, his one hand resting just below my waistline and the other gripping my arm. Why is he still holding me like that? Is he waiting for the lights to come back on? I'm utterly ashamed to say that I actually shudder. *Shudder*, for Christ's sake. I'm not proud of it, but it happens.

"Cold?" he says. I can tell he's grinning by the way his voice tightens.

Pushing him away, I find my footing and back up a step, finally free of his dizzying touch. "No. I'm fine. Just clumsy.

Thanks. I have to go." I turn and head in the direction of the EXIT sign, hoping to the good Lord that my path is clear.

"Be careful, Beck," he calls behind me. "It's dark as shit in here."

I make good progress in the general direction of the door. I think I found the aisle. Great.

"All good," I call back, confident of my impending escape.

The glow of the EXIT sign guides me, and I'm nearly home free. That is, until I plow into the snack table, sans Sheila's delicious gluten-free peanut butter cookies. The metal legs scrape loudly against the hardwood floor, and a colorful array of curses flies uncontrollably out of my mouth. I recover quickly enough and finally push through the door, Jax's needling snickers following me the whole way.

# CHAPTER FOURTEEN

# Jaxon

Tiffany's lips are so soft. She smells so good. Her skin is like silk. So why the hell am I thinking about someone else? I stop kissing her.

She pulls away and looks at me. "Is something wrong?"

I lay my head on the pillow and sigh. "Sorry. It's just this thing with my moms has me a little preoccupied." Liar.

Tiffany rests her head in the crook of my shoulder and laces her fingers in mine. We're in my bedroom, because Tiffany's mom is always home, and these days my moms are never home.

"How long have you lived here?" she asks, tweaking my nipple and scanning my room.

"Since my moms adopted me when I was seven," I say. "Why?"

She punches me in my side. "Because your room is always so . . . neat."

I chuckle. "What can I say? I like things to be orderly."

"Do you remember your real home?"

I lose my smile. "This is my real home."

"I meant your birth parents," she says.

I lie there quiet for a moment, trying desperately *not* to remember—the screaming, the crying, living in a constant state of fear. "No," I finally say. "I don't remember them at all."

"Oh." Tiffany pushes my leg off hers without pressing further. "Let me up. I have to pee."

"Sexy."

"Shut up." She bounces up off the bed and shakes her ass all the way into my bathroom. I know what she's doing, but it's just not working today for some reason.

I look over at the clock on the nightstand to check the time, but instead I zero in on the framed picture sitting beside it. It's the one of my moms and me at Lake Marion three summers ago. I'm floating in that ratty old inner tube from the cabin, and they're hanging off the sides, laughing like they're going to tip me over. I think they actually did. We always had so much fun on those trips.

"Bobby said you had a visitor in the weight room the other day," Tiffany calls from the bathroom.

My face flushes with heat. Goddamn Bobby Jenkins.

"Huh?" I call back. Weak. "Don't know what he's talking about."

She sticks her head out. "Beckett Gaines?"

"Oh, him," I say like the asshole I am. "We have calculus together and had a test that morning. He was just returning my study sheet." Lying to her is getting too easy. I grab my phone off the nightstand and check for texts, hoping that if I don't respond she'll drop it.

"Okay, I'm sorry. But it's just not normal," Tiffany calls to me.

Shit. I can't ignore her again. She'll get suspicious. "What's not normal?" I say with a sigh, putting my phone down.

"That your room is so much cleaner than mine."

I look up. Wearing nothing but her pink bra and microscopic panties, she stands in the doorway of the bathroom. I swallow. Hard. She struts around the room, running the tip of her index finger over all my shit. My books, my football gear, my Tom Brady poster, and my neatly racked dumbbells—she even does some suggestive handling of my baseball bat. Her body is sick. Tanned, toned, and perfect. She knows exactly what to do with it too, and it's working. Jax Junior is suddenly wide awake and ready for a playdate. Tiffany slinks over to the foot of the bed and gets on her hands and knees as she crawls on top of me.

"Damn, girl," I say. "You ain't playing around."

She grins and giggles as she unties the drawstring on my gym shorts. Jax Junior is not being the least bit shy, practically forcing his way right through the fabric. When she finally frees him and takes me in her mouth, I lie back, close my eyes, and exhale through the initial shock of pleasure. Tiffany is freaking talented. I mean, like the best. It feels amazing. Of course it does.

So why the hell can't I stop thinking about Beckett Gaines?

# CHAPTER FIFTEEN

# Beckett

It feels like we've been on I-20 for days, but it's only been about an hour. The drive west from Florence to Columbia is an uninspiring one, to say the least. South Carolina definitely has its bright spots—the Grand Strand beaches, Charleston, Hilton Head, and the mountains near the North Carolina border. But the swath of earth in the center of the state is a wasteland of dying small towns where the inhabitants seem to subsist on nothing more than pecan log rolls and boiled peanuts, judging by the billboards. We stop only once for snacks and to pee. We sing and laugh the rest of the way. Actually, this little mindless mini adventure is just what I need before I meet Jax later tonight.

"So, Fussy," Connie asks, "who are you going to ask to the Rainbow Prom?"

In honor of Shelby's eighteenth birthday, I'm treating her to a spa day at the world famous Queefy Le Pew's Pussycat Parlor and Day Spa in Columbia. Sure, there are salons and day spas in Florence, but none staffed entirely by drag queens. And in keeping with that theme, we've decided to address each other only with our drag names for the entire day. Connie Lingus about peed herself when I told her what I had planned for her. She's always been a little apprehensive about getting a makeover, but throw in a few drag queens and complimentary anal bleaching and the girl was all over it.

"To be honest," I say, turning down the Rihanna, "I'm so used to not having a date for these kinds of things that I haven't even thought about it."

"Well, I know one smitten junior who's dying for you to ask him," she says, ripping into a pack of peanuts. She pours the entire bag into her Pepsi and covers the top of the bottle with her mouth so the salty fizz doesn't erupt all over my car. It looks disgusting, but I can't blame her. It's just about the best thing you can put in your mouth.

"Everyone in school expects you and gay Frodo to hook up at some point," Connie says before taking a big swig of peanut Pepsi.

*Note to self: Trademark Peanut Pepsie. Add the e on the end to avoid a copyright infringement lawsuit.*

"So just because we're both gay and out, Carter's my only choice?"

"I don't make the rules," she says, lowering her window a few inches and burping. She blows the peanut Pepsi stink outside because we have manners. "But I'll bet if you don't ask him soon, he'll be asking you."

"Sweet baby Jesus," I say. "Me and Carter Treadwell on a date? Why don't you just usher in the gay apocalypse while you're at it? Sorry. Not happening. What about you, birthday girl? You going to finally grow a pair and ask Chevy to the prom?"

"Not funny, Fussy," she says, staring out the window at the nothingness of central South Carolina. Shelby only ever avoids eye contact when she doesn't want you to see the vulnerability pooling in her eyes. It would be bad for her don't-give-a-fuck rep.

"Why not?" I say, slapping the steering wheel once. "You are Shelby Fucking Timmons, for Christ's sake. The baddest bitch in school and, judging by your erotic short stories, a bona fide freak in the bedroom."

She looks over at me. "Mrs. Davidson gave me an F on those and called my mother."

"Well, you *were* only in the seventh grade, sweetie, but that's beside the point. I'll bet Chevy would love to go to the prom with you," I say, crossing all my toes, hoping I'm right.

"Then why hasn't he asked me?"

I cut my eyes at her. "Connie. *Girl.* You barely breathe when he's around, much less say anything that sounds remotely human."

She doesn't respond. Just stares out at a pasture of catatonic cows.

"Hey," I say, trying to lure her out of this gloomy trance. "What's going on? Really."

She sighs and looks over at me. "Guess what my mom wants to get me for my eighteenth birthday?"

I shrug.

"Lap-Band surgery," she says, looking back out the window. "Fucking Lap-Band surgery."

I grip the steering wheel so hard the leather squeaks, imagining it's her bitch mother's neck.

"I mean, what an awesome way to start your eighteenth birthday, right?" she says. "Does wonders for your self-esteem."

I glance her way. "You're not actually going to—"

"Hell no," she says, looking over at me. "But I told her I'd consider it if she went to rehab."

"Oh no, you—"

"Oh yes, the fuck I did."

Her sly, rosy grin is back, and we high-five each other. It even feels dorky when we're alone.

I turn Rihanna back up to full blast and yell over to Connie. "Don't you worry, Miss Lingus. A fierce new 'do and a freshly bleached anus will do wonders for your self-esteem."

Thanks to the GPS gods and Rihanna, "we found love in a hopeless place" called the Vista along the banks of the Congaree River about thirty minutes later. Actually, it wasn't hopeless-looking at all. The area was much nicer than I'd imagined, with lots of trendy shops, restaurants, and art galleries. We parked in a prepaid lot a couple of blocks away and easily found our destination.

The moment we push through the silver sequined front door, we know we're not in Kansas anymore. The walls of the reception area are completely lined with black and white fur, the hardwood floors painted black with a single white stripe down the middle, and a reception desk along the far wall has a giant set of whiskers on the front. A platinum blonde drag queen wearing six-inch heels and about as big around as one of my legs greets us with a polite smile. She wears a little black dress so tight it looks like it was painted on. Her makeup is flawless and I've never seen such a tiny waist on a man or a woman. It doesn't even seem possible. Like where the hell are her hips and ribs? And her penis, for that matter?

"You must be Connie Lingus and Fussy Bottoms," she says, looking at her computer screen. She glances up at us. "So who's who?"

"I'm the fussy bottom," I say.

"Fussy Bottoms," Connie corrects me with a closed-mouth smile like a ventriloquist. "Not *the* fussy bottom."

I know that, I just got a little tongue-tied looking up at this radiant, magical creature behind the reception counter.

"Well, welcome to Queefy Le Pew's," she says. "I'm Aida Cox and I'll be your concierge today."

I look over at Connie. "Our concierge. Baller."

Another drag queen comes in from the back, and this one I recognize right away. She's quite a bit shorter than Aida Cox and a lot thicker all over. She practically makes Shelby look petite by comparison. She's wearing a black kimono robe thing with a wide white stripe down the back and a wig she must have stolen right out of the Chasing Rainbows Museum at Dollywood. Her face lights up when she sees me.

"Beckett," she says, coming over and kissing me on both cheeks, I'm sure leaving ruby red lipstick marks. "We've been expecting you."

"Thanks, Miss Queefy, but today I'm Fussy Bottoms," I say proudly.

"Well, of course you are, honey," she says, patting me on

the shoulder and stepping behind the counter beside Aida Cox.

"And this is the birthday girl," I say. "Connie Lingus."

Queefy rests her chin on her fist and looks Connie up and down. "We do love a challenge, and you are one big beautiful blank canvas. Don't you worry, honey, when we're done with you, you're going to feel like a queen."

I look over at Connie. I've never seen such a huge and genuine smile on her face. So far, so good.

Queefy checks the computer screen and slaps at the keyboard. "Roger called earlier and gave me his credit card number, so you guys are all set."

Connie looks over at me, her face twisted in confusion. "Roger?"

"Dad and I went to Myrtle Beach last summer to see the tour of *Golden Girls Live*. It's an all drag production based on the show. Queefy played the part of Blanche and she was *a-ma-zing*. We got her autograph after the show. Dad went all fangirl on her and insisted on buying Queefy a drink."

"The things I could do to that man if he wasn't straight," Queefy says, looking up in a wistful daze.

Aida gives her a sideways glance and a neck roll. "Never stopped you before, girl."

"True," Queefy says.

"Are you in anything now?" I say.

"Well, I just auditioned to play Truvy in the all drag production of *Steel Magnolias* in Atlanta," she says. "But the director said I might be a little too *on point*."

"You'd make a *fabulous* Truvy," I say, and she really would.

"We'll see," she says, waving off the compliment. "Okay, Connie girl, you're scheduled for a Brazilian wax and then we have some work to do with you in the salon."

Connie gives me a sharp look. "A Brazilian wax?" She puts her hands on her hips. "Hooker, you know I already keep my shit tight!"

"Tight enough for international relations?" I say.

She ponders this for a silent moment while we all await the verdict. Finally, she sighs. "Well, I guess I do want to be a good ambassador for our country."

I smile, relieved, and Queefy nods her approval.

"And I have you both down for a complimentary anal bleaching," Queefy says, looking up with an eyelash batting smile.

"Oh no," I say. "The complimentary anal bleaching was just for the birthday girl. My anus is just great, thanks."

"Suit yourself, honey," Queefy says. "Aida will take you back."

Aida Cox leads us down a hall and into a unisex bathroom/locker room. We change into our black and white, skunk inspired robes and wait in the small lounge as instructed. There's a snack table that Connie inspects more out of wonder than hunger. We don't see a lot of tiny cucumber sandwiches and petits fours in Florence. Hell, I only know what petits fours are because of my gayness. We're born with the knowledge of such things. I can't explain it.

My massage is performed by a giant black drag queen whose name tag reads KLEENYA BUTTS. This makes me a little self-conscious as I'm buck naked on her table with my ass in her face.

129

*Note to self: Always douche before a massage.*

It's the first professional massage I've ever had, and I find it hard to relax. I'm stiff as a board for at least the first half hour. Kleenya is extremely professional though. She keeps my junk properly covered with a sheet as she works me over like I'm a giant blob of pizza dough. I may not be able to walk for a week. I'm not surprised when I hear Connie's bloodcurdling scream from somewhere down the hall. She has a low tolerance for pain, and she's never been waxed anywhere—much less anywhere near the vicinity of her cooch. I bet she'll be cursing like a motherfucker any minute now.

A string of colorful curses echoes down the hall outside as if on cue. *And scene.*

"Okay, on your knees, sweetie," Kleenya says to me when the hour is almost up.

"Huh?" This doesn't sound good.

"Just get on your knees and keep your head on the table."

I'm too intimidated by Kleenya's size and domineering personality to refuse, so I do as I'm told, pulling the sheet up to keep my ass covered. I look over as Kleenya pulls a couple of exam gloves out of what looks like a tissue box. Oh shit. If she lubes up her finger with K-Y jelly, I'm out of here. What the hell is this, the complimentary prostate exam? But she doesn't grab any K-Y jelly. She douses a cotton ball with some kind of clear liquid, lifts the sheet, and proceeds to rub the stuff all over my ass. I mean, this queen is *all* up in my candy. I want to ask her about ten times what the fuck she's doing, but she works with such confidence, efficiency, and detached clinical professionalism that I feel like questioning her bizarre postmassage methods would be an insult and extremely immature of me. After all, I've never had a massage before, so maybe this is normal. Besides, her name *is* Kleenya Butts. Maybe this is just her signature end-of-massage cleaning.

Next, she rubs a cold cream all up and down my crack—over and around my hole. I am so freaking embarrassed that I close my eyes and pretend I'm in the doctor's office getting treated for ass cancer or something. That makes it all seem less intrusive. The creaming of my asshole is over almost as quickly as it started, thank God. Kleenya wipes the area down with more cotton balls. A minute later she tells me that I'm all done and to take my time getting dressed. I can meet Connie in the salon when I'm ready. I don't waste any time getting off the table and putting my robe back on over my creamy ass.

Aida Cox meets me in the hallway outside the massage room and leads me into a bright, spacious salon area. Four drag queens of varying sizes, shapes, and colors work on clients' hair and makeup while passing barbs back and forth at one another that would make Amy Schumer blush. Connie Lingus sits in a chair on the end with a black apron tied around her neck. Her hair is matted wet and lies flat against her skull. I'm thrilled to find her stylist, a curvy Latina queen, plucking away at Connie's eyebrows. It's like Christmas morning for me. I want to jump up and down and squeal with joy, but I don't think Connie would be amused.

She glares at me. "Calm down, hooker. Get over here and tell me about your massage."

"It was great. How was the Brazilian?"

Connie huffs. "My cooch looks like a giant, angry marshmallow."

I slap my hand over my mouth to keep from laughing in her face.

"The redness will go away, mami," her stylist says. "Just temporary pussy trauma."

"Sorry," I manage to get out with only a squeak of laughter before I pull it together. "If it makes you feel any better, I got my ass disinfected by a queen named Kleenya Butts."

Both Connie and her stylist gawk at me.

"That was the anal bleaching," Connie says, and then loses her shit.

I stand there, clinching my creamy ass cheeks under my robe. *Ew.*

"Don't worry, papi," the stylist says, smiling. "When the cream dries up your cha-cha will be pretty as a peach."

Connie shakes her head and nods at the stylist. "This is Amanda Rimmer. And she says when she's done with me, Frenchy won't be able to keep his hands off of me."

I take her hand and squeeze it, giving her the most sincere face I can muster. "Let's just hope Chevy likes roasted marshmallows."

I spend the next hour getting a manicure, trading lines from *The Golden Girls* with Queefy while she does my eyes, and bending over in front of the full-length mirror in the bathroom with my head between my legs, trying to get a look at my anus. It's not flour white like I expected. Just pretty and pink from stem to stern. I can't believe I waited seventeen years to get my asshole bleached. I wonder what other beauty secrets are being hoarded within the drag community.

When I head back into the salon, Amanda Rimmer is just finishing blowing out Connie, and all I can think is *wow*. Connie's hair has a fresh, golden copper shine and falls in luscious waves around her shoulders. Her cheeks are no longer splotchy, and her face is a single even shade, for once. And I never even realized what beautiful amber eyes she has. Her lips are hooker red—*appropriate*—and even her nose looks thinner. The magic of drag makeup, I guess. And finally, she has two completely separate and normal-sized eyebrows. Connie stares at herself in the mirror in silence, inspecting Amanda's handiwork. She's not smiling and she's not frowning, so I don't know what she thinks about the transformation. She doesn't even see me standing behind her at first, she's so mesmerized by the change.

Finally, she glances up and catches my gaze in the mirror. Her lips slowly curl into a smile, and I can finally breathe. She doesn't hate it. Actually, just the opposite. I can see it in her sparkling amber eyes and in that full faced smile. Connie Lingus, aka my best friend, Shelby Timmons, finally feels as fierce on the outside as she does on the inside.

I bow my head and say a quick prayer for Chevy. He's going to need it.

# CHAPTER SIXTEEN

# Jaxon

As the RideShare driver pulls into a packed parking lot, I peer out the window, wondering if Beck is punking me. A sizable, nondescript building sits at the far end of the lot, with white Christmas lights dangling from its roofline. The trailer mounted LED sign by the road flashes a block lettered message:

COLLEGE NIGHT

2 FOR 1 BEER WITH STUDENT ID

"Is this it?" the driver asks, nodding toward the entrance. "I can drive you up to the door if you want."

"No, this is fine," I say, reaching for the door handle, my palm sweaty and my heart pounding. "I'm not even sure this is the right place." I don't really believe that.

He eyes me in the rearview mirror. "Want me to wait?"

I get out of the car and peek back in at him. "No, that's okay." Because I have a sneaking suspicion that it *is* the right place.

As I close the door, the driver gives me a half-interested

wave and pulls back out into the street, leaving me stranded miles out of my comfort zone. The muted driving beats coming from inside the club draw me in the direction of the entrance. I pass a couple of older guys sitting on the hood of a car, kissing and passing a joint between them. Their brazen inspection of me is thorough, and though all my *parts* are covered in jeans and a pullover shirt, I might as well be completely naked. I lower my gaze and pick up my pace until I reach the door. Emblazoned on the faded red awning above the main entrance is what I can only assume is the name of this fine establishment.

RUFF RIDERS

Great. What the hell has Beck gotten me into? And how does he even expect us to get into a club? A couple of guys push past me, and I realize that I'm blocking the entrance. I move to the side, nodding an apology. They're college aged and their jeans and T-shirts look like they were spray-painted on, accentuating every muscle and curve of their well maintained bodies. They hold hands, and one of them winks at me as they pass. For a moment it actually feels kind of normal and cool, and a small pang of jealousy pinches in my gut. This *is* normal for them.

Also, the obvious has been confirmed. This is a gay bar. I didn't even know there *was* a gay bar in Florence. I mean, of course, there would be, and *should* be, for that matter, but it's just not the kind of place a local high school quarterback/student body president should be seen in. Bad for business. My business, that is. For a split second, I consider pulling up my RideShare app and getting the hell out of there. The glass door opens in front of me and Beck stands there.

He waves me in. "What are you doing standing around out there? Come on."

I try to make my feet move, but all I can do is stare at his long, bare torso and smooth stomach. His nipples are small, slightly oval, and his belly button is flat. His skin glistens with a thin sheen of sweat and his pants sit low on his hips. I don't recall ever seeing Beck without a shirt, and it's especially jarring in this setting. He's also sporting guyliner, something I never understood the concept of until now, seeing it on him. It frames his eyes and adds an air of smoky sexiness to his look. I have to admit, it's hot. So are those tight, black leather pants he's wearing. They hug his ass like a second skin and draw my gaze to a noticeable protrusion in the front.

"Jax," he says, snapping his fingers in my face, rousing me from my gaping inspection.

My feet finally relent, moving me toward him and into a wall of thumping EDM. I nod down at his lower half. "Jesus, how did you get those pants on?"

I could be wrong, but I think I detect the slightest hint of a smile. Either he likes that I noticed how he's rocking those pants, or he just likes that *anybody* notices. The small lobby is dark—black walls, black ceiling, black curtains separating us from the main room. Beck guides me over to a counter illuminated only by one of those old green and bronze banker's lamps. I thought the gays had better decorating skills. Behind the counter sits an entity—part human, part grizzly bear, I think. His muscled, hairy chest is twice the size of mine, and black leather straps frame his furry pecs.

"Ooo," he purrs at me. "Hey there, handsome. ID and shirt, please."

I reach for my wallet. "I'm sorry. ID and what?"

Beck points to a small black and white sign propped by the lamp.

COLLEGE NIGHT

NO SHIRTS ALLOWED

"Seriously?" I say to Beck. Looking around the room, I see that all the guys in the line forming behind us have either already removed or are in the process of removing their shirts.

"Do you think I normally prance around like this?" Beck says, resting his elbow on the counter.

I don't know if he does or not, but as tight, toned, and tanned as he is, he certainly should. I hand the grizzly bear my driver's license and pull my shirt over my head, tucking it in the waist of my jeans in the back. Beck glances at my chest and quickly looks away, which makes me smile. The bouncer hands my ID back to me and snaps a pink armband onto my left wrist.

"So the bartender knows we're underage and can't buy alcohol," Beck explains, tapping his matching wristband with an eye roll. Like the law is such an inconvenience to his Saturday night out on the town.

"Welcome to Ruff Riders, stud," the grizzly bear says to me. "If you get bored with those twinks in there, you can come back out here and keep me company." He smiles and winks. I can tell he's handsome under all that facial hair, but he looks like he could break me in half.

I follow Beck through the parted black curtains and grab

him by the arm when we emerge on the other side. "If anyone finds out I came here—"

"Jax," he says, facing me. "None of the guys here care who you are, just what you look like. And if one of your buddies from school sees you here, why don't you ask him what the hell *he's* doing here?"

When he's right, he's right. "Good point."

Beck turns and disappears in the crowd. I'm right behind him, maneuvering through a virtual sea of toned and muscled man flesh, which is both terrifying and exhilarating. There are so many hands on my skin as I push my way through the mosh of gays that I feel I need a cigarette by the time I catch up to Beck at the bar.

"Well, that was interesting," I say, my cheeks warming. "I think I got about five mammograms and a couple prostate exams just crossing the room."

Beck lets one of those rare grins slip loose. "Fresh meat. They can smell it coming a mile away."

I lean against the bar, facing him. "Do you come here a lot?" Beck rolls his eyes at me and I chuckle. "You know what I mean."

"I've been here a few times on college night," Beck says, scanning the crowd. "Otherwise it's strictly twenty-one and over. It's a fun place. For a queer kid in Florence, it's like gay Disneyland."

I look down at my pink wristband. "Well, I need a drink, and this isn't going to help."

Beck looks around the bar area and suddenly slips away. I follow the crown of his head until he stops at a high top table a few feet away and starts chatting up three guys who look old enough to be his dad. Beck really is something to watch—the way he turns on the charm, touches a shoulder, leans in when he laughs. Within thirty seconds, I can tell by the way six eyes molest him that he has them in the palm of his hand.

One of the guys rests a hand on Beck's hip and gestures down to his pants with the blue cocktail in his other hand. Beck stands back and poses for the table with his hands on hips. He even turns and gives them a lingering rear view. The guys look impressed, as well they should. After a few more laughs and a couple of ass grazes, Beck's back with two shot glasses filled with dark liquid.

He hands me one and raises the other. "Bottoms up!"

I raise my glass in response. "Don't say that too loud in here."

Beck's instant laugh lights his whole face. I like it even better than the sly grin he sometimes sports. By the time we down the shots—tequila—one of Beck's admirers drops two more off. The guy doesn't give me a second look as he moves on. Beck, on the other hand, gets a wink. Judging by the ease with which he flirts, I assume Beck has a lot of experience with guys like that. What's more bothersome is how the thought of that makes me feel. The next time one of them touches his ass, they may lose a hand.

"You make friends fast," I say, leaning into him.

He looks over at the older guys and shrugs. "It seems to be my demographic."

Of course he's being modest. I'm sure he could hold the attention of any age appropriate frat boy in the place, if he wanted.

"Where do all these people come from? There can't be *that* many gay guys at Francis Marion," I say, referring to our local mini university.

"Everyone's home for the weekend. College of Charleston, Carolina, Clemson . . ."

His voice trails off as the volume of the music increases. I move a little closer so I don't have to shout. My hand brushes his, but I pretend not to notice. "So why are *we* here? Getting busted for underaged drinking isn't going to help my scholarship chances."

Beck looks back at me, his eyes looking bigger than ever highlighted in black eyeliner. He points to the deejay booth above the crowded dance floor. "That deejay up there is Justin Black."

When I shake my head and shrug, Beck rolls his eyes at me.

"*Justin Black*," he says, like repeating the name will jog my memory. It doesn't. "He's world-class. He's worked with Beyoncé, Rihanna, Ellie Goulding, you name it. He plays the biggest clubs and parties in the world, but he grew up in Florence. Got his start right here in this club, so he spins here unbilled when he's in town. He's between tours right now. If we can get him to deejay the PFLAG prom, it'll be a huge draw. Trust me."

I nod. "Okay. So do you know the guy or something?"

Beck's eyes go wide. "Me?" He shakes his head and smirks. "No. Not at all. But I've watched him when he's been here before. He's extremely picky about who he invites up to the booth, and you are *exactly* his type. If anybody on the dance floor can get his attention, it's you."

Wow. I'm incredibly flattered and monumentally offended all at the same time. Beck thinks I'm hot. I mean, he didn't come out and say it, but the implication was clear. On the other hand, apparently he thinks my only bankable assets are my face, my muscles, and my ass. It's familiar territory that I am sick to death of.

"Oh hell, no," I say, turning my back to the dance floor. "I'm not shaking my ass just to get noticed by some douchey, Eurotrash deejay."

Beck rolls his eyes at me. "He's from *this* Florence, not Italy."

This guy thinks I'm an idiot. "I know what you meant, Beck. I'm just not comfortable being dangled as sex bait. Especially since, oh, I don't know, *I'm not gay*."

"Exactly. Be sure you tell him that. He has a whole section on his blog filled with sexy pics of half-naked, *straight* jocks. It's his greatest weakness."

I lean in so he'll hear me over the pounding music. "I'm also not a whore."

Beck scrunches his face. "I never said you're a whore." He waves a hand in front of my chest. "But, look at you, for shit sake. If I looked like you, I would walk to class every day butt-ass naked."

I fail to suppress a grin spawned by the mental image of Beckett Gaines strutting down the halls of East Florence High School wearing nothing but that snarky smile, some guyliner, and kicks. *That* I would pay to see.

Beck returns my grin and raises an eyebrow. "Sorry. I just assumed that you were used to using your looks to your advantage."

The blood drains from my face and a flood of heat replaces it. Beckett obviously witnesses my change in color, because his eyes widen.

"That didn't come out right," he says, practically shouting over the music. "I just meant—"

"Wow," I say, turning away from him, my blood coming to an instant boil. "So that's what you think I'm all about. Fine. I guess I'd better get to work and earn my keep."

I don't know what pisses me off more—that he said it, or that it might be true. My anger heating me from within, I down my shot, grab his, and scarf it down too. Either that's three, or I'm already losing count. The tequila burns going down my throat, but its effect is nearly instantaneous and gives me the courage I need. I pound the shot glass down on the table. Yank my shirt out of the waist of my jeans and fling it at Beck. With his mouth hanging open and my shirt draped over his shoulder, I leave him there. Pushing my way through the crush of very tipsy and handsy guys, I head straight to the dance floor.

# CHAPTER SEVENTEEN

# Beckett

Damn. I have to hand it to him. *The Great* Jaxon Parker has some moves. I'm not the only one who notices Florence's own little Magic Mike either. Jax has the attention of practically every guy on the dance floor. The forest of shirtless torsos around him grows so thick that I lose track of him from my vantage point in the bar. Slipping through the crowd, I head up the stairs that lead to the balcony overlooking the dance floor. A cheer erupts from down below just as I reach the top step. I rush over to the railing to see what all the fuss is about. Oh. Of course. They released the soap suds. If these boys *had* shirts on, they would be coming off right about now. But they don't. So they start shedding the only significant piece of clothing they have left—their pants. *Well played, Ruff Riders. Well played.*

Jax's eyes are closed, so he doesn't know that he's surrounded by a soapy sea of thonged cocks. When he finally opens his eyes, he's visibly taken aback. He glances up and we lock gazes. His face hardens, sending a chill down my spine. It's quite clear that I pissed him off royally and he blames me 100 percent for his current predicament. Surprisingly, I do feel a tad guilty. Just a tad.

Jax runs his thumbs down inside the waist of his jeans, unbuttoning and unzipping them with the seductive finesse of a Chippendales dancer. The men around him rub soapsuds all over one another. It looks like Mr. Clean threw an orgy and Jax is ground zero. When he raises his hands in the air, his jeans slide down, exposing white, Calvin Klein boxer briefs filled to capacity in the front and the back.

*Note to self: Cash in college fund and invest it all in Calvin Klein.*

With his jeans bunched around his knees and suds rising around him, Jax runs a hand down his sweaty chest, over glistening abs, and under the waistline of his underwear. His hips and ass grind their way through the sea of flesh like they have a mind of their own. It's just about the sexiest damn thing I've ever seen. And he looks completely comfortable with all the guys dancing around him and ogling his body. For a *straight* guy, anyway. *Interesting.*

A bald, monster of a guy dressed in black pants and a tight black tee slips up behind Jax and immediately my protective nature kicks in. Mr. Clean taps him on the shoulder and motions for Jax to follow him. Jax shoots me a quick look and pulls up his jeans as he follows the guy, much to the dismay of everyone on the dance floor. For a moment I think the bouncer is throwing him out of the club, but instead he leads Jax over to the stairs to the deejay booth. Well, I'll be damned if I wasn't right. He got Justin's attention in record time. And really, how the hell could he not?

I head down the stairs and push my way to the edge of the dance floor as close to the booth as I can get. I want to be sure Jax sees me so he can call me up to close the deal with Justin Black. Jax climbs the stairs, using one hand to hold his jeans up over his crotch. He hasn't bothered to zip or fasten them yet. Smart move. He glances over my way, catching my gaze, and I wave like a freaking dork. He looks straight at me, but his expression doesn't change and he quickly looks away. *What the hell?*

At the top of the stairs, deejay Justin Black slinks over to Jax and offers his hand with a predatory grin. Jax smiles back with every bright, shiny tooth in his head, accepting Justin's hand with the one he was using to hold up his jeans, so down they go. Brilliant move. This guy has skills. Justin's not shy at all about checking out the goods presented to him. Jax leans in and gives the deejay a hug. Okay, wow. Straight boy is going a little overboard here, but I can appreciate the effort. I crane my neck forward so Jax will be able to see me and call me up there. He sees me, all right. He bores a hole right through me as Justin holds their bodies close together and slips a hand under the waistband of Jax's Calvin Kleins and down over the cleft of his ass. Justin's not shy about grabbing a handful of muscled glute, either.

Without warning, a Blanche Deveraux caliber jealous rage shoots through me and I want to rip every spiked hair out of Justin Black's perfectly coiffed head. The reaction surprises the shit out of me, but I can't help it. Watching the guy pawing Jax like that sends me into an unexpected tailspin. Jax doesn't shrink away from Justin's touch. On the contrary. He throws his head back like Justin just said the funniest thing he's ever heard. He must have learned that move from Tiffany, because I've seen her do it a hundred times.

Justin's hand stays glued to Jax's ass cheek. I want to scream at the top of my lungs, *He's in high school, you perv!* But not only does Jax seem fine with the public fondling, when he pulls back from Justin, the bulge in the front of his boxer briefs has grown considerably. Holy shit. *The Great* and *straight* Jaxon Parker has a boner. It doesn't go unnoticed by Justin, either, who gazes down at Jax's crotch and reaches for it. Jax grabs the guy's wrist and a scowl flashes across his face. Before Justin looks back up at him, though, Jax replaces it with a smile, shakes his head, and wags a finger as if to say, *No, no, no, you naughty little boy.*

Interesting. Jaxon Parker is just full of surprises. After a little more techno-drowned conversation to which I wish I'd been privy, Justin and Jax pull out their phones and swap. I can only assume they're exchanging contact information, and at least the activity forces Justin to remove his hands from Jax's ass. Jax uses the opportunity to pull up his jeans, fasten, and zip them. Justin holds up Jax's phone with the screen facing them, drapes his arm around Jax's neck, and grips one of his pecs. They both smile and look at the phone until a flash of light cements their selfie. After they trade phones back and share another sweaty, full-body hug, Jax is finally on his way down the steps. And it's a good thing too, because I am completely worn out just watching it all from the sidelines. Jax looks at me and nods toward the bar. When we finally meet there, he won't look me in the eye.

"Jesus," I say. "You were better at that than I thought you'd be."

"Got the job done, didn't I? Earned my keep?" He holds out his hand and raises his eyebrows. "My shirt?"

His shirt. Shit. I forgot all about it, and it's no longer hanging off my shoulder. I bend down and scan the floor. "I must have dropped it. I'll find it."

"Forget it," Jax says, pulling me up by the arm and practically dragging me toward the door. "Let's get the hell out of here." He glances over his shoulder at me with a haze of disgust clouding his normally bright blue eyes. "I need a shower."

# Jaxon

We don't speak at all for most of the ride home. Beck offered to drive me, so rather than standing shirtless and on display in the parking lot of Ruff Riders waiting for RideShare, I accepted. Beck has barely even looked at me since we got in the car, which is fine with me. I just want to get home and forget this night ever happened. I can still feel that deejay creep's hand on my ass, and my skin is sticky with soapy residue.

I shove my hands in my pockets and slouch down in the seat as much as I can, like I'm trying to hide my nakedness in the leather. "Beck, if you ever tell anyone about that . . ." Fuck. I didn't mean for it to come out like a threat.

Beck stares straight ahead at the road, the passing streetlamps lighting one side of his face. The other side remains a dark mystery. "Tell who about what?"

Cool. He gets it. No need to talk about it.

"About you dancing in your underwear with a hundred or

so horny guys drooling over you, or how Justin Black molested you in the deejay booth?"

I guess we *are* talking about it. "He didn't *molest* me. Jesus. He just grabbed my ass a couple of times."

"I asked you to get his attention, not have his baby."

"Oh, for shit's sake. Do you think I enjoyed having that guy's hands all over me?"

Beck rolls his eyes and mutters under his breath. "Sure looked like you did."

Shit. He saw my boner. "Just please, can we keep tonight between us?"

"Why haven't you told anyone you like dick yet? Tiffany might like to know something like that."

My face heats, and I want to put my fist through the window. He's purposefully badgering me. He could have said "guys," but no, he said "dick." I keep my voice low and restrained. "I've told you already. *I'm not gay.*"

"Yeah, that's what you keep saying. But tonight your junk was saying otherwise."

I could go with the argument that, *Hey, I'm seventeen. A strong breeze can give me a hard-on*—which is true, actually. But maybe if I tell him, he'll understand and keep his mouth shut.

He shakes his head. "What I can't figure out is how someone with two moms, who you apparently love and adore, can be ashamed of being gay."

*Just say it*, I tell myself. *Maybe then he'll quit calling me gay.* "Trust me, Beck. I *love* girls. I love having *sex* with girls." I could leave it there and see if that's the end of it, but I really doubt it will be. The words tumble out of my mouth before I can stop them. "But I'm also attracted to guys."

Beck looks over at me for the first time since we got into the car. If he's shocked by my revelation, I can't tell. His face is like stone.

He raises an eyebrow. "So you're bi?"

I shrug. "I don't know. I guess. Maybe. It's mostly been curiosity and crushes till now. I know I'm not *totally* gay, but I guess I'm not one hundred percent straight, either. Maybe I'm just a very sexual person. Maybe I'll grow out of it. I don't know. Why do I have to put a label on it?"

"Maybe you'll *grow out of it*?" He shakes his head and looks back at the road. "People like labels, Jax. It makes things easier to understand."

"Well, think of me as bi if you want, but *please*, just don't tell anyone. Other than my moms, you're the only one who knows."

"You mean your moms, me, and all the guys you've fucked."

There go my fingers curling into a fist again. "You know, I'm really not the total whore you apparently think I am. I've never *fucked* a guy before, okay? Sure, I've fooled around here and there, at summer camp, on vacations—no one at school though. And it was all pretty PG-13."

Beck brakes at a red light and glances over at me. "Then how do you know you're really bi? Maybe you were just curious. A lot of horny straight guys experiment when they're young."

"Believe me," I say. "I've jacked off enough times watching *Magic Mike* to know it's more than just curiosity."

His lips curl into a grin and he refocuses on the road. A few moments of uncomfortable silence pass before he says anything.

"How many times have you seen it?"

I lower my head and relax my hand. "Probably a dozen."

"Amateur," Beck mutters, and huffs. He jabs his thumb into his chest. "Twenty-three."

My whole face tightens into a grin. "Whoa, dude. That's a lot of wasted swimmers. I'll bet your dad spends a small fortune on paper towels."

"Wet wipes."

"Nice," I say, raising an eyebrow and nodding at him, impressed. "Never thought about that."

Beck shifts in his seat and smiles. "I've been at this a long time. Learned a few tricks along the way."

My lighthearted chuckle fades as I stare out the window. We've stopped at the intersection in front of the Florence Holiness Tabernacle—and me without my gasoline and matches. I glance over at Beck. His eyes are peeled on the stoplight, and he's going on about the various options for masturbatory maintenance like I've never done it before.

I tune him out and gaze down the alley on the right side of the church, spotting a massive black SUV with one of those Jesus fish decals on the back. Only a single lamp hanging over the side door of the building lights it. The door opens and a thin, blond man emerges. He's nice-looking and smartly dressed, maybe in his thirties. He looks side to side and then ducks into the passenger side of the vehicle. Not a second later, a tall, broad man exits the building and locks the door behind him. I recognize him from television. It's Pastor Doug. At least that's what his flock of crazies calls him. *Pastor Doug.* What the hell is that, anyway? I mean, I don't go around introducing myself as Quarterback Jax. Ma doesn't introduce herself as Plumber JoJo. Without his signature send-me-that-twenty-dollar-bill-and-receive-your-blessing TV smile, *Pastor* Doug's countenance is more severe, even a little scary. He jumps into the driver's side of the SUV and starts the engine. The noise draws Beck's attention. He squints, watching the SUV drive away.

The light changes, but he doesn't see it because he's still staring over at the SUV as it disappears around the corner.

"Light," I say.

He looks back at the road and presses the gas pedal. "Oh, sorry. Well, you definitely had a Magic Mike thing going on at Ruff Riders tonight. Where the hell did you learn to dance like that?"

Pride curls my lips before I can stop it. "Not bad, huh?"

"Oh. Way better than not bad. You had those guys jizzing all over themselves. Good thing there was plenty of soap floating around."

I chuckle and relax a little more. "My moms had me in hip-hop dance classes from the time I was nine years old. I got pretty good. Then I started playing sports in middle school and liked that a lot better. A lot less teasing at school too."

The way Beck's face suddenly darkens on a dime unnerves me. Part leftover smile and part fresh scowl. Probably the words "middle school" and "teasing" triggered something.

"Is that why you did it?" he says evenly.

Are we really doing this again? He brings it up, then he doesn't want to talk about it, and then he *does* want to talk about it. It's like I have two Tiffanys in my life.

"Did what, exactly?" I say, trying to keep my shit together. "I'm sorry, but I really don't know what you're talking about. If that makes me a dick, then I guess I'm a dick."

Beck turns his attention back to the road as we pull into my neighborhood. I guide him left, then right, then left again. He doesn't say anything else until he pulls into the driveway and kills the engine.

He turns his body toward me and looks me in the eye. "Before eighth grade, you and I weren't really friends, but you were always nice to me, at least."

I don't say anything. He obviously needs to get something off his chest.

"Then you started hanging around the jocks, and some of those guys made middle school *hell* for me. Called me every hateful name their tiny little brains could come up with and sent me home with more than a few black eyes, just because I was who I was and didn't give a shit what anyone thought about it. Then *you* became part of that group. And you weren't so nice to me anymore."

"Beck, I *never* called you a name, and I certainly never laid a hand on you. I would never do that."

"No. But you were there, and you did nothing."

The words hang in the air between us like three bullets traveling in slow motion. Aimed at me. *You did nothing.*

"Actually, you did do something," he says with a crack in his voice that resonates in my chest. "You laughed. When they called me names like 'skinny little faggot,' you laughed. When they pushed me around, you did something too. You walked away. You were the rising star of the JV team and becoming one of the most popular kids in school. All those guys looked up to you. Hell, *I* looked up to you. *And* you have two moms. Of all people, I thought *you* would stand up for me. But you never did."

My heart plunges to my stomach. The memories flood my brain in one giant tidal wave of shame. All the names. All the roughhousing. Jesus. I'd convinced myself it was all harmless fun. But it wasn't fun, not for Beck. And I didn't *do* anything to stop it, which is almost worse than if I smacked him around myself. After what I went through as a little kid, how could I stand by and watch that happen to someone else?

"You're right," I say, my voice wobbly. I glance down at my hands, because like the coward that I am, I can't look at him right now. A dozen excuses rise in my throat and rush to the tip of my tongue, but that's where they stall out and die.

*I was trying to fit in.*

*I wanted to be friends with the jocks because they made me feel safe and strong.*

*Yes, I had two moms, but I didn't want to bring attention to that.*

*If I took up for you, they would have thought that I liked you—which I did.*

But those are all just empty excuses. So I swallow them back down.

"Beck, I don't know what to say. I'm sorry." There's so much more I *should* say, but I leave it at that. I have to look at him now. He deserves that at least. When I finally do, the tears pooling in his eyes break me. He wipes them away. Fast. Like my sudden inspection reminds him of their presence. Beck sits forward in his seat, staring out the windshield. I can almost see the protective veneer being reapplied to his face like makeup. His eyes dry quickly. His jawline tightens. His lips are a thin line across his face. I can tell that my feeble apology did little to quiet his inner demons. He has to withdraw now—put up walls to protect himself. I can certainly understand that. Poor guy. Just like in the gym, I have the urge to reach over and hug him. But just like in the gym, I don't.

"Thanks." The crack in his voice lingers. He clears his throat to extinguish it.

"Jesus," I say, touching his knee. "Don't *thank* me for apologizing for being such a dick to you."

He glances down at my hand with a raised eyebrow and I withdraw it. "Sorry." I guess we're back to him being repelled by me.

"So who's this Doris woman you rubbed in Tracee's face at the PFLAG meeting?" he asks, abruptly changing the subject.

I take a deep breath and exhale all the tension of the past five minutes out of my lungs. "Doris is a cop. And she's also an ex of my mom's."

Beck looks over at me. "Tracee?"

I nod. "They were together for about a year, back in the day. Florence's lesbian community is small, so it was inevitable that Doris's and JoJo's paths would cross eventually. They actually hit it off pretty well, which really gets Mom's panties in a wad. She thinks Doris has a thing for JoJo."

Beck nods. "Lesbians can get hella jealous."

I shake my head at him. "I've seen the way Doris looks at JoJo, and I think Mom is right." I shrug. "It couldn't hurt to have a police presence at the Rainbow Prom, right? In case those Jesus freaks get out of hand."

Beck grins. Finally.

"If JoJo and Doris are at the prom together," I say, "it'll send my mom into a royal tizzy. Then your dad will see that she'll always be hung up on women. Just need to find a way to get JoJo and Doris together again. And soon."

"Wow," Beck says with a nod of approval. "That's actually a decent plan. So now we have to get Doris the cop and Tom the mayor to come to the prom. He's the one person that would send my dad into a jealous rage, or at least my dad's version of a jealous rage."

"How are you going to get to the mayor?" I say. "He doesn't exactly just stroll around town."

Beck grips the steering wheel at ten and two. "Can you meet me at the Crusty Cup tomorrow morning at eleven?"

I nod and shrug. "I guess so."

Beck nods me toward the door, a not so subtle hint that it's time for me to go. I open it and pry myself out of his miniature car.

"Dress nice," he says, leaning over and restarting the car, which barely registers any sound.

I lean down and peer inside. "Why? Where're we going?"

A mischievous grin stretches across Beck's face. "Church."

## CHAPTER NINETEEN

# Beckett

Living in the ass crack of the Bible Belt, you can't throw a rock without hitting a church, and Florence is no exception. As I sit on the bench in front of the Crusty Cup, sipping my tea and waiting for Jax, I spot three just in my current line of sight.

A couple of blocks down on my left sits Palmetto United Methodist, one of the oldest congregations in town both in structure and demographics. Facing off with PUM on the opposite side of the street is the less stuffy and more modern construction of Christ Assembly of God, where Cassidy Charles goes. And just across the street to my right sits First Baptist of Florence, a beacon of sophisticated Southern religion and status. All the *right* people go to First Baptist, including Florence's wealthiest families—the Winthrops, the Danielses, and even our newly elected mayor, Tom Davenport.

Since Justin Black moved away, the mayor is our only *real* local celebrity. He's famous more for his family name, fortune, and his future political ambitions, though. Everyone believes he'll be living in the governor's mansion in a few years before moving on to Washington. More important, there's history between the mayor and my mom. Although I don't know *any* of the details, the mere mention of that history makes my dad squirm like Donald Trump at Taco Bell.

I haven't talked to Shelby since we got back from Columbia yesterday, so I shoot her a quick text.

*Do it tomorrow.*

Her reply comes immediately.

*Do what?*

Ugh. She knows what the hell I mean.

*Ask him.*

She doesn't reply for a full minute. Then a message pops up.

*Sorry. Mom's drunk on Bloody Marys.*

*Hmmm,* I type. *No Lap-Band surgery for you!*

She replies with a wink emoji, which means she has to go. Poor girl. Her mom is one hot mess.

A red pickup rambles down the road, drawing my attention. Lesbian mom number two, JoJo, pulls up to the curb, leans forward, and waves at me through the front windshield. We've never actually met, but she has a nice face—thick, round, and a sweet smile that stretches the width of it. With just a glance I decide I like her and wave back. Maybe it's because she looks like a Tonka truck in a town full of Matchbox cars. I can certainly relate to sticking out like a sore thumb around here. Or maybe I feel sorry for her, because I know that her wife walked out on her and is now screwing my dad. To be cheated on is one thing, but to be cheated on with someone sporting body parts you can't fully compete with must be a real kick in the cooch.

*Note to self: Google strap-ons.*

Jax hops out of the truck and pushes the door closed. He waves back at his mom as she pulls away. He's dressed in typical Carolina boy, dressy-casual attire—a starched-within-an-inch-of-its-life white polo button-down with a red tie, khakis, and shiny cordovan loafers—sans pennies. Though I wear a similar ensemble, the way Jax's body fills out his clothes makes me feel sloppy and like I will be a sexual disappointment the rest of my life.

"Sorry I'm late," he says. "Had to catch a ride with JoJo. Punctuality is not exactly her strong suit lately."

I stand and check the time on my phone. "The service has probably started." I look up at him, pocketing my phone. "You don't have a car?" I didn't mean it as an accusation, but it comes out like one.

Jax's cheeks redden and he shakes his head. "No. Money's a little tight right now. Maybe I'll be able to get something used to take to college, *if* I get the football scholarship."

Though I don't see how there is room for them, he shoves his hands in his pants pockets and looks down. I feel like I've embarrassed him, which really wasn't my intention. He's just the kind of guy you assume has a new Beemer sitting in the school parking lot, but that apparently couldn't be further from the truth. Apparently, I don't know as much about *The Great* Jaxon Parker as I thought I did. He's actually sort of like a real person.

"We'd better get in there," I say, tossing my cup in the trash.

He touches my arm. "Beck, I just wanted to say how sorry I am about middle school."

"You apologized last night," I say, retucking my shirt as an excuse to pull my arm away from him. I don't want to talk about this again, and I don't know why it feels like a thousand tiny needles pricking my skin when he touches me, but it startles me every time. I nod in the direction of the church. "We're late."

He sighs and relents. "I never knew you went to church," he says, crossing the street beside me.

"I don't."

I allow two smartly dressed older ladies to pass in front of us. Organ music and a chorus of singing voices spill out of the front door of the church when the ladies reach the top of the steps and enter.

"So what are we doing here?" Jax asks.

I stop a step above him and turn to face him. His eyes sparkle like blue diamonds in the bright morning sun. *Damn him.*

"The new mayor goes here," I say.

Jax smiles. "You want to ambush him at church?"

"He talked about equality a lot in his campaign. What better way to show his support for the LGBT community than to make an appearance at the first ever Rainbow Prom?"

I turn, but Jax grabs my arm and I flinch. There go those damn needles again.

As I turn back to face him, he pushes his fingers through his hair. It falls dutifully back into place. Even his hair is annoyingly perfect.

"What?"

He smirks. "You're pretty good at this."

I wave him away. "Oh please. This is *Golden Girls* 101. Watch and learn."

"Golden what?"

I cock my head at him, incredulous. *"The Golden Girls."*

Jax shakes his head and shrugs.

I turn and climb the steps. "I can't even look at you right now."

Jax snickers behind me—an amused snicker, not a mean one—and I fight the smile curling my lips. As we step inside the vestibule of the church, we're greeted with the rousing sound of a few hundred voices belting out "How Great Thou Art" at the top of their lungs just beyond two swinging doors. A cheerful older man stands guard, looking fit and dapper in a gray suit with an official-looking black name tag. It says his name is Usher, like the singer. Extremely cool name for an old white dude.

Usher gives us a broad smile and pulls open the sanctuary door. That's the thing I notice right away about the congregants of First Baptist. They smile. *A lot.* It's a stark difference from the scowling faces and turned up noses you see coming out of the Florence Holiness Tabernacle on Sunday mornings. Those people look like someone ate a lot of asparagus and then pissed in their offering plates.

Just inside the sanctuary, a much younger man in a sharp suit and also named Usher—must be related—hands us each a bulletin and points us in the direction of the back row, where a few empty seats remain. The place is packed. People stand holding hymnals and singing with varying degrees of commitment. Jax follows me as I step into the row and stand next to an elderly woman with a fabulous crown of swept up gray hair. She smiles at me and offers to share her hymnal. When I accept, she pats my arm with grandmotherly affection. By the fourth verse, I'm feeling more relaxed than I thought I would in a place like this. I glance over at Jax. His hair drips with sweat.

I lean over and whisper in his ear. "You okay?"

He stares straight ahead and nods. Weird. Maybe churches make hot people nervous. Like God knows they sold their soul to Satan in exchange for six-pack abs and a chiseled jawline.

*Note to self: Check Jax's scalp for the mark of the beast.*

After what feels like forty-eight verses, the song finally ends, and we sit on the thickly padded pews. A pleasant-looking man with salt-and-pepper hair approaches the pulpit. The minister, I assume, though I expected fancy robes, not a navy suit. Apparently, the Baptists don't roll that way.

As the minister rattles off a laundry list of announcements, I scan the sea of well coiffed heads, searching for the mayor. Unfortunately it's not a very diverse looking group of people and not a great vantage point here on the back row. I give up for the moment and glance over at Jax again. With his eyes peeled on the minister, he dabs his forehead with the back of his hand, and for a second I wonder if he's going to faint. The nice lady beside me reaches across and offers him a tissue. Jax accepts with a nod and a weak smile. She gives my arm a feeble squeeze, and I get all gooey inside. I can tell this woman is a baller Christian, like the real kind. They're like unicorns in this town.

Jax wipes his face with the tissue and steals a glance to his left. I follow his gaze, spotting the subject of his discomfort, and it *definitely* ain't Jesus. Tiffany Daniels sits on the end of a pew a few rows down, staring at us over her shoulder with a mix of confusion and horror marring her face. Jax's worlds are colliding, and I'm like the huge, pink meteor locked on a crash course.

I lean over and whisper in his ear, "Do you want to leave?"

Tiffany's eyes widen, and I half expect steam to shoot from her ears any second now. What the hell does she think I'm doing? Telling him how I want to lick his balls while the minister reads John 3:16?

Jax gives a quick shake of his head, so I continue my fruitless search for the mayor while the minister drones on about compassion and acceptance. Only bits and pieces of the sermon seep into my uninterested brain, but I get the gist of it. Toward the end of the twenty minute sermon, I finally spot the mayor's handsome profile one row in front of us, but on the other side of the sanctuary. *Gotcha.* I keep my eyes peeled on him until we're directed to stand for the final hymn.

Jax looks over at me. "Stay here."

It clearly wasn't meant as a suggestion. He stands and slips out the back door with little fuss. Tiffany is immediately on her feet and follows him through the door held open for her by old Mr. Usher.

As soon as the minister says "Amen" at the end of the benediction, I set my sights on the mayor and turn to leave. The nice lady grabs my arm, drawing my attention. She smiles at me, her eyes glassy with tears, and my heart breaks. I never want this sweet old lady to cry again.

"I hope you will come back to visit us," she says with a weak and crackled voice, dabbing the corner of her eyes with a tissue.

I think she genuinely means it too. I just wish I knew why she was so sad.

"And if you do, I usually sit right here." She winks at me, letting me know not to worry about her tears. I don't know what's come over me, but I hug her. I'm not a hugger, mind you—only with Mom and Dad. Hopefully, I'll enjoy hugging my first boyfriend when I finally meet him. I guess I should probably also hug the guy who pops my cherry, just out of the sheer relief and gratitude. That would be the least I could do, I suppose. But I probably shouldn't be thinking about that while standing in church hugging this sweet old lady. As I pull away, I smile back at her and then make a beeline toward Tom Davenport.

A swarm of people have already surrounded him. Everyone wants to shake hands with the new mayor and presumed future governor. He probably goes through this every single Sunday. What a pain in the ass that would be. As I wait my turn to kiss his ring, or his ass, or whatever protocol requires, I glance over my shoulder to the back of the sanctuary. No sign of Homeo and Julie Wet. There must be trouble in paradise.

"Tom Davenport."

When I look back, the mayor stands right in front of me, holding out his hand. I look down at it like he has leprosy before coming to my senses and accepting it. He smiles with like 185 sparkling white teeth while giving my hand a firm squeeze that actually makes me wince a little. His close-cropped hair shows only the slightest signs of graying around the edges. His face is kind and campaign poster ready with what Mom used to call "bedroom eyes."

"Hello," I say, forcing myself to let go of the man's hand so the Secret Service doesn't tackle me to the ground or something. I don't know if it's the piercing gaze of those hazel eyes, or the fact that the mayor of Florence is a total DILF, but I feel an oral purge coming on, and I'm helpless to stop it.

"I'm Beckett Gaines, and I was wondering if I could talk to you about the upcoming PFLAG prom on the twenty-third—actually, they're calling it the Rainbow Prom, but I wasn't consulted on that—it's going to be amazing, by the way—we're pretty close to locking down Justin Black to deejay—he's a bit of a sleazebag, but he's like the hottest deejay spinning right now—but the Holiness Tabernacle whackadoos are planning to protest at the prom, and we just want the queer kids to feel safe and have a good time—so I was wondering if you could possibly come—you know, have sort of a mayoral presence, let the city know that you don't think gay kids are freaks, or that fags will burn in hell like the Jesus tweakers will be shouting at them—I mean, everyone thinks you're so bae and everything, and it would send a really strong message if you came."

I force my mouth closed. Purge over. Shit. I just called the mayor "bae." I don't know how long that grin has been resting in the corner of his mouth. Actually, I think I blacked out about forty-five seconds ago and just went on autopilot. But if I've offended him in any way, there's no trace of it on his stylishly stubbled face.

He squints one eye at me and asks the impatient old fart

tapping him on the shoulder to give us a minute. "What did you say your name was?"

I clear my throat and try to find my voice down in there somewhere. "Beckett. Beckett Gaines."

Something sparkles in his eyes. If he weren't so good-looking, I might even call it shifty or pervy.

"You're Lana's son."

*Bingo!* I give him my mom's big, squinty smile and cock my head like she would, just to seal the deal. I manage to stop myself before I sling her imaginary long hair over my shoulder. "Yes. Yes, I am."

He nods and scans my face like a dermatologist in search of blackheads. He's probably looking for traces of Mom.

"I haven't seen Lana in a long time," he says. "How is she?"

"She's fine," I say, and *thank you very much for the opening.* "She's actually back in town."

He cocks an eyebrow. "Really? I would love to see her sometime." A dimple forms in his left cheek like a Disney animator just drew it there. "We went to high school together. We used to be . . . close."

"Wow," I say, feigning surprise. "Really? She never mentioned that."

The dimple disappears and the sparkle in his eyes fades. Shit.

"I mean, she never talks much about life before my dad," I say, trying to recover. "I guess out of respect for him. They're divorced now, though."

His corneal spark flickers back to life. Cue the dimple animators.

"She'll be at the Rainbow Prom." I haven't actually asked her yet, but I know she'll be the easy one, as much as she wants to jump back into my life with both feet.

The mayor's dimple does, in fact, return. He looks me up and down, but not in a pedophile kind of way. "How old are you, Beckett?"

"Seventeen," I say.

He nods and waves to some guy who pats him on the back as he passes. "Seventeen," he says, crossing his arms over his chest. "How in the world were you able to get Justin Black to deejay this prom of yours?"

I shove my hands in my pockets and cock my head at him like we're friends now. "You know who Justin Black is?"

He glances down and chuckles, shifting his weight to one side. "I'm not *that* old. I know he's a Florence native, and I do have a daughter around your age. She's a freshman at Furman. I know she'd love to meet Justin Black."

I already know he has a daughter at Furman. I Google-stalked him this morning. Her name is Sloane. He's a single dad. A widower. Voter catnip.

"Oh, really? I didn't know," I lie. The minister is circling. I have to wrap this up. "So you'll come? And absolutely bring your daughter. I'll make sure she gets to meet Justin. It's Saturday the twenty-third. East Florence High gym."

He squints his eyes as he studies me. "I would definitely win Dad of the Year if Sloane got to meet Justin Black." His smile broadens and he sighs. "I'll check my calendar. I didn't even know we had a PFLAG chapter in Florence, but I'd be honored to lend my support." He must feel the minister's presence bearing down on him, because he takes a step closer to me and squeezes my shoulder. The toothy campaign smile has been replaced by a sincere and pleasant stare. "If you need anything else to make this Rainbow Prom a success, feel free to drop by my office. I'm there pretty much every day right now, even weekends. And tell your mother I said hello."

As Mayor Tom Davenport turns to greet the minister, his parting wink tells me he'll move heaven and hell to be at the prom to see Mom. I turn and walk up the aisle toward the exit, feeling quite pleased with how things are coming together. One mom down. One Tonka truck to go.

# CHAPTER TWENTY

Jaxon

"I just don't get it, Jax," Tiffany says, getting red in the face. "First the coffeehouse and now church? What the hell is going on between you and Beckett Gaines? What aren't you telling me? And don't lie to me."

We stand at the bottom of the steps outside the church as people file out. I try to keep my voice contained. "You're acting ridiculous, Tiff. Like I can't even go to church with a friend without you losing your shit."

She cocks her head at me. "Since when are you and that little fag friends?"

The word stings. It's not like I haven't heard her use it before, but it's different now. We're at church. And she's talking about Beck.

"Oh my God," she says, planting her hands on her hips. "Are you gay?"

"No," I say, a little too quickly for my own comfort and wishing she would keep her voice down. I smile at a lady passing by. "I'm not gay." I shake my head, like I am about to break a confidence, but it's the only thing I think she'll buy at this point. "As crazy as it sounds, his dad and my mom are dating."

Tiff does a double take. "But your mom's married. To another *lesbian*. And you said this separation of theirs was just temporary."

"Yeah, I'm not so sure now," I say, hanging my head and trying to look as dour as possible to encourage sympathy. I glance down and fake a sniffle. Shameless.

"Oh my God, Jax," she says. "I'm so sorry."

I look up at her. "I haven't given up on them just yet."

I tell her about Mom and Roger dating and about JoJo possibly taking a job in Greenville. But I *don't* tell her about the Rainbow Prom, or Ruff Riders, or getting caught cruising around on a gay hookup app.

She takes a step closer to me and puts a hand on my arm, squeezing my bicep. "Is there anything I can do?"

Translation: *Do I want to have sex with her*? It's her answer for everything. Not that I ever minded in the past.

I shake my head and glance over at the door, looking for Beck in the crowd. "No. I'll be fine."

When I look back, her face has hardened again. Tiffany isn't used to rejection. "That still doesn't explain why you came to *my* church with Beckett Gaines. I mean, what would the guys on the team think if they saw you hanging out with that nellie queen?"

Heat floods my cheeks and I turn to face her, a hard edge framing my voice. "Lay off him, Tiff. He's a sweet guy who hasn't had it as easy as we have."

Tiffany's eyes widen to the size of golf balls. "He's *sweet*?"

"Jesus!" I say, throwing my hands up. "Stop twisting my words."

I get a few inquiring-mind stares shot my way as people file past us and down the steps. Beck exits the church and heads in our direction. Terrific.

"Hey, Tiffany," he says cautiously as he approaches.

Tiffany crosses her arms, creating a physical barrier between them, and gives Beck the only greeting she can manage—her Sunday morning version of the stink eye. It's the same as usual, but she's wearing nicer clothes. A moment of awkward silence hovers over our little triangle. Thank God Tiffany's mom calls out to her.

Tiffany gives Beck a final once-over, silently judging his appearance like I've seen her do to her friends a thousand times. Then she narrows her judgmental gaze on me. "I have to go. Call me later. We're not finished with this." She turns on her heel and marches down the sidewalk toward her parents, her arms crossed tightly over her chest the whole way.

"Everything okay?" Beck asks, shoving his hands in his pockets.

"Just typical Tiffany shit."

"Is it about me?"

I hedge. "Don't worry about Tiffany."

Beck slings his hair out of his eyes. "Sorry."

"You don't have anything to be sorry about," I say. It comes out sounding a lot more intimate than I'd intended, so I change the subject. "Did you talk to the mayor? Is he coming to the prom?"

171

"I think so, but we have to deliver on Justin Black. Have you heard from him yet?"

I pull out my phone and check my texts. "Nothing yet. I'll text him again."

"No," Beck says a notch too loud. He looks around, realizing it himself. "I'm sure he'll text you if he can do it."

Well I'll be damned. I think he's jealous.

"So what's the deal between you and Tiffany, anyway?" Beck asks, changing the subject abruptly. "She's your girlfriend, right?"

"I know it sounds stupid, but *it's complicated*," I say, using air quotes.

Beck hangs his head and chuckles. "It does sound kind of stupid," he says. "Everyone at school assumes you guys are a couple."

"I know. We are, I guess."

He looks up again. "You guess?"

I flatten my voice. "Like I said, it's complicated."

He raises his hands in surrender. "Sorry. Didn't mean to pry."

The old woman who sat next to him in church walks by and blows him a kiss. Beckett mines grabbing the kiss out of the air and throwing it back at her. Her whole face lights up, and she waves good-bye. I totally get what she feels. Beck seems to have that effect on people. He has that effect on me.

"I think now *you* have a girlfriend," I say, nudging him playfully in the arm with my elbow.

Beck shakes his head and looks away. I could swear his cheeks redden. He heads down the sidewalk, and I follow after him. "Hey. Do you have plans tonight?"

"Just hoping I don't have to spend it with Tracee," he says over his shoulder. "No offense."

"None taken. I feel the same about your dad. I'm having dinner with JoJo. She Crock-Pots a mean roast. Want to join us?"

Beck stops on the sidewalk and turns to face me, his face twisted with confusion or surprise. Maybe both. "Okay. I guess so."

I take a step closer to him and lower my voice. "Can you see if Shelby is free too?"

"That'd be okay with your mom?"

"I didn't mean for her to join us for dinner, exactly," I say. "I have an idea that requires an accomplice."

Beck smiles. "Look, don't get me wrong, I *love* Shelby. But she's not the best at following basic instructions."

"Can she throw a rock through a window?"

He raises an eyebrow. "Now that, I'm pretty sure she can do."

"Good," I say, slapping him on the back. "Then give her a call."

He starts walking again. "How does this have anything to do with breaking up your mom and my dad?"

"I may not be a Golden Girl, or whatever," I say. "But I have a few tricks up my sleeve. I'm not just brawn and beauty, you know." Jesus. I hope he knows that was a joke.

There it is. The faintest hint of a smile creeps up on his face even as he fights to snuff it out.

# CHAPTER TWENTY-ONE

# Beckett

As I follow her into the dining area of her double-wide, I feed JoJo the line. "Where are our seats?"

If there is a God, she will get it. Surely she will. Much to Jax's dismay, it's all we've been talking about for the last half hour.

JoJo stops, turns to face me, and plants a hand on her hip. Slipping into character with a snarky but sexy Southern drawl, she says, "I don't know. If history teaches us anything, mine will be next to a baby who smokes."

It's official. There is a God.

JoJo and I erupt into laughter. Jax looks at us like he'll be calling the men in white with the straitjackets at any moment. He hit the jackpot with *this* mom—she's so much better than Tracee. Not only is she sweet and funny, but apparently, she watches TV Land at least as much as Dad and I do. She loves *Golden Girls* too, but *Designing Women* is her jam, and she can quote lines from it until she's blue in the face.

Jax still looks lost. I cock my head at him. "Come on. Julia Sugarbaker? Really? Nothing?"

He shrugs his shoulders and shakes his head.

JoJo pulls out a chair for me. "Don't bother, Beck. Jax only watches football and plays video games. He has no idea who the Sugarbakers are."

I sit and make the sign of the cross over my chest even though I'm not Catholic. "Forgive him, Lord."

"I'm in the room, you know," Jax says, taking a chair directly across the table from me.

I check my phone for the time and then set it to silent. We got out of that living room just in the nick of time. I kept hinting about how good the roast smelled, but I had JoJo spellbound with my Suzanne Sugarbaker impression, so it's understandable that she didn't pick up on my fake hints of hunger. Maybe I should have just said, *Hey, y'all, we need to get up out of this living room before a huge-ass rock comes crashing through that lovely bay window and knocks one of us the hell out.* If Shelby doesn't flake, that is.

"Hey, Ma," Jax says. "Have you given any more thought to going to the Rainbow Prom?"

Like a bull in a china shop, this one. A bull with a face like Brad Pitt's secret love child, that is. I jump in to help Jax out before he blows our cover.

"They need more chaperones. We're expecting a bigger crowd now that Justin Black is on board." I keep saying that Justin Black is *on board*. Jax hasn't actually heard from the guy yet, but I'm trying to stay positive.

Jax unfolds his napkin and drops it in his lap. "He's this big deejay—"

"I know who Justin Black is, Jax," JoJo says. "I don't live under a rock."

She passes him a platter of roast cut into several succulent chunks, drenched in au jus and sitting on a bed of carrots, potatoes, pearl onions, and celery. Southern food porn.

"Yeah, Jax," I say under my breath. "*Everyone* knows who your buddy Justin is." I glance into the living room, as if we might not have heard the bay window shattering. Shelby's late. I give JoJo my most sincere, sympathetic pout. "I get that it might be uncomfortable for you at the prom with Tracee there. I just think it would be great for Jax if *both* his moms were there."

Jax cocks his head, glares at me across the table, and speaks very slowly. "I told you I'm not going to the prom."

I plaster on a smile and grit my teeth at him, matching the drag of his words. "Why the hell would you expect her to go if you aren't there?"

JoJo holds a fork full of meat in the air and glances back and forth between us before landing on Jax. "He's right. The only reason I would go is to support you."

An awkward silence settles over the table. Jax shifts in his chair and squares his shoulders. JoJo chews her meat slowly and lets him squirm. *Baller mom.*

She waves her fork in my direction but stares at her son. "Does he know?"

Jax looks down at his plate and nods.

She puts her fork down and wipes her mouth as a smile

spreads across her face. "Is this a meet-my-mom date?"

"Jesus, Ma," Jax says, a little louder than necessary. "No. We're just friends."

His answer isn't a shock, or even mildly surprising. Still, the way he says it stings, like it's the most ridiculous idea ever conceived. Not that I would ever want more than a friendship with Jaxon Parker. I'm not sure he even deserves my friendship after the way he treated me in middle school. Forgiveness is one thing. Forgetting is something else entirely. I never forget.

"But you told him about the bi thing, apparently," JoJo says.

"He told me," I say, fortifying my voice so Jax knows that I don't give a shit that he thinks just the idea of us being more than friends is preposterous. "He likes cooch with a side of sausage. No big whoop."

JoJo nearly chokes trying not to spit carrots and potatoes all over my face. Jax kicks my leg under the table.

I flinch and wince. "Ow! Jesus. What?"

JoJo waves at him to leave me alone as she dry-heave laughs. Speaking of dry heaves, what the hell is keeping Shelby? We should be cleaning up glass and calling Officer Doris by now. Unfortunately, Shelby is about as dependable as a wet dream.

"Sorry," I offer halfheartedly, and stab my meat with the fork.

"It's fine, Beck," JoJo says, patting my arm. "I don't know if Jax told you or not, but I'm actually the irreverent one in the family." She smiles apologetically to Jax. "Sorry, sweetie.

I didn't mean to jump to conclusions. But just so you know, I'm all for this union, whether it's just as friends or something more. You need someone like Beck in your life."

I'm as speechless and dumbfounded as Jax appears to be.

"Your sexual orientation aside, if you went to that prom, it would send a strong message," she says to Jax. "You're so well liked in school and your teammates look up to you."

Jax shakes his head. "It's not that simple, Ma. It's different in the locker room, where guys call everything 'gay,' like it's some all encompassing derogatory slam, and everyone laughs like we're all on the same page about it all. Plus, I'm their quarterback and this is still the Deep South, for Christ's sake. I mean, it's hard enough having two moms. All bets are off if they find out I'm bi."

JoJo nods her head and leans back in her chair, her sweet face drawn. She reaches over and takes his hand in hers. I feel like I'm intruding on something personal, and now Shelby's ten minutes late.

JoJo sighs. "I know it's not the same and it's scary, but don't sell yourself short, Jax. Or your friends, for that matter. They just might surprise you, and I'm positive that you'll surprise yourself. You're the most resilient person I know. You're a survivor."

Jax nods and hangs his head. At this point I can't tell if he's acting or really emotional. I busy myself by slipping my phone out of my pocket and glancing at it under the table. No text from Shelby. I hope she's okay. Outside in the distance, the low, husky bark of a dog sounds, urgent and agitated. Like Lassie trying to tell someone that Timmy fell down in the well. Now I'm worried. JoJo's double-wide sits on top of a hill. The front yard slopes down at a pretty steep clip, and the law of gravity has not been kind to Shelby over the years.

Jax clears his throat, regaining my attention. "How did you know you were gay before you had sex with a guy for the first time?"

I chuckle and pocket my phone. "How did you know you were attracted to girls before you first had sex with one?"

Jax shifts in his seat uncomfortably and glances over at JoJo. "I just knew."

I shrug at him. "Same with me being gay. I just know— even though I'm technically still a virgin."

Shit. The damn word rolled right off my tongue before I could stop it.

*Note to self: Invent Imodium for the mouth. Think of a catchier name for it.*

"*You're* a virgin?" Jax raises his eyebrows like they're reaching for the ceiling.

"Jax," JoJo says with a hand on his forearm.

I lean back in my chair and cross my arms over my chest, trying to ignore the incessant barking outside. "Is that so hard to believe?"

"Well, yeah," he says, crossing his arms, mimicking my posture but adding a smirk. "It is, actually. You seem so confident in your gayness and all."

That hits me the wrong way. Or the right way. At the moment, I'm not sure of the difference. I lean forward and rest my elbows on the table. "Being gay is who I *am*. Not who I *do*."

That silences him. His crinkled brow and downcast eyes tell me that whether he fully understands it or not, at least he really heard me.

The sudden spray of glass covers the entire table before the crash of sound even registers in my ear. A softball-sized rock lands in the middle of the roast platter, splattering meat juice onto the walls as well as our faces. JoJo stands and fires off an impressive round of curses. Jax jumps to his feet, wiping his eyes with his napkin. My right ear stings with the lingering graze of the rock, and I wonder if I'm like one of those soldiers in war movies walking around with half my head blown off, but I don't know it yet. I hope not. Bloody bits of brain would be a bitch to get out of this beige shag carpet. Jax is a terrible actor. He holds his hands out to his sides and looks around the room like, *What the fuck could have done this? I was so not expecting that at all!*

I wasn't expecting it either. Not in the middle of the dining room table, *Shelby*. Jesus, the girl doesn't even know what a bay window is? She could've killed me, for Christ's sake. A familiar scream sounds outside. Jumping out of my chair, I run over and stick my head out the gaping window, trying to make sense of the scene. Looking like a toppled Teletubbie, Shelby rolls boobs over back down the hill with her hands raised over her head. A large German shepherd runs beside her, its jaws clamped down on her shirt. The dog yanks at it and wags his tail like he's having the time of his life. The shirt bottles up around Shelby's neck, and her bra is coming off. Not my girl's finest moment.

"Do you see anything, Beck?" JoJo yells out behind me.

I glance over my shoulder at Jax, who stands behind his mom and shrugs as that annoying grin forms on his face.

"I can't really tell," I say, stretching out the lie to give Shelby time to roll away. "I'll go out and take a look." I glare at Jax, who's so miserably fallen down on the job. "Maybe you should, I don't know, *call the police or something*?"

His eyes widen. "Oh, right. We should do that."

JoJo joins me at the window and peers out. Luckily, Shelby has cleared the neighboring trailer and is safely out of sight, though the sounds of her struggle with the amorous canine still echo in the dark.

"No use calling 911 for this," I recite my lines as rehearsed. "Probably just some kids." Okay, that sounded a little too *Scooby-Doo* out loud.

"Beck's right," Jax drones robotically. He grabs JoJo's arm and leads her away from the window. "But remember those Tabernacle rednecks at the Crusty Cup the other day? Maybe they found out where you live. You should at least call down to the police station to file a report. Don't you have a friend down there?"

We have to get this boy into some drama classes. Stat!

JoJo nods. "Doris. She did say to call her if I ever had any trouble out here. Maybe you're right." She grabs her phone and heads into the kitchen.

I sidle up to Jax and peek around the corner to make sure JoJo is out of earshot. "I'd better go check on Shelby. Last I saw her, she was being dragged down the hill by a frisky German shepherd."

"Shit," Jax says, running fingers through his hair. "That's

the neighbor's dog, Rocky. I forgot all about him. He's harm-less, though."

"Maybe. But Shelby's not."

Jax's eyes widen. "Oh, right." He shoves me into the living room and out the front door. "Hurry before she kills him."

I'm out the door and down the hill in a matter of seconds. In the distance I spot Shelby running down the middle of the road, tits to the wind. She screams obscenities and chases one overly delighted German shepherd with her bra hanging from his jaws.

I stop running, frame my mouth with my hands, and yell at the top of my lungs. "Run, Rocky, run!"

# CHAPTER TWENTY-TWO

Jaxon

The sun beats down on us, but Coach Wayne doesn't seem to notice. He calls drill after drill like we're training for the Super Bowl. And the way Tiffany glares at me from the sidelines, I know she's not done with our little chat at church yesterday. She barks at her squad, leading them through a series of sexually charged dance routines that drain my guys of their focus. Not that I'm any better. Our drills look like shit, and Coach is about to blow a gasket. He finally gives up and tells us to take ten.

On the bench, I dig my phone out of my bag and check my texts. There are two. The first one is from Beck and the second from . . . *bingo* . . . Justin Black. I swipe right with my thumb, and the deejay's message populates the screen.

*Hey, stud. I'm in. Hit my girl up with details and save me a dance. JB.* There's an emoji wink face and an out-of-state phone number at the bottom.

"Fuck, yeah," I mutter, though I'm not sure if I'm excited

because I feel somewhat responsible for snagging one of the hottest deejays in the country for our sad little gay prom, or because I know Beck will be stoked about it. For some reason I think it's the latter. I really don't give a shit about the prom, but it'll be cool to give Beck the good news. After all, it was his idea to go after Justin Black in the first place.

"What're you grinning at? Pussy pics? Let me see."

I look up and find Bobby Jenkins standing there.

"Just a text from a friend," I say, quickly dropping my phone in my bag.

"A friend, huh?" His crooked stare is unusually psychotic today. Suddenly I'm ready for our break to be over. Bobby looks down his nose at me. "This a friend you made at the fag bar last weekend?"

My face goes instantly hot. *Shit. How the fucking hell?* I take a quick calming breath, look up, and cock my head at him. "What?"

*Really, Jaxon?* I chide myself internally. *That's all you got? Monumentally weak.*

He caught me off guard. I add a little annoyed heft to my voice, trying to recover. "What the fuck are you talking about, Bobby?" I look away, over at the cheerleading squad. Yeah. That seems the right thing to do when you've just been accused of going to a gay bar. Stare at some USDA approved cheerleader ass.

"My fag cousin from Darlington goes to that club over on South Cashua," Bobby says. "He swears he saw the star quarterback of the East Florence Tigers there last Saturday night, dancing around in his underwear and getting real cozy with all the queers."

I may not be a big talker, but I don't think I've ever been actually speechless until this moment. It's like I'm physically incapable of joining words together and pushing them out of my mouth with a sufficient amount of air. Seems a little naive of me now, though. The club was packed that night.

"Fuck off, Bobby," I manage to get out, trying to sound unconcerned and disinterested.

Bobby hocks a loogie on the ground. He rests the back of his hand on his hip, shifting his massive weight to one side. His crooked sneer is dangerous and unreadable.

"Yeah, I told him all that cum he swallows must be affecting his eyesight." He nods over at Tiffany. "Because I know you're hittin' *that* on a regular basis." He looks back at me and grins. "Sorry, bro. Tiff fucks and tells, but from what I hear, she ain't got no complaints."

He knocks me on the shoulder with his helmet and snickers, but I can't tell if he believes I was at Ruff Riders or not. I don't know what to say, so I laugh and assume he doesn't. "Damn right."

There. That wasn't a lie or a denial. I'm relatively pleased with my answer. So why do I feel like a steaming pile of shit with a cherry on top? Tiffany and her girls head off to the locker room. She looks my way and gives me a tentative wave, which Bobby catches as well.

He grunts, leering at Tiffany. "Shit, Jax. If you ever *do* decide to go gay, I will be more than happy to—"

"Easy, Bobby." My tone is firm, and I mean it. He's out of line. Pushing my buttons just to see if I'll react.

Bobby grins one of those good-old-boy grins where you

don't know if he wants to hug you or put his fist through your face. "Sorry, bro." He knocks my shoulder again with his helmet. A little harder this time. "Just messin' with you. Don't worry. I told my cocksucker cousin he had it all wrong, because Jaxon Parker is all man. Ain't that right?"

I grit my teeth at him and stand. "That is exactly right, Bobby."

Another truth, but I still feel like shit.

"Goddamn right." He puts on his helmet. "Ain't no faggots on this team. I'll make sure of that."

Was that a threat? I take a step forward, and my fingers curl into a fist at my side. I want to nail this fucker so bad. Or maybe my anger is misdirected. Maybe it's my own spineless ass I want to kick. Someone slips an arm between us and pulls me back. It's Terry, the most levelheaded guy on the team. The look in his eye tells me I need to back off, and Terry knows me better than anyone.

"We good here?" Terry asks, and gives me a firm nod, feeding me the answer he wants to hear.

I smile at Bobby. "Abso-fucking-lutely good. Right, Bobby?"

Bobby shoots me something between a smile and a sneer. "All good, bro."

"Cool," Terry says, lowering his arm. "Coach called us back. Let's go."

Bobby gives me one last smile/sneer and runs out onto the field.

Terry steps in front of me, the sun reflecting off his dark skin. "What the hell was that about? You looked like you were about to let loose on his redneck ass. And let's be honest, bruh, that probably wouldn't have gone down the way you saw it happening in that pretty little head of yours." He raps my skull with his knuckles and laughs.

I flex my fingers and smile back at him. "It was nothing. Really."

"You sure?" Terry says, holding his helmet in front of him. "You've been a little scattered lately. Things still bad between your moms?"

I nod, thankful that I can throw my moms under the bus and blame all my questionable behavior on their breakup. I wonder how far I can ride that train. "Yeah. But there may be hope."

Terry punches my arm and flashes me that million-dollar smile of his. "That's amazing. Fingers crossed, right?"

"Fingers crossed," I say, picking my helmet up off the bench.

I take a deep breath. Crisis averted and no one's the wiser. Still feel like shit, though. When Terry steps out of the way, who do I find standing there with the worst timing in the history of American high school football?

Beckett Gaines.

Terry looks at him with a mixture of confusion and kindness battling for control of his face. "'Sup."

Beck glances over at him and nods up once. "Hey, Terry."

I don't know how long the awkward silence lasts, but it feels like weeks. I can feel the heat of Bobby Jenkins's stare on the back of my neck.

Finally, Terry nods over to the field. "We better hit it, Jax.

Later, Beckett." He waves at Beck with his helmet and sprints away.

"Wow," Beck says, his eyebrows rising. "I didn't think he even knew my name."

I've tried, but I can't contain my anxiety, and the more anxious I get, the more I chide myself internally for being that way. One minute I'm thinking about the guy while my girl is blowing me and next he's the last person in the world I want to see. "What're you doing here?" God. My tone. I'm such an asshole, hypocrite jerk.

Beck's face darkens a little. "I was just wondering what happened last night after I left. I texted you but you never answered. Did Angie Dykenson show up and save the day?"

I cock my head at him. "Angie who?"

Beck rolls his eyes at me. *"Doris."*

"Oh. Yeah. She came. Ma got more and more freaked out when she started thinking the Tabernacle nuts had her address. Maybe a rock through the window wasn't the best idea. But it worked, I guess." I glance nervously over my shoulder. Both Bobby and Coach Wayne are boring a hole through me, though I'm sure for different reasons. I need to wrap this up. "She stayed for about an hour. Filled out a report. Talked to JoJo and calmed her down. Maybe a little too much."

"What do you mean?"

"I'm not sure if JoJo really noticed last night, because she was a little shaken up, but Doris is *really* into her. I hope our plan doesn't backfire."

Beck rests a hand on his hip, shifting his weight to one side and doing so a tad too effeminately for my current level of comfort. The simple move looks entirely different on him than it did on Bobby. If it were just the two of us standing there, it wouldn't bother me a bit, I swear. But we have about a dozen sets of eyes on us right now. Sweat scurries down from the base of my skull to the crack of my ass.

"Did you ask Doris about having a police presence at the prom?"

I lift my helmet, hoping that will indicate that *I really need to go*. "Oh yeah. She said she'd talk to her captain about it. She was all about keeping the gay kids safe."

"And JoJo? Is she coming too?"

"I'm working on it, Beck, okay?" There's that tone again. The flash of hurt in his eyes is obvious. Why am I being such a dick to him?

"Hey, Parker," Bobby calls from the field. "What are you doing over there, getting your hair done?"

*That's why.*

Several snickers drift over from the field. Beck's face goes completely white, and I . . . well, I say nothing. Again.

"Cut the shit, Bobby." Sai's voice. Not mine. Should've been mine.

I can barely stand to look into Beck's eyes, they're so muddy with . . . I don't know . . . hurt, betrayal, judgment. He recovers pretty quickly though. Holds his head up high and flips Bobby off—which elicits a muted symphony of whistles and taunts in return. Without another look in my direction, he turns on his heel and walks away.

I feel about two inches tall.

# CHAPTER TWENTY-THREE

# Beckett

I guide the Prius through our neighborhood like I'm on auto-pilot. Other than the fact that I haven't cried since I left the football field, I feel like I'm right back in eighth grade, and that pisses me off more than anything. I never let guys like Bobby Jenkins get to me. Not anymore. But when Jax just stood there with his hypocritical thumb up his ass, *again*, that hurt. I thought we were at least becoming friends. Hell, I was even beginning to think there could possibly be something more. I can't deny that the butterflies I feel when I'm around him aren't just about the way he looks. He gets to me in ways I never expected. Anyway, I won't make that mistake again. I know he's been texting me, because my phone has been pulsating in my pocket like a vibrator in heat.

A car is parked in front of our house, but I'm so distracted that it doesn't even click that it's the same car that was there the night Mom showed up on our doorstep. Not until I get inside and find her sitting in the living room across from my dad, does it register. *And they're laughing.* It trails off when I enter the room.

I plop down on the sofa beside Dad. "What's so funny?"

"Just reminiscing about when you were little," he says, squeezing my shoulder. "You were so sassy, even way back then."

Mom laughs. "Do you remember the time when you were five, and I came out in my new Sunday dress, so proud? I said, 'Hey honey, how do you like Mommy's new dress?' You were eating cereal at the kitchen table and you looked up at me, horrified. You said that it made me look frumpy. I mean, what five-year-old uses the word 'frumpy'?"

They chuckle again. It's nice to see them laughing together. I guess. For a moment it's like she never left. Like she never just decided one day that she didn't love Dad anymore or feel like she was suffocating in this town. But she did.

"That dress was hideous," I say with a sigh, pushing my hair out of my eyes.

Dad pats my knee. "How was school today, bud?"

I look back and forth between them. This is so damn surreal. "Actually, it sucked ass."

Mom crinkles her brow and leans forward. "What happened, sweetie?"

I'm not exactly sure why it flies all over me. She's just showing concern. Just being nice. Just doing what mothers do. I guess it's because she's stepping back into the role she abandoned so easily like she still holds some claim to it.

"I don't want to talk about it," I say, waving my hand in the air.

Dad squeezes my knee once. It's like our own private code. One long squeeze like that means *We can talk about it later*. He gets that I'm not comfortable sharing with Mom right away. He gets me in general, thank God. He's the only one who ever has, other than Shelby, and I start to wonder why I even want him and Mom back together if I'm harboring some deep-seated anger against her. I'm sure it'll get easier with time. I remind myself, it's about what's best for Dad, not me. It's just hard getting used to her being so . . . *here*.

"Did you tell Mom about the PFLAG prom?" I say.

Dad withdraws his hand. Oops. That's another code. Not a good one.

Mom sits back and crosses her leg. "What's PFLAG?"

Okay, that flies all over me too. I need to get a handle on this anger bubbling just under the surface. But, come on, how could a liberal mom of a gay kid not know about PFLAG?

Dad pats my knee twice. Code for *He's got me*. "It's the Parents and Friends of Lesbians and Gays," he says. "I joined the chapter here in Florence."

"And there's a gay prom planned for the queer kids and our straight allies," I say, trying to get back in my groove. Remember the end game. This is about Dad. Not me. "You should come."

Dad coughs into his hand. "Your mom probably already has plans, Beck. It's only a couple of weeks away."

"When is it?" she asks, matter of fact.

"The twenty-third," I chime in. "Seven o'clock at the East Florence gym."

"Wow. I haven't been back there in a long time." She raises

her eyebrows and pushes her hair back over her shoulder. "You must be expecting a large crowd to have it at the gym."

"A large crowd of crazies," Dad mutters.

"What's that?" she says.

I jump in. "Florence Holiness Tabernacle is planning one of its charming Fags Burn in Hell demonstrations, good Christians that they are and all."

"That sounds dangerous," Mom says, looking genuinely concerned.

"We have it under control, Lana," Dad replies with an edge in his voice. Sounds like he's feeling some of the same things I am. "Don't feel like you have to come."

Mom does a double take like she's just been highly offended. "I don't feel like I *have* to come, Roger. I *want* to come. I'm Beck's mother, after all. I want to support him."

The tension in the room is to be expected, I guess, but it makes me wonder if the two of them would ever be able to get over the past and move forward together. Maybe that was just wishful thinking.

Dad's face finally softens. "Of course, you're welcome to come. It's just that—"

"His girlfriend Tracee will be there," I interject, firmly back in the game. "That's two *e*'s. No *y*. That's *extremely* important."

Mom waves her hand in front of her. "I'm not here to cause trouble or to cramp your style, Roger. But don't you think it would be nice for both of Beck's parents to be there to support him and his friends?"

Dad sighs. "If that's what Beck wants."

They both look at me with eyebrows and hopes raised for

me to support their differing agendas. Of course I want her to be there. It's the whole point of inviting her old squeeze, Tom Davenport: to make Dad jealous. I know he'll feel betrayed if I don't back him up, but I have to be the responsible one here. The one who looks to the future when they can't see the forest for the trees. I have to be the Dorothy.

"Actually, it would be great if both of you were there," I say, feigning the innocence of an eight-year-old. "If that's okay with you guys." *You guys*? When the hell do I ever say "you guys"? I can't look at Dad.

Mom's mouth spreads into a smile. "Then it's settled. I'll get a new dress and everything."

"Oh Lord," I say.

"Exactly. So you should go with me and help me pick one out," she says, pointing at me. "Saturday morning?"

I nod. "Oh, but can Shelby come with us? She needs one too, and when it comes to fashion, I don't trust her judgment either."

Mom waves her hand at me. "Of course Shelby can come."

Actually, I'm quite pleased with myself, but feeling a little shitty that I had to take sides against Dad. Seems like I brought the room down when I came in, so maybe I should give them some privacy.

"I've got a ton of lyrics to memorize for choir." I stand, go over, and kiss Mom on the cheek.

"See you Saturday, sweetie," she says. "I'll come by at ten and then we'll go pick up Shelby. Okay?"

"Great." I look over at Dad. "Don't you have a date tonight?" Might as well plant some seeds of jealousy in Mom, too.

"I do," Dad says, blushing slightly. "I'll be leaving soon."

"Tell Tracee I said hello." And I'm out. Let them stew in that for a minute or two.

Heading upstairs, I fish my phone out of my pocket. The damn thing vibrated on my thigh like a dozen times just since I got home. I feel like I need a cigarette. I close the door behind me, plop down on my bed, and look at the home screen. It's filled from top to bottom with notifications. Jesus. Four texts from Jax, three from Shelby, one InstaPic DM, one from Quickchat, and two from Bangr.

I start with Shelby's texts.

First text: *I have grass stains on my tits. They won't come out.*

Second text: *Is bleach bad for tit skin?*

Third text: *Shit. I accidentally bleached one of my nipples white. Now it matches your anus. Will InstaPic to you.*

Okay. Skipping over the InstaPic DM, I open up Quickchat. *Oh, sweet baby Jesus*, it's from Carter Treadwell.

*Hey, Beckett.* I imagine Kim Kardashian's voice saying it. *I was just wondering. Do you have a date for the Rainbow Prom?*

Delete. Delete. Delete. I'll just pretend I never saw that.

I exit Quickchat and hurry over to the Bangr app. The first DM is from CockyInSC.

*Why'd you run off the other night? You're cute. Still need your cherry popped? I'll be gentle. Unless you don't want me to.* 😊 😜 😜

*Ew.* I feel the need to Lysol my phone down. I hit delete and block him. I click on the two new messages, and a little jolt of excitement shoots through me when I see that they are both from Brock. And there are actual *words*. Not just winks and ass grabs. We have officially moved to third base, skipping right over the dick squeezes.

*Hey.*

Wow. A real talker here. I recheck his profile pic—a close-up of his curvy pecs and ripped abs. No face. I open the second message.

*You there? Wanna chat?*

I'm not sure if he means on the phone or via the safety of the direct messaging. My last hookup on Bangr didn't end well, but after dealing with those homophobic assholes at school today, I could use a little virtual flirting with a hot guy. Well, I assume he's hot anyway, with a body like that.

I thumb a quick hello to Brock and hit send.

A response pops up within seconds. *Hey! Glad you hit me back.*

I'm not playing games again. *Is that profile pic real?*

*LOL. Promise. 100%. Why no pic 4U?*

*I'm shy.* I type. I don't add, *and too young to be trolling around on Bangr.*

*LOL. I doubt that. What you lookin' for on here?*

Why is this so damn exhilarating? I could literally be flirting with a serial killer and not even know it. Thank God there was no Bangr when Jeffrey Dahmer was around. But I don't want to get into another potential dog park rape scenario.

*Just a friend*, I type.

The reply comes quick.

*I'll be your friend. If you'll let me.*

Damn, this serial killer is good. It's fun, even if it is just a fantasy—my imaginary friend Brock. I sigh, as if he can hear me, and type. *You can be my friend as long as you don't hunt me down and murder me.*

*LMFAO. You're funny. Bet you're cute, too.*

Okay, tiger, calm down. That's enough for our first date. I type, *Gotta go.*

A sad face emoji appears on the screen. Then another. Then another.

*Bye*, I reply, and add an emoji wink. And another. And another.

*Bye, Beckett.*

Whoa. Seeing my real name in a DM from a complete stranger on a fuck app is a bit unsettling after the CockyInSC debacle. I need to change that in my profile ASAP.

Another messages pops up. *You should add a profile pic. I bet you have a killer smile.*

I sit there staring at Brock's last message, tapping the screen with my index finger. It takes me a full minute to make the decision. I go to my profile page and click on *add profile pic*. I scroll through my photo library searching for a selfie that shows some of my face, but nothing full frontal. Got it. My hair hangs in my eyes, I'm serving up Mom's smile, and my head's turned to the side. Perfect. Cute but not too revealing. I upload the picture and then scroll down the page to my personal information. There it sits, the whole damn thing. *Beckett Gaines*. Jesus. Why didn't I just include my address, phone number, and SAT scores?

I delete my name and stare up at the ceiling. It seems so obvious when it finally comes to me that I'm a little embarrassed it took me more than ten seconds to think of it. In the name field I type,

*D. Zbornak*

I feel good about my Bangr presence now that I'm incognito and meeting new people. It'll be nice to chat with faceless pervs from time to time. Maybe I can help with their rehabilitation. Like social work. Suddenly, in my mind anyway, Bangr is a respectable app with noble intentions. At least that's the way I intend to use it. I drop my phone on the bed and let out a long sigh. Who am I kidding? Other than Shelby, I have no *real* friends. Certainly not Jaxon Parker. My phone vibrates beside me. I pick it up and unlock the home screen. Another text from guess who—Jax. Jesus Christ already. Feel like a dick much? I relent and scroll through Jax's texts.

First text: *I'm sorry.*

You should be.

Second text: *Like I said. I'm a coward.*

Yes, you are.

Third text: *I suck.*

Agreed.

Fourth text: *I'm trying to be better. Call me.*

No chance in hell.

Newest text: *U left today before I could tell U. Heard from Justin Black.*

I can't hit the CALL BACK button fast enough.

# CHAPTER TWENTY-FOUR

# Jaxon

Seeing Roger's car in the driveway for the second night in a row is the shit icing on the cake of one very shit day. I totally blanked on a history pop quiz, Bobby Jenkins is like a dog with a bone with this me-being-spotted-at-a-gay-club thing, and Coach Wayne ripped me a new one at practice for my half-assed performance. He says I don't have my head in the game. Can't say that I disagree with him.

Terry guides his SUV into our driveway and stops behind Roger's car. "Looks like you have company."

"Yeah," I say. "Lucky me."

He looks over at me. "Oh. Your mom's new guy?"

I nod.

Terry shakes his head. "She's always been with women and suddenly she wants a dude. I mean, whatever makes her happy, but I don't get it."

"Me either," I say.

I have the urge to call Beck and tell him his dad's at my

house, but I'm not sure he wants to hear from me. He was so stoked about landing Justin Black for the Rainbow Prom. I almost thought it made up for the way I acted at practice yesterday. But he avoided me at school all day, so I'm beginning to doubt that. Tiffany won't let up about a double date this weekend with Terry and Molly. I guess I'll go even though I know I need to break it off with her. That will *not* be pretty, but I can't lie to her anymore. My heart's just not in it. And lately Jax Junior really isn't either, which kind of freaks me the hell out.

Terry shoves the gear stick into park and turns to face me. "So are we doing Saturday night with the girls or not? Molly keeps asking."

"I guess so," I say. "Don't have anything better to do."

"Well shit, bruh, don't get too excited about it," he says with a sarcastic chuckle. "You know you'll at least get oral out of it."

He punches me in the shoulder, and I shrug. "I don't know. I guess. Let's just plan on it," I say, opening the door and getting out. "I need to talk to Tiff anyway. Thanks for the ride."

Terry waves as he backs down the driveway. So I just decided to break up with my girlfriend because my head's all twisted over a guy. This bisexual thing is exhausting. Inside, I find Mom and Roger giggling in the kitchen. The sound grates on me like nails on a chalkboard. Thankfully, my presence settles on them like a wet blanket.

"Sorry for interrupting," I say, though I'm not in the least.

"Hey, hon," Mom says, slipping her arm around Roger's waist as he leans against the counter.

"Jax," he says with a wink, like we're old pals or something.

"Did Beck tell you?" I say to Roger. "We found a deejay for the dance. Justin Black. He's like one of the biggest out there right now."

Mom comes over and hugs me. "That's amazing, Jaxon. You and Beck did that?"

I shrug and nod. "It was all Beck's idea, though."

Roger shoots me a look I really can't read, but Beck's name triggered it.

"Justin knows it won't be like the clubs he usually plays," I say. "But he grew up around here and apparently was bullied quite a bit when he was a kid for being gay. He's between tours, so he's doing it for free to support your PFLAG chapter."

"Well, he sounds like a doll," Mom says, returning to Roger's side.

She probably wouldn't be saying that if she knew how handsy Justin was with me at Ruff Riders.

Roger shifts his weight uncomfortably. "I just hope there're no surprises before the big night."

"What do you mean?" I say.

Roger sighs. "A student filed a complaint with the school board about using the East Florence gym for the Rainbow Prom. Religious freedom violation, they said."

"Let me guess," I say. "Cassidy Charles."

"Religious freedom, my sweet patoot," Mom says with real anger in her eyes. But she doesn't curse. That's my and JoJo's department.

"What about everyone else's freedom?" she says.

"Well, hopefully nothing will come of it," Roger says.

"I hope you're right," Mom says, her smile back in full force. She looks over at me. "We're just heading out to meet the prom planning committee for a drink to discuss backup plans. Want me to make you something to eat before I leave?"

"No, thanks. I'm good."

"Okay then," she says, and touches Roger's shoulder. "Let me go check my face and change shoes. I'll be ready in a few."

Certainly she's not going to just leave me in here with him. But she glides right out of the room without a second look. Shit. What the hell am I supposed to say to this guy?

Roger crosses his arms over his chest and his legs at the ankles. Wow. I wonder if he knows what kind of message he's sending me with that body language right now. Apparently, he sees me as much as the adversary as I see him. Maybe now's the perfect time to plant those seeds of doubt that Beck was talking about.

Roger opens the door quite nicely for me. "Your mom's really great."

I plaster on a fake smile. "Yep. She's the bomb. *Both* my moms are, actually. Have you ever met JoJo?"

Roger looks down. "Look, Jax. I can appreciate that this is hard on you. No kid wants their parents to split up. But I really like Tracee. She's sweet. Loving. She makes me laugh. I'm not going to hurt her, I promise. And I would *never* try to replace JoJo in your life."

"You do know my mom is a lesbian, right?"

I know it's a little bold and completely steers my interaction with Roger in a whole other direction. But I really don't give a shit at this point.

He takes a deep breath and cocks his head at me. "Well, I don't think it's that simple, Jax. I've always believed that women are more evolved than men in some ways."

I chuckle under my breath and shake my head. "If that's what you need to tell yourself."

I cross the room and open the fridge. I'm not hungry. I just needed to move. I pull out the orange juice, unscrew the lid, and take a big, long chug. Normally, I would never drink right out of the container. Both my moms would lose their shit if they saw me. But it feels defiant, and I want Roger to witness that defiance, lame as it may be.

I put the juice away, close the door, and face him. Widen my stance and cross my arms over my chest. "Look, Roger. I'm sure you're a perfectly decent guy. Beck thinks you're the shit, and he seems like a pretty good judge of character. So I say this for your own good."

Rogers narrows his eyes on me and tightens the fold of his arms. "What's that?"

I take a step toward him and square my shoulders like we're facing each other on the line of scrimmage.

"I know a little about Mom's history before JoJo," I say, feigning concern for him. "Yeah, she had a boyfriend or two back in the day, but they never lasted. When it came to long-term relationships, she always ended up with a woman. Every. Single. Time. Trust me, *Mr. Gaines*, this is temporary."

Roger stares at me, his eyes cloudy and his lips a thin line across his face. I got to him. I know I did. Mom's timing could not have been better.

"Roger," she calls from the living room. "I'm ready."

"Be right there," he calls back, his steely gaze locked on me.

He uncrosses his arms and walks right up to me. Stands nose to nose with me and straightens his spine, giving him another inch of height over me. I'm not the least bit intimidated, but I brace myself for the backlash.

"I appreciate your concern, Jax," he says calmly, "but don't you worry about me. I'm a big boy and I can take care of myself."

After an uncomfortable moment where I actually wondered if we could come to blows, he finally holsters his penetrating gaze and moves toward the door. Before he slips out, he turns back to me.

"By the way. Your mom told me about catching you on that gay app."

Every muscle in my body tenses up, and I just hope it doesn't show on my face. Jesus Christ, why doesn't Mom just put an announcement in the *Florence Morning News* and be done with it?

"I can appreciate that you may be questioning your sexual orientation, or experimenting or whatever," Roger says with no trace of his usual amiable tone. "And I want you to know that I completely understand and support you in that, one hundred percent. I'm not your enemy, Jax. But if you hurt my son, or play with his heart, I will be."

Roger turns and leaves me standing there with my mouth hanging open and my dick in my hand.

# CHAPTER TWENTY-FIVE

# Beckett

Dress shopping all day with Mom and Shelby was actually kind of nice, like old times—the good ones. But I didn't get any information out of Mom about Tom Davenport. The couple of times I brought up his name, she changed the subject, so I finally gave up. I guess I don't have to know all the gory details about their past, as long as his presence at the prom sparks a jealous rage in Dad. At least Mom and Shelby found Beckett-approved dresses for the prom, though Shelby has yet to ask Chevy to go with her. I worry she's waited too long. He might already have a date. I made her promise to ask him tonight.

I look around and wonder how I ended up back here— at City Park on a Saturday night with the scent of dog shit tickling my nose. At least I'm not cruising the parking lot, peddling my virginity again. This time I sit on a bench at the end of the dock, watching the ducks and waiting not for a pedophile in a Barneymobile, but for Jax. If I hadn't agreed to meet him, I don't think he'd ever stop texting me. I think a few days of the silent treatment really got to him, though I can't imagine why. Why the hell would he even care? Maybe he's just obsessed with breaking up my dad and his mom and thinks I'm bailing on him. I'm not. But I'm sure as hell not doing it for him. Today with Mom was nice. I wouldn't mind more of that.

As dusk settles in around me, a few lights scattered throughout the park flicker on. The place is a tad creepy as day fades into night. There aren't any clandestine hookups happening in the parking lot yet. It's too early for that. Too much light still. The place is just empty and lonely with only the crickets, cicadas, and quacking ducks to keep me company. The solitude is familiar. Too familiar.

My phone vibrates in my hands, and I glance down at it expecting to see a text from Jax explaining why he's late. Instead, it's another Bangr DM from Brock. He's been quiet the last few days, and I really wasn't sure if I'd hear from him again. I tap the message and it opens up on my screen.

*D. Zbornak. Golden Girls, right?*

Well, well, well. Color me intrigued.

*I'm impressed*, I type.

*I call foul on the profile pic, though. Not enough face.*

I consider my response carefully, because I don't want another Barneymobile situation. But Jax is late, so what the hell.

*Told you. I'm shy. How old are you? Don't lie.*

I wait. It takes nearly a minute for the reply to come, so I expect a lie.

*Old enough. Lol.*

A bit sketchy but not overly suspicious. Might as well get right to the brass tacks. I type, *How many people have you murdered?*

*I've lost count.*

Okay. A sense of humor. Points. Unless he's actually telling the truth. That would be more my luck.

*What are you doing?*

I type, *Waiting for a friend.*

*Just a "friend"?* 😊

*Hardly even that*, I type without hesitation, but I can't bring myself to hit send. The truth is, I don't know what Jax and I are to each other. Friends, enemies, just partners in crime. Even though he's been a major asshole in the past, I can't get the guy out of my head, and it's making me a little cray-cray. I hit the backspace button until all the letters vanish. The phone vibrates again and a new message appears.

*More than a friend?*

*Ha*, I type. *Nope. Virgin here.*

Several seconds pass, and I wonder if I've scared him off. His response finally pops up on my screen.

*Sorry. Not what I was asking. But save yourself for someone worthy of you. You're worth it.*

I stare at the words, soaking them in. Typeless. *You're worth it.* I've only ever heard words like that from my dad, and I usually respond to him with an eye roll. But hearing or seeing them from someone whose DNA I don't share, from a total stranger who could either be a fifty-year-old skinhead in a prison in Iowa using a contraband phone he keeps hidden under the lid of his toilet, or a lonely boy my age somewhere in Florence, hits me in a different place entirely. Is Brock implying that *he's* worthy of me?

Someone touches my shoulder, and I nearly drop my phone into the water.

"Shit!"

Jax scoots around the bench, laughing, and plops down beside me.

"That's not funny," I say, holding my chest. "I could've had a heart attack."

*Note to self: Start taking one baby aspirin every day.*

"What're you doing?" he asks, peeking over at my phone.

I clear the screen with a swipe and wonder if he saw the Bangr icon. "Nothing." I slip the phone into the pocket of my jeans, where Brock can vibrate sweet nothings close to my crotch.

I glance over my shoulder just as Jax's RideShare car pulls away, a very quiet Prius like mine. When I look back at Jax, his smile fades and he bumps me with his shoulder. He's sitting closer than I expected. I like it, and I hate that I like it.

"Thanks for meeting me," he says. "I can't stay long."

"Tiffany awaits?" I say, with a small dose of Zbornak sarcasm.

Jax diverts his gaze. "Something like that."

I wait for him to look back up at me. He smells good. Like a combination of cucumber soap and coconut body lotion. Freshly showered. Hair still a bit damp on the ends. Something about it makes him looks innocent. Vulnerable. Adorable.

"So? Why are we here?" I ask before I get totally lost in his damn alluring aura.

Jax sighs and stares out across the pond. "Apparently, someone recognized me at Ruff Riders and told Bobby. That had me really rattled that day on the practice field. But still, I'm sorry I didn't shut him down when he started in on you."

I huff. "Sai Patel showed more balls. Probably because he knows what it's like growing up different in this town."

"Maybe so, but that's no excuse," Jax says, and looks over at me. "You're my friend and you deserve better than that. I should have stood up for you. I'm sorry, Beck."

A lump clogs the base of my throat. He seems so sincere. Like he's disappointed in himself and sad that I was hurt. If my eyes start itching . . . goddamn it, there they go. Thank God Brock vibrates on my dick, providing a needed distraction.

Jax's baby blue eyes refuse to be muted even by dusk. Why does he have to be so fucking gorgeous? And now he's gone and apologized and called me his friend and said nice things and shit. My head is spinning.

I sniff a wad of snot back up my nose. *Sexy.* "So we're *friends* now?"

Jax's face sags. "I thought that was a given." He's quiet for a moment and then sighs. His knee brushes against mine, igniting an army of goose bumps all over my body. God, I wish he didn't have that effect on me. But he does. And no. It's not *just* about the way he looks. It's all so damn confusing.

He shrugs and shakes his head. "It's not always easy for me to say what's on my mind, or in my heart, or whatever. But I want to be different. I don't want to go through life . . . afraid."

"Afraid?"

He sighs. A heavy sigh. "Afraid of living, afraid of what people think of me, afraid of being alone. Afraid of the past."

I cock my head at him. "Wow. I didn't think *The Great Jaxon Parker* was afraid of anything."

He raises an eyebrow at me and chuckles. "I'm not that great, Beck, trust me."

He knows I was mocking him, right? He reaches into the front pocket of his jeans, pulls out his phone, and stares down at the screen.

"Shit. No bars," he says, tossing it onto the bench beside him and gazing out over the dark surface of the pond. He rests the weight of his leg a little more against mine. It feels almost natural. Comfortable. Brock vibrates on my crotch again. *Calm down, girl. I'm busy.*

"I've never told anyone this," he says, watching a family of ducks swim by. "I was seven when my moms adopted me," Jax says. "Well, first they fostered me. The state removed me from the home of my biological parents. I don't remember too much of it. I think I blocked most of it out. But I remember some—mostly about Carl. That's the douche bag who impregnated the woman who gave birth to me."

"That's an interesting way of referring to your biological mom and dad," I say, softening my tone a little.

Jax returns his gaze to the water and shakes his head. "I'll never call those people Mom and Dad. Not ever."

I tread cautiously. "What do you remember about them?"

Jax hangs his head. "Nothing good. My own screams. Pain. Bruises. Tears. Rehearsed explanations about accidents and falling down stairs. Carl was a violent dude. I went to this shrink when I started having nightmares about it all. I guess it would've been around the time we were in middle school. The therapist said I could have *emotional scars* the rest of my life."

I swallow back the new lump in my throat for a couple of reasons. *One*—because I would have never in a million years pegged Jaxon Parker as someone who would see a therapist. *And two*—that he went to one while we were in middle school. I had no idea of the scary shit he was dealing with back then.

"And the woman?" I say cautiously.

He looks over at me and shrugs. "Peggy. Don't know too much about her. Other than the fact that she was a junkie and Carl beat the shit out of her and me on a regular basis. Among other things."

My eyes begin to itch again, and I hedge the encroaching tears. *Among other things.* I have the sudden urge to hug him. And then run home and hug my dad and even my mom.

"Thankfully, a neighbor reported the abuse and DSS got me out of there. I bounced around to a few not-*quite*-as-bad-but-not-so-great-either foster homes for about a year or so. Lucky for me Tracee and JoJo were the last foster parents I ever had. They said it took some doing and Peggy fought them, but they were finally able to adopt me." He glances over at me. "They saved my life."

I just stare at him. I can't imagine what he went through. My heart breaks for him.

"Playing sports and getting jacked made me feel strong and safe. The tough guys I surround myself with, the constant working out, the asshole veneer, the overachieving bullshit, it's all just . . . protection. Like a shield. I'll never let anyone hurt me like that again."

Suddenly, it all makes sense—his desire to please, to be liked, to be accepted. Why he needs his moms back together so badly. They're his safety net, his security blanket. The only thing that's ever made any sense in his life. I rest my hand on his knee, not knowing if he'll recoil, swat it away, or kick my ass. But I do it anyway because I need to touch him. I want him to feel safe.

He looks down at my hand and covers it with his own, knocking the wind right out of me. His skin is warm and a little rough. And those fucking needles are back in full force, but now they join the goose bumps covering my entire body. Jax turns my hand over. Presses his palm against mine and rubs them together, heating our skin instantly. I can barely breathe. Our fingers entwine like a reunion of old friends who've been separated for a very long time. It's scary and exciting as hell. New and familiar at the same time. I squeeze his hand. He squeezes back and gently scrapes my skin with the tip of his index finger. I press my thumb into the center of his palm. It's like our hands move independently of our bodies. Speaking a language only they understand. Actually, our hands need to get a fucking room.

Jax looks up at me and leans in. Our faces are so close I feel the heat of his breath on my lips. "Can I kiss you, Beckett Gaines?"

No one has ever asked if they could kiss me in my entire life. I'm stunned not only by the question, but because I don't think I know the answer. Do I want him to kiss me? On the one hand I've always wanted to chew on that juicy bottom lip of his and taste his Jolly Rancher breath. On the other hand, it's *The Great* Jaxon Parker. And on the other, other hand, it's Jax. Brock vibrates a third time against my crotch. I ignore it. In this moment, no one else exists in the world but me and Jax as I try to figure this out. It's bizarre. Surreal. But I think it's going to happen. And the craziest thing is, it feels . . . right.

I must nod, though I don't remember sending such a command to my brain, because Jax leans in and presses his lips against mine. I don't think anymore. I just go with it. I close my eyes and finally understand what people mean when they say they *see stars*, because the moment his tongue parts my lips, it's like a Fourth of July fireworks show on the back of my eyelids. If Shelby saw me right now she'd probably sling holy water at us and try to cast the demons of *what the fuck* out of me. And I couldn't blame her, the way I've vilified Jax all these years. But now with my mouth full of him, everything is somehow different. He pushes deeper inside me, covering my whole mouth with his. His kiss is urgent. Desperate. Like the way I used to kiss my Thor action figure when I was eight. I don't know how long we stay attached like that, but I never want to be separated from him—*this* Jax. This new and improved Jax. Sensitive. Sweet. And a little broken.

But a car horn ruins it all only a moment later. Jax pulls back with a start, and we look over our shoulders toward the parking lot. Someone stands backlit in the crosshairs of headlight beams. I can't tell who it is, but a familiar voice brings us crashing back to reality.

"Jax?" Tiffany calls out. "Is that you?"

Jax jumps to his feet and backs away from me like I have gay cooties or something.

"Tiffany," he calls out, his voice drenched in desperation. "It's not what you think."

His words knock the wind right out of me. I stand and step away from him, because I can't believe my ears.

"It's not what she thinks?" My ears burn and my heart pounds like a jackhammer in my chest. "You spineless motherfucker."

He looks over and reaches for my arm. "No . . . Beck . . . that's not what I meant."

I back away and raise my hands. "Jesus! I can't believe I fell for your bullshit, and your eyes, and your fucking green apple, Jolly Rancher breath."

"Jax?" Terry Fox calls from the parking lot. "You okay? What's going on?"

Jax's face goes white as a ghost as he steps back. He doesn't see how close he is to the edge of the dock, but I do. Do I feel the urge to warn him? *Hell* no.

"I'll be right there," he calls out.

"Fuck this," Tiffany shouts. "Take me home, Terry." A door slams.

"Tiffany! Just wait, goddammit. I can explain," Jax yells.

I can't believe what I'm hearing. *He can explain? I need to be explained?*

He looks over at me, still edging back. "Beck, I'm sorry . . . I have to—"

He makes a pretty big splash, but the water's so dark now I can barely see his blond head go under. The engine of

Terry's SUV revs in the parking lot. I look over my shoulder just in time to see them spin out and pull away, Terry Fox, Molly Kim, and Tiffany Daniels inside. Actually Tiffany hangs out the back window shooting me the bird and instructing me in all manner of creative ways that I can go fuck myself. I don't need this shit. I'm out of here. Let the bastard drown.

I storm down the dock toward the parking lot to the sounds of Jax thrashing about in the water behind me. Surely to God, the asshole knows how to swim. *The Great* Jaxon Parker can do *everything*. After a few more steps, a gargled scream stops me in my tracks. I take a deep breath and rub my temples, contemplating if I can live with the guilt if he drowns. Pretty quickly I determine that *yes*, in fact, I *can*. But sweet JoJo would be devastated. And even I wouldn't want Tracee to suffer the loss of a child.

"Shit," I yell at the stars, and shake my fist at . . . the moon, I guess, for lack of a better target. I turn and sprint back down to the water's edge.

# CHAPTER TWENTY-SIX

# Jaxon

They're all over me. Webbed feet and feathered wings splash water all around me, attacking from all sides as a chorus of angry screeches echoes in my ears. There must be dozens of them. A bill grazes my arm, and I scream about two octaves higher than I thought possible. Pond water pools in the base of my throat as I search for the bottom with my foot. I take in another mouthful of scummy water and cough it right back out. I can't see the dock. All I see are hundreds of angry, beady eyes surrounding me. Closing in on me. Trying to *drown* me.

I look up. An arm, a *human* arm, reaches down to me. I grab on to it, digging my fingers into the skin and praying that I make it out before I'm eaten alive. With my free hand, I grab on to the edge of the dock and pull myself up, collapsing on the wooden planks, facedown and coughing the shit water up and out of my lungs. Labored breathing on my left guides the turn of my head. Beckett is on hands and knees, his chest heaving.

I glance back down into the dark, watery grave from which he just saved me. Three medium-sized ducks swim around, nipping at the water and quacking like they're laughing their feathered asses off at me. Dirty bastards.

Holding his arm where I must have grabbed him too hard, Beck stands and glares at me. "I probably should have let you drown." He turns and hurries down the dock toward the parking lot.

"Beck, wait," I say, but I'm too out of breath to explain. I curl my fingers into a fist and slam it down onto the wood. "Goddammit!"

Lifting my head, I look back at the parking lot just as Beck's car pulls out, nearly clipping a streetlight. Terry's SUV is nowhere in sight. I know I was late getting to Tiff's, but I just didn't want to leave Beck. Even soaked in scummy pond water, I can still taste him on my lips. Now he thinks . . . they think . . . shit! How the hell did they know where to find me, anyway?

I drag myself up and onto my feet. Water oozes out of every crevice of my clothes. My jeans feel like they weigh a hundred pounds, and my T-shirt clings to my chest like a slimy second skin. I grab my phone off the bench. Still no bars. I trudge down the dock, holding my phone up in the air, trying to get bars. No luck, and there's not a soul in sight who might have better cell coverage than my shitty plan.

I peel my shirt off and wring it out, feeling just as defeated as the shirt looks. Slinging it over my shoulder, I hold the phone up and walk a little farther. One bar! My heart races.

But who knows how long it'll last. I could use it to pull up the RideShare app or I could call Beck. If I could just talk to him and explain. But really, what's the use? It's not like he'll ever talk to me again anyway.

Maybe he'll talk to Brock.

# CHAPTER TWENTY-SEVEN

# Beckett

I slam the front door behind me. Head straight up the stairs to my room. That door gets a nice slam as well. Dad's text said he went to the office to pick up something, so I can slam the shit out of every door in this goddamned house if I want.

Plopping down in the middle of my bed, I stare up at the ceiling, trying to calm myself before I explode. My hands shook the entire drive home from the park. I don't even remember making the turns that brought me here. I should've let that bastard drown. How much of a loser do I have to be to keep falling for his bullshit?

My phone vibrates in my pocket, drawing me out of my conflicted head. I take a deep breath and fish it out. Surely, he's not dumb enough to actually ever text me again. Not after tonight. I hold the phone up in the air at arm's length. That's when I notice the bruises on the inside of my arm where Jax clamped down on me like a vise grip when I pulled him out. Great. Now I have to walk around looking like Julia Roberts in that movie from Dad's vintage DVD collection, *Sleeping with the Enemy.*

*Note to self: Canned vegetables cabinet needs organizing. Labels to the front!*

I tap my four digit passcode into my phone to unlock the home screen. What I expect to find are all the Bangr DM messages left by Brock while I was at the park. But turns out it wasn't my imaginary friend vibrating against my boner while I was sucking face with Satan, after all. It was Shelby. There are four texts, and I start swiping left.

First text: *Meet me at the Crusty Cup after you're done at the park with Pretty Boy 'Roid?*

Second text: *At CC and OMG Frenchy's here studying with Anya. Did you get the InstaPic of my bleached nipple?*

Third text: *Warning. HBIC of evil has landed. Tiffany's here with Terry and Korean Beyoncè. Terry is so f-ing hot. Would bang that brotha so hard. Actually said hello and asked where u were. Btw Anya said she, Asa, Chevy, and couple others are sharing limo to the RP. They want us to ride them. WITH them. Ok??? Did I mention Chevy would be there???*

Damn. That kind of sidelines Shelby's plan to ask Chevy to the prom. But maybe a group thing would be easier for her. And it's not like I have a date anyway.

Fourth text: *Incoming! Get out of there. They're on the way!*

Well, my girl tried to warn me, got to give her that. Even though she played right into Terry's hand and probably told him right where to find me. Shelby wouldn't have thought Terry would assume Jax was with me. But Tiffany sure as hell would. I hit reply and type,

*Thanks for the heads-up, but got it too late. And how did they know where we were???????? Drama, Mama. Tell you later. I'm a mess. Limo sounds fun.*

And I am a mess. I don't know what was all over that dock—other than duck shit—but it stuck to me like some kind of nasty-ass glue. I need a shower. Springing up off the bed, I lose my clothes faster than Tiffany Daniels on a Saturday night and trot down the hall, buck naked.

While the shower is warming up, I check myself in the full-length mirror. Honestly, I don't understand how I'm still a virgin, because I think my body looks reasonably above average. And, of course, my ass gets high marks. I can't imagine why no one has wanted to tap that yet. Oh well, maybe I should just get a cat, live with my dad forever, and call it a day. The hot water feels amazing on my skin, washing all the Jaxon Parker right off me. I swear, I could kick myself for letting that prick mess with my head. And just when I was starting to think he wasn't an evil cyborg under that hot outer human shell. Just when I thought we were friends. Just when he made me feel like . . . well, something *more* than friends.

I mock his voice in my head. *I'm straight. I'm not one hundred percent straight. I'm attracted to guys. I think I'm bisexual.*

Jesus, he's exhausting. Go practice on someone else and just leave me alone. It feels right when I think it in my head, so why can't I bring myself to wash him off my lips? I can still feel his lips pressed against mine. Just the memory of it stiffens me in an instant. I wash my lower stomach with sudsy hands, letting my fingers fall and lightly graze my shaft. My dick rises to meet my touch—*an invitation*. I take it into my hand and close my fingers around its thickening girth, stroking it gently and getting it nice and slippery . . . I mean, clean.

I swear the more I think about Jax, the madder I get and the dirtier my penis feels in my hand. It needs a thorough scrubbing, and that's just what I give it. With every sudsy tug, I try to dispel the memory of Jax's tongue parting my lips and pushing down into my mouth. I tighten my grip and scrub the sudsy shaft back and forth. Back and forth. With that hand fully engaged, the deep disgust I feel for Jaxon Parker drives the index finger of my other hand to find its way between my legs, over my taint, and to the rim of my hole. It's good to be thorough when showering, especially in your nether regions. I ease my soapy finger inside, and a moan rumbles up from my throat. God, I hate that asshole. Jax, not *my* asshole. I'm quite fond of my own freshly bleached asshole, especially right now.

"Oh fuck!" I groan. The ensuing orgasm comes quick and seizes in every muscle. My whole body jerks and buckles in what feels like one long never-ending full-body spasm. My knees finally give out, and I crumple down onto the floor of the stall as I unload in a succession of shivers and spastic kicks.

If anyone saw me right now, they'd be shoving a spoon into my mouth to hold my tongue down so I don't bite it off. Jesus, now I can't stop thinking about biting my tongue off. After what feels like hours, but I know could only have been a few seconds, the herky-jerky shower stall dance slows and so does my racing heart. I roll over on my back with my legs bent at the knees, letting the hot water beat down on my stomach, washing the last remnants of Jaxon Parker off my skin.

Jesus. How long has it been? Sex with myself has *never* been *that* good. I'm an adequate self-gratifier at best. Damn that Jaxon Parker. Damn him for kissing me one minute, rejecting me the next, and then dominating my masturbatory thoughts, leaving me a sticky mess in the bottom of my shower stall after the best solo sex of my life.

Once I regain the use of my spaghetti legs, I pull myself up, finish showering, and dry off. Feeling completely spent and exhausted, I drape the towel over my head and muss my hair dry as I stroll back down the hall to my room. The house is still quiet. Dad will probably be home soon, though. I step into my room, letting the towel drop to the floor, and what do I find sitting on the edge of my bed? Big Titties. It's such a foreign sight that I completely forget about my momentary state of nakedness. Tracee looks up at me and seems distracted by my junk—*naturally*—but her inspection is brief and oddly maternal.

"Beck," she says, raising a hand to shield her eyes. "Why is your penis so red?"

I look down. She's right. It looks like a stalk of Twizzler. I snap to my senses, snatch the towel off the floor, and cover my candy. I'm sure my face is as red as my penis.

"What are you doing in my room?" I ask with no small dose of irritation as I tie the towel securely around my midsection. I don't even like this woman seeing my cute naked belly button. If the towel were big enough, I'd tie it around my chest and wear it like a one-piece swimsuit so she couldn't see my nips, either.

She peeks through her fingers and frowns. "I heard you in the shower. Can you put something on, please?"

*It's my fucking room and I didn't invite you in here, Boulder Tits*, I want to say as I hurry over to the basket of folded laundry on my bed and fish out some Andrew Christian bikini briefs. I shimmy into them under the towel and remind myself that my anger at Tracee is somewhat misdirected. But she did invite herself into my room without my permission.

"Not to be rude"—*hint, hint*—"but can I ask what you are doing here?" I quickly slip a T-shirt over my head and pull on a pair of khaki shorts all before discarding the towel. "Is Dad home?"

She lowers her hand from her eyes and shakes her head. "No. I have a key."

I purse my lips to keep from spewing obscenities like a purge of vomit. Why the hell did Dad give this woman a key to our house, and why is she in my room getting all up in my Kool-Aid?

"I've got some bad news," she says, resting her elbows on her knees. "About the Rainbow Prom. Sorry to barge in, but I thought you'd both want to know."

I stand in front of her and plant my hands on my hips. "What bad news?"

Tracee runs her fingers through her hair. "The school board voted. They're not going to let us use the gym."

Heat rises from the tips of my toes to the rims of my ears in about two seconds flat. Damn that Cassidy Charles and her holier-than-thou mother. "That is total bullshit."

Tracee nods. "The very definition of it, I agree. But what can we do about it? It's too late to find another venue."

I sit down next to her, feeling slightly bad for being rude.

The prom meant a lot to Tracee. "How can they do this? Was there a public hearing or something?"

She shakes her head. "It was all hush-hush and behind closed doors. That pastor from the Holiness Tabernacle was in on it too. Snakes, all of them. Principal Healy called the chair of the PFLAG chapter this afternoon to give her the news."

She hangs her head like she just heard someone died. Tracee put a lot of work into this prom, and it's sad to see her looking so defeated. And I had a lot riding on it too. But even more than that, I think about how disappointed Carter Treadwell and all the queer kids in Florence County will be when they're once again told that there's something wrong with them. That they're not good enough for normal things like a prom where they can feel safe being themselves.

"There *has* to be another place," I say, the take-charge Dorothy in me rising strong.

Tracee just shakes her head. "We made some calls. Everything within our budget is already booked."

My mind races, flipping through a slide show of possible solutions, but not landing on any solid option.

"Maybe there's a way to get the school board to reconsider," I say, thinking of one slight possibility.

"I doubt it—" Tracee stops and touches my arm, causing me to flinch a little. She furrows her brow and her eyes go cold. "Beckett, what happened to your arm?"

"What?"

"You have bruises on your arm. Did someone hurt you? Are you getting bullied again?"

Several possible responses run through my head all at once.

*I just saved your spineless prick of a son from drowning in a duck pond.*

*It's a self-inflicted wound from beating the hell out of my meat in the shower.*

*When you're near me, my bodily organs begin to shut down, so you have to move far away from here. Out of state would be the safest for me, if that's not too much to ask.*

Or, I could take the planting-seeds-of-doubt part of the breakup plan to a whole other level. It's diabolical, and Jax would kill me if he finds out, but *fuck him very much*. I look into Tracee's big, round, cow eyes, and remind myself that this woman is as flighty as a 747—not to mention a tried-and-true carpet muncher who *will* end up leaving my dad in a puddle of Xanax for the next power tool lesbian that makes her fat nipples hard.

I yank my arm away with a put-on wince. Hide it under my shirt and pretend to have a hard time looking her in the eye. It's not much of a stretch, but I'm a trained actor, so I hold myself to a higher standard—which also means producing tears on cue. It's not really that hard. I just think of things that make me really sad.

*Man buns. Cargo shorts. Speedos on anyone other than Olympic divers. Duck face selfies. Carbohydrates.*

It's working. With my whole body withdrawn like a scared child, I look up at her. Lip quiver, *check*. Pooling tears, *check*. Crack in voice, *check*.

"I fell down the stairs?" The words alone might not be convincing enough for a DSS worker, but the way I lifted that last word into a question . . . move over, Meryl, Kate, J.Law, and don't be hatin' bitches.

It works like a charm. The alarm in Tracee's eyes can't even be hidden by mounds of cakey mascara. Actually, she looks so horrified, I immediately feel like shit for using what I know about Jax's childhood to manipulate her. Maybe I crossed the line. *You think?* But I don't stop her from thinking the worst about my dad. I remind myself that this is for his own good. He will understand that one day.

She stands up and takes a deep breath. "I need to go find your father. Right now."

"He went to the office to pick up something," I say, and rattle off the address without a moment's hesitation.

"I know where it is," she says, nodding and touching my shoulder with such a sincere I've-got-you look that I want to hurl all over her Payless pumps. Dad is going to kill me. I can live with that—which I realize makes absolutely no sense. Tracee is out the door in a blur of boobs and hairspray. It's official. The Florence Holiness Tabernacle crazies are right. Just put me on a spit and slather me with BBQ sauce, because I'm going to burn in hell. But not for the reason they think.

After a quick check of the time on my phone, I scrounge around on the floor, searching for something nicer to wear. If I hurry, I may be able to catch him in his office. He said he's there practically every day of the week. I lose the khaki shorts and step into a pair of dark jeans. I pull on a light blue button-down over my T-shirt and tuck it in as my phone buzzes. I grab it and check the home screen. A DM from Brock. Hmm. I'm in a hurry because I have to save the gay prom, but I'm compelled to answer my imaginary boyfriend. Wow. Look how quickly Brock got promoted from imaginary *friend* to imaginary *boyfriend.* I'm so easy it's hard to believe I'm still a virgin.

*Let's meet*, his message reads.

That didn't work out so well for me last time I found Mr. Right Now on Bangr. No way in hell I'm doing that again.

*When and where?* I type. I'm pathetic.

*Rainbow Prom?*

If I can get the hell out of here and go save it. I step into my penny loafers and run my fingers through my damp hair.

*Maybe. Will let you know*, I type, regaining some modicum of virtue.

*K. Hope so. Gotta run. Bye, Beckett.*

It's still a little creepy when he uses my real name. Too intimate. I rather he call me *D* like my profile says, because I feel like a massive Dorothy right now. Fixing shit and taking names. As I plow down the stairs and out the front door, all that's missing is a bright, floral printed caftan flowing behind me like a *Golden Girls* superhero cape.

# CHAPTER TWENTY-EIGHT

# Jaxon

I need to come clean to Beck about Brock soon, and I will at the Rainbow Prom if he agrees to meet me . . . or Brock. No RideShare driver was going to pick me up in the state I'm in, so I walked the whole way to Tiffany's house—water sloshing in my shoes and my clothes reeking of duck shit. God, I hate ducks. Okay, I'm terrified of ducks. They freak me the hell out as all birdlike creatures do. Chickens, peacocks, cockatoos, the entire avian family—spawn of Satan, all of them. And yes, maybe I lost my shit a little when I fell into the pond, but they were flapping and quacking all over me like some kind of crazed flock of demonic waterfowl. I'm positive one of them tried to bite me. Thank God, Beck came back and helped me out of there. I know he needs time to cool off, so I figure I'll start my damage control tour with Tiffany. Thankfully, she lives only a mile or so from the park. Terry's SUV is parked in the driveway, which is good. Hopefully, he'll have my back, but his girlfriend Molly *is* Tiff's best friend.

As I start up the front steps, the door opens and Tiffany stands there in a white crop top and shorts, with steam practically coming out of her ears. She looks me up and down. "Well, for once you look like the pond scum you are. I'd hoped you'd drowned. What the fuck do you want, Jax?"

I stop on the bottom step and shove my hands in my pockets. Water drizzles out and down the legs of my jeans. "Can I talk to you a minute?"

Tiffany steps forward and leans against one of the soaring, white columns of the porch. She crosses her arms over her chest. "About what?" she says. "About you letting that fag kiss you? Because you didn't look like you were fighting him off too hard."

Terry steps through the open doorway with his arm around Molly's shoulder. Molly scowls at me.

"Hey, bruh," Terry says, grinning and covering his mouth with his fist to keep from busting a gut when he sees me. "Rough night?"

I nod up at him. "Not my best. Hey, I need to talk to Tiff. Okay, guys?"

Terry nods and leads a still scowling Molly back inside, closing the door behind them. I climb the steps slowly and stop about three below the landing where Tiffany is perched.

"That queer made a pass at you," she says with her eyes narrowed on me suspiciously. "*He kissed you*. Why didn't you kick his ass, Jax? You're too nice. I knew once you started spending time with that freak that this would happen. That he would develop some kind of sick crush on you and eventually cross the line and—"

"I kissed *him*, Tiff," I say, interrupting her.

Her mouth hangs open and she furrows her eyebrows as much as the Botox will allow. Even though she looks stunned, I know that somewhere deep down, she already knew. She just didn't want it confirmed. She needs to paint Beck as the predator and me as the victim. *That* she can wrap her head around. Not the truth.

"What do you mean *you* kissed *him*?"

I look down, like a coward, breaking eye contact. "I didn't want you to misunderstand what happened and go around telling everyone that Beckett made some kind of desperate pass at me." I force myself to look up at her again, searching for any trace of compassion in her eyes—not that I deserve any. "I want you to know the truth. I kissed him. I *wanted* to kiss him. And I'm not sorry about it—except that I hurt you. I'm just sorry I wasn't honest with you sooner."

Tiffany shakes her head, rejecting my words. "Jax, you don't have to protect him. The other day at church when I asked you if you're gay, I didn't mean it. You're too good at sex to be gay. I was just angry at that little fag."

I take a deep breath, trying to contain my anger. "Please stop saying that word. Especially when you're talking about Beck."

Tiffany pushes off the column. Her nostrils flare and her eyes widen. "Jesus, Jax. Are you in love with him? Is that what this is about? You *are* gay, aren't you?"

I shake my head. "I'm not gay. I guess I'm bi. But that's not the point." To make the distinction sounds idiotic and weak the moment it leaves my mouth.

"Not the point?" Tiffany shifts her weight to one side and plants her hands on her hips. "Wow." She narrows her eyes on me. "So all those times you took me from behind, you were thinking about doing *guys*? Were you thinking about *him* the last time I sucked your dick? Is that why you came so hard?"

*Yes* and *yes*, but that's probably best left unsaid at the moment. "Tiff, I just wanted to come here and say that I'm sorry. Sorry for sending you mixed signals, for using you. Hell, I didn't even know I was doing it at the time. That's why I don't think we should hang out anymore. Not like that, anyway. I don't want to lead you on, and I certainly don't want to hurt you."

She shoots me a glare that could melt steel. Her neck becomes an abstract canvas of red splotches and protruding veins.

"You goddammed piece of shit!" she screams at the top of her lungs. I swear they heard that two streets away. "*You* want to break up with *me*? Oh hell, no, asshole. *I* am breaking up with *your* cock loving ass. And, trust me, everyone at school will know why. So you can get the fuck off our property now. I don't ever want to see you again."

That would be nearly impossible unless one of us changes schools, but again . . . not the time to point out logistics. The front door opens, and Terry and Molly spill out onto the porch.

"What the hell's going on?" Molly asks, moving to Tiffany's side and placing a hand on her shoulder. "You okay, Tiff?"

Tiffany points at me, eyes red and swollen with tears. "He wants to fuck dudes. Hell, he probably already has. Did you fuck Terry, Jax?"

Molly whips her head around in Terry's direction.

Terry looks down at me, mouth hanging open and lips curling on end. He glances back and forth from Tiffany to me, and back to Molly. His bottom lip quivers with barely contained laughter. Who kissed whom, or whether or I want to fuck guys, girls, or Hot Pockets are details that don't matter to Terry right now. I know he thinks this whole situation is hysterical, but the eye daggers he's taking from Molly keep him in check for the moment.

"I've never wanted to fuck Terry, Tiff," I say with a conciliatory sigh.

Terry coughs out a chuckle and glances over at me. "Um, thanks, bruh. I guess. But what the hell is she talking about?"

Tiffany points at me again. "Jax *wanted* to kiss that fag in the park. Apparently, we interrupted some kind of secret fag rendezvous."

"Tiffany," I say, as calmly as possible. "I understand that you're upset, so I'll ask you one more time. Please don't use that word when you're talking about Beck."

Molly gasps. "So it's true, Jax? You like dudes?"

"Look," I say, backing down the steps. "I just wanted you all to know that Beck's not some kind of sleazy predator. He's just a gay kid who's not ashamed of who he is. I came to set the record straight and to apologize to Tiff. I'll go now."

"And to break up with me," Tiffany says, crossing her arms again.

I cock my head at her. "Come on, Tiff. You know that's been a long time coming, and it has nothing to do with Beck or about me being attracted to guys or girls."

Terry walks slowly down the steps toward me. "So let me

get this straight . . . so to speak. Are you saying that you *do* like guys?"

I inhale a deep, cleansing breath and exhale slowly. It feels right to say it now. Here. Out loud. I'm so tired of hiding. "Yes, Terry. I'm attracted to both girls and guys. I'm bisexual."

Terry cocks his head and stares right through me, his face devoid of expression. I don't know what he's going to do, but in those few seconds I wonder if I know Terry Fox the way I thought I did. He stops on the step above me and lowers his voice, even though it would be impossible for the girls not to hear him.

"Dude. Why didn't you ever tell me?" There's a hint of disappointment in Terry's voice. "You know I'll always have your back, right?"

A flood of relief washes over me, but now is not the time for a bro-fest. I nod over in Tiff's direction. "Thanks, man. But let's talk later, okay? Kind of in the middle of something here."

"You're not in the middle of anything, Jax," Tiffany says, moving to the center of the landing. "We're done. And by the time you get to school Monday morning, you will be too."

She turns on her heel and stalks off into the house with Molly right behind her. Molly looks back and flips me off with a scowl as she slams the door closed behind them. Terry and I stand there in silence, staring at each other.

He joins me on the bottom step and puts his hand on my shoulder. "You gonna be okay?"

I shove my hands back into damp, slimy pockets. "Is it true what you said? You really got me on this?"

Terry lowers his head. "You know, it hurts that you even

have to ask." He looks back up at me. "You're my best friend. *Of course* I've got your back. Just like you've had mine ever since we were kids and I had every racist slur imaginable hurled at me."

In that moment I don't think there's anyone on earth— man or woman or Hot Pocket—that I love more than Terry Fox. We sit on the step, side by side, and I wrap my arms around my knees.

"You think she's really going to tell everyone at school?"

Terry looks over at me and rests his forearms on his knees. "Your truth? No. Her truth? Most definitely." He knocks my shoulder with an elbow. "You know you need to get ahead of this with the team, right? Better they hear it from you than in the cafeteria or on Quickchat."

I sigh and shake my head. "But if I tell them I'm bisexual, all they're going to hear is 'gay.'"

Terry falls silent. He knows I'm right. He's probably already thought it himself.

"Fuck them," he finally says. "You can't control what those fools hear *or* think. All you can do is tell your truth. Just be honest with them. They'll respect you for it. At least some of them will. Maybe more than you think."

I look over at him and rear my head back in surprise. "When did your dumb ass get so wise?"

His smile consumes his whole face. You'd think I just compared him to the baby Jesus.

"I don't know what I'm doing here, dude," I say. "I wouldn't even know what to say to the guys."

Terry drapes his arm around my neck. "You told me a while

back that your moms were the two bravest people you've ever known. Right?"

I nod. "That I did. And it's true. They've never been ashamed of who they are, even living in this narrow-minded town."

Terry nods as if his point has been made for him. "Then maybe try leading by their example, Jax. And have a little faith in people." He squeezes my shoulder and stands. "I'll say good-bye to Molly and then drive you home."

I look over my shoulder as he disappears into the house, my mind and my heart at war with his words and no clear victor emerging.

# CHAPTER TWENTY-NINE

Beckett

What the Florence city-county complex lacks in stately South-ern charm, it makes up for in retro, utilitarian design. The ten-story cinder block box with windows looks as if it was plucked right out of Cold War era Moscow. It being Saturday, the lobby is like a graveyard, and with no metal detectors or security guards on hand to add any heft, my first impression of our city government is more than a little disappointing.

I was relieved to find a sleek, black Beemer sitting in the mayor's reserved spot in the parking lot. I hope he really meant it when he offered me that open invitation. As the ele-vator carries me up to the tenth floor to the mayor's office suite, I wonder what kind of skeletons they'll find in his closet when they start digging. They always find something, and this guy seems way too good to be true. But if we're going to find a venue for the prom in one week, with the school board and a church full of bigoted whack jobs fighting us every step of the way, Mayor Tom Davenport is probably our best hope.

The elevator door opens onto a tastefully decorated lobby where a curvy receptionist with flawless dark skin and a warm smile sits.

"Hi. I'm here to see the mayor," I say, walking up to her desk without waiting for her to greet me.

Her pretty smile fades a little, and her forehead crinkles as she gives me a once-over. "He doesn't usually take meetings on Saturday. Is he expecting you?"

Feeling a tad underdressed all of a sudden in my wrinkled button-down, I shove my hands into the pockets of my jeans. Maybe I should have thrown on a blazer.

"Not exactly," I say. "But he did tell me to come by anytime. So is he? Here? It's an emergency." *Calm down, girl*, I chide myself. *Emergency* is a bit of a stretch.

The woman purses her lips and picks up the handset of the phone. "Let me see if he's available. Your name?"

"Beckett Gaines," I say, turning away to give her some privacy.

"Yes, sir," she says behind me. "There's a young man here to see you. He doesn't have an appointment but says it's an emergency. His name is Becket Gaines?" Slight pause. "Okay, will do."

As I turn back to face her, the woman stands. Her smile has returned. "I'll show you the way."

She leads me down a long hallway lined with outdated wallpaper and large, ornately framed portraits of past mayors. I feel just a tad drunk with power. I mean, what seventeen-year-old kid just shows up at city hall on a Saturday and is escorted right into the mayor's office without an appointment? That's pretty baller, if I do say so myself. His office door is open, and the receptionist raps her knuckles on it as she glides in.

"Sir, Beckett Gaines," she says, and waves me in.

I like the sound of that. Sir Beckett Gaines.

*Note to self: Get knighted.*

Tom Davenport stands behind his desk at the far end of the room, looking classically handsome and smartly pressed. It's not a huge office, but a stately contrast to the exterior of the building, with dark hardwood floors, antique furniture, heavy drapes, and built-in shelves filled with books. It looks like old Davenport money threw up all over this office. I can't wait to see what he does with the White House.

"Beckett," he says, rounding the desk in expertly tailored navy slacks and a white polo button-down. "What a nice surprise." He holds out his hand to me. "I hope everything's okay."

Oh, right. The *emergency*. I shake his hand, and he motions for me to sit in a squeaky leather wingback chair facing his desk. *Baller*. I wouldn't be surprised if he offered me a cigar and some brandy. I should probably politely decline. It wouldn't look good if the *National Enquirer* got ahold of something like that. I can just see the headline:

*Hot Mayor "Entertains" Underage Boy in Clandestine After-hours Meeting*

As he heads back to his chair, he looks up at the receptionist. "Thanks, Jeanette. Sorry to have kept you so late. I'll lock up. You can head home."

Jeanette nods and closes the door behind her as she leaves. The mayor's smile is wide, genuine, and infectious. I can't help but return it, though I don't know why we're sitting here grinning at each other. He entwines his fingers into a ball on the desk in front of him. I don't think he's going to offer me that brandy.

"So? What's this emergency that brings you all the way down here on a Saturday?"

I scoot to the edge of my seat, lean forward, and rest my elbows on my knees, like we're old friends. "Actually, it concerns the Rainbow Prom I told you about."

He furrows his brow. "Yes. I heard about the school board vote."

"Do you think you could talk to them? Make them reconsider?"

"I'm sorry, Beckett," he says, leaning back in his chair. "The school board is an elected body and I don't have any authority over them. Believe me, if there was anything I could do about that, I would."

I stare at him, wishing I didn't hear him right. I thought *Supermayor* could do anything. I guess I was wrong.

I shake my head. "We only have a week to find another place to hold the prom or we'll have to cancel it. We have kids coming from all the high schools in Florence, Darlington, Marion, Timmonsville . . . I mean, shouldn't everyone have a fun and safe prom experience, no matter who they are or who they love?"

Tom Davenport looks at me like he's studying every inch of my face. After several seconds of intense inspection, he finally smiles and rests his body weight on the armrest of his chair.

"You know, when I was seventeen, I wasn't thinking about anyone but myself. Which girl I wanted to date, which college I wanted to go to, how much money I wanted to make. Unfortunately, I don't think I gave too much thought to the needs of other people. That's something I had to learn over time. But to be so young and understand it already . . . you have to be born with that kind of compassion. It's an admirable quality."

I shrug. "It doesn't feel admirable, it just feels right. I guess being gay gives me a different perspective than you had when you were my age, that's all." I lean back in my chair.

He nods slowly. "Can I ask you a personal question, Beckett? You don't have to answer it if it makes you uncomfortable."

I shrug again. I really need to stop doing that, especially in the presence of a future world leader. I sit up straight and nod.

The mayor picks up a pen and taps it once on the desk. "When did you first know you were gay?"

I don't hesitate with my response. "When did you first know you were straight?"

He huffs a slight chuckle. "Touché. Sorry. I wasn't challenging you or your sexual orientation." He pauses and stares at me. "I just meant I'm glad you had supportive, loving parents when you came out."

I break his gaze and glance down. "My dad's always been there for me."

When I look back up at him, his brow is wrinkled. "I'm sure your mom loves you just as much as your dad. But I'm sorry she left you. I'm sure she had her reasons, as hard as those might be to understand." He stares at me a full minute before looking away and rubbing his misty eyes with the back of his hand. Maybe he misses his wife. Or a life with my mom that might have been. Maybe he sees me as the son he and Mom could've had together. Whatever it is, he recovers pretty quickly.

"Sorry." His million-dollar campaign smile returns. "I think I have an idea," he says. "What about the Beacon?" He raises an expectant eyebrow. "That I can do with a phone call."

I stare at him, my mind in a footrace with my heart. The Beacon is the sickest hotel from Columbia to Charleston. Far too swanky for Florence. I don't even know how they stay in business around here.

"How—"

The mayor chuckles. "My family owns it. The grand ballroom is quite nice. I'm sure we could move some things around to accommodate your prom."

"You own the Beacon Hotel?" So that's how they stay in business.

He puts on a pair of stylish red-framed glasses and picks up his phone. "That would be better than a school gymnasium anyway, don't you think?" He thumbs a number into the screen as I sit there with my mouth hanging open.

"We could have the Rainbow Prom at the Beacon Hotel? But the PFLAG chapter can't afford—"

He raises a finger up to put me on hold and says hello to someone named Kelly. He asks Kelly about the date of our prom and if some event could be moved to another ballroom. He waits a few seconds for an answer and then smiles. After a brief description of our event and some particulars about how the food, beverage, and the ballroom rental fee itself should all be *comped*, he thanks Kelly for taking care of the details and ends the call. Just like that.

"Yes. You can have your prom at the Beacon Hotel."

"Wow," I say, shaking my head in disbelief. "That's so . . . so generous of you."

He gives me the warmest smile I have ever seen on a future president of the United States, seemingly tickled to death that he was able to help me.

Tom Davenport drops his phone on his desk like he has a hundred of them in a junk drawer at home. "Just glad I could help."

"But the Tabernacle," I say. "They can still apply for a permit to protest, can't they?"

He nods and leans forward on the desk. "Unfortunately, they can. But they can't stop the prom from happening at the Beacon, and I can delay their permit as long as legally possible. In the end, though, they do have their rights, just like everyone else."

I stand because I have taken up way too much of the mayor's time and his generosity makes me giddy and uncomfortable all at the same time. "I don't know what to say, other than thank you."

He pops up out of his chair and rounds the desk, retucking his shirt. "Well, this isn't free, you know. Remember you owe my daughter that introduction to Justin Black."

"Done," I say, shaking his hand. "But tell her to keep her expectations low. He's kind of a dick."

He laughs, hard, and guides me over to the door, his hand on the small of my back.

"Thanks again, Mr. Mayor," I say, not even sure that's the proper way to address him. *Your Honor? Your Honorable Hotness?*

"Please," he says, opening the door for me. "Call me Tom."

I melt a little inside. He's so handsome it warms the back of my neck. Mom has baller taste in men. My dad included, of course.

"And Beckett—"

"Beck," I say. If I can call the mayor Tom, he can at least call me Beck.

"Okay, Beck," he says with a smile. "I meant what I said about how glad I am you were raised by such great parents. Your dad *and* your mom. I'm sure they're both very proud of you."

I don't really know how to respond to his endless cheerleading for my mom, so I just nod, look away, and make an abrupt beeline for the lobby.

# CHAPTER THIRTY

Jaxon

Other than Bobby Jenkins being his normal asshole self, running off at the mouth and *playfully* knocking guys around, there seems to be a calm, even jovial, vibe in the locker room as the guys strip down and head for the showers. It's been five days since the breakup, and things have been relatively quiet at school. Hurricane Tiffany petered out early, I guess, because she hasn't posted anything on Quickchat that would cast any doubt on either our relationship status or my presumed heterosexuality. I wonder if I have my best friend to thank for that. Maybe Terry spoke words of wisdom to her in that soothing voice of his and talked some sense into her, or at least bought me some time. If he did, he's not taking credit for it.

And as much as the way I left things with Beck gnaws at me, I'm trying to give him some space—not that he'll answer my texts anyway. When I left him in the park Saturday night, the hurt in his eyes was obvious, and the last thing I want to do is cause the guy any more pain. For now, I'm just glad he's talking to *Brock*. Setting things straight with Tiff was a huge first step in the getting-my-shit-together department, but I still need to talk to the team. This is high school, after all. My secret *will* get out eventually. Today was the last practice of the week, and I've put it off as long as I can. I just don't know how to broach the subject with the guys.

When I step out of my jockstrap, a small chorus of snickers and whistles erupts behind me. Well, I guess it's been decided for me. *Great. Let the games begin.* I turn around without bothering to cover my junk. Why should I? Never have before. It's not like these guys haven't seen me buck naked a thousand times, and it's not like I have anything to be shy about. Bobby Jenkins stands there facing me, wearing nothing more than a smirk and a bushy jockstrap.

He tosses a set of kneepads on the floor in front of me. "Better put these on before you hit the showers, Parker. You might need them."

Flanking Bobby, his dim-witted posse snickers and slaps him on the back. Rick, Billy, and Trey have shared one brain since third grade, and there's not nearly enough of it to go around. This is not the way I wanted this to go down, but it's my own fault for putting it off so long. I struggle to keep my calm. Ever the peacemaker, Terry steps in front of me in white tube socks, a Gamecocks ball cap, and nothing else. He picks up the kneepads and walks them back over to Bobby. Even I have to admit that this impromptu dick-off is a little cliché, but hey, we use what God gave us, and God gave Terry a lot to work with.

"I think you dropped these, Bobby," he says calmly, tossing the pads on the bench. "Because I know you didn't mean to disrespect your quarterback. Right?"

Bobby is a couple of inches taller than Terry, and the rage brimming in his eyes is fueled by his well documented racism. And while everyone knows that Terry Fox is as levelheaded as they come, that's a pot you do *not* want to stir.

I step up and stand beside Terry. "It's okay, Ter. Bobby was just fucking around, that's all."

The locker room has grown silent. In various states of undress, the other guys fall into an unofficial huddle around the confrontation. Bobby glares at Terry, a racial slur visibly forming on his lips. This could get ugly fast. Best to divert focus.

"He probably heard a rumor that I like dick," I say. "So he's having some fun at my expense. Right, Bobby?"

Bobby breaks his threatening gaze on Terry and glances over at me. "I heard it's more than just a rumor."

"And where'd you hear that?"

A sneer twists his lips. "Last night when I was fucking your *ex*-girlfriend."

Stifled chuckles and snickers snake their way through the room. No wonder it's been so calm around school. It was the eye of the storm. Hurricane Tiffany made landfall last night with a very targeted wallop. I'm impressed and a little disgusted.

Bobby takes a step closer to me. "You deny it, Jax?"

I know that Bobby said the words, but it's Beckett's voice I hear in my head asking the question. I look Bobby directly in the eye and close the remaining distance between us. We stand nose to nose. Clarifying the differences between the words "gay" and "bisexual" seems unimportant, to say the least.

"So what if I do like dick, Bobby?" I say through gritted teeth, heat rising to my ears. "Your little pecker need sucking? Your bitch ass need fucking?"

Okay. So not my most eloquent and inspiring QB pep talk ever, but it does elicit some nice support from the peanut gallery. In the locker room, you're only as badass as your last dis, and that one stung Bobby big-time. He's speechless, his face is red and puffy, and he's literally seething.

Terry steps up to him, third leg swinging happily in the breeze. "Take a beat, Bobby." Terry looks over his shoulder and shoots me a scolding glare. He expects more from me, as he should.

"Look, guys," I say, picking up a towel and tying it around my waist. I think this would be more effective without all my junk on display. "I don't want to lie to you, okay? What Bobby says, it's true. I'm attracted to dudes. But not to any of your ugly asses, that's for sure, so don't get it twisted."

There. I said it. It's out there and I can't take it back. It's just too bad the levity I added fell flat. The silence in the room is immediate and deafening. My heartbeat accelerates and my hands become slick with sweat.

"So you're gay?"

I glance over my shoulder. Coach Wayne stands in the doorway behind me, his stone face unreadable. I didn't even hear him walk in. *Shit.*

I turn to face him, squaring my shoulders. "Bisexual, Coach."

He stares at me for a full minute, chewing on a toothpick that dangles from the corner of his mouth. Finally, he exhales deeply and scans the room. "Anybody got a problem with your quarterback's sexual orientation?"

His tone is flat and matter-of-fact, like he's bored of the distraction already. At first, no one says anything, which seems too good to be true. So I wait, knowing it will come.

"Yeah. I got a problem with it, Coach." And there it is. Bobby crosses his arms over his chest and widens his stance, which looks kind of silly with him standing there in a jock-strap a size too small. Billy, Rick, and Trey mimic Bobby's posture but don't say anything.

"Of course you do, Jenkins," Coach mutters, and plants his hands on his hips.

Bobby lowers his arms and curls his fingers into fists at his side. "Pastor Doug says it's a sin, Coach. It ain't normal. And I ain't playing with no faggot."

A chorus of oh-no-you-didn't whistles sail around the room.

Coach takes a step toward us, automatically silencing everyone. "Well, Bobby," he says. "You certainly have a right to your opinions."

Bobby grins and nods at me like he's won.

"But you do not have the right to use that kind of inflammatory language, not in this locker room, not on the field, not even at home on your own goddamned shitter," Coach says, his voice rising with every word. "This is not a fucking democracy. Clean out your locker and turn in your gear on your way out."

Bobby's eyes go wide as golf balls. "What the fuck, Coach?"

"If you'd like this suspension to be permanent," Coach says, his voice coated in a familiar growl, "that can certainly be arranged."

They stare at each other in a silent showdown, the challenge hanging in the air between them. Bobby pushes more air through his nose than it seems it can handle. His face is so red I seriously worry that he's going to pass out. He glares over at me one last time before taking a step back and stalking over to his locker at the end of the row. He makes plenty of noise getting dressed and cleaning it out, and Terry stands right beside him the whole time, keeping him in check, like a hot, naked security guard escorting a fired employee out of the building.

Coach Wayne walks over to Billy, Rick, and Trey. "You boys got anything to add to this illuminating discussion?"

They shake their heads, grab towels, and scurry off to the showers. With the tension in the room dying down quickly and the shit-stirrers gone, the other guys either return to their lockers or head to the showers. But on their way, every single one of them comes over and gives me a supportive slap on the ass. I can't imagine how red it is right now, and thank God I have a towel wrapped around my waist to soften the blows a little. I just stand there, grin, and bear it. I never thought getting my ass slapped by so many naked and semi-naked guys would cause a lump to form in my *throat* of all places. I hold my shit together, though, and thank each one of them by name as they pass.

Terry is the last one, and his slap is the hardest and loudest. "I told you, I got you, bruh." We lock arms as he leans in, touching his forehead to mine.

"Thanks, bud," I say, and knock a pesky tear out of my eye with the back of my hand.

"No need for that now," Terry says, smiling at me.

I wave him off. "Naw. It's all good. I just wish Beck was here to see this. Some of these guys probably don't even remember how they bullied him when we were younger. And now this . . . it's like no big deal to them."

"What did I tell you?" Terry says. "People can change."

"And times change," Coach says, joining us. "Like they say, things do get better. Hey, you should make one of them videos, Jax. It'd be good for local kids who're too scared to be themselves to see."

I shake my head at him. "I gotta say, Coach. I never in a million years thought you'd react like this."

Coach tucks his thumbs in the elastic waistband of his shorts and sighs. "I had a gay brother. You think you have it rough now, imagine what it was like for him thirty years ago. He was bullied, picked on, beat up. But the worst were the church folks. Convinced him he was an abomination and going straight to hell. He couldn't handle it. One day he took my dad's shotgun, walked out to the barn, and ended it once and for all."

"Jesus, Coach," Terry says. "That's terrible."

Coach nods. "And such a goddamned waste."

"I'm afraid gay kids around here are still getting that same message," I say.

Coach cocks his head and squints an eye at me. "What's going on, Parker?"

"There's this dance, or a prom, this Saturday for LGBT kids. But some people in this town would rather they stay in the shadows or, God forbid, do what your brother did. They plan to make some noise and show their asses at the prom."

"Let me guess," Coach says. "Pastor Doug and the Tabernacle of Hate."

Terry and I nod at him.

Coach shakes his head and scratches the back of his neck. "They're planning one of their protests?"

"Afraid so," I say.

"Well, that's just complete and utter bullshit," Coach blusters. "Those kids shouldn't be subjected to that." He narrows his eyes on us and then nods once. "You boys hit the showers and then stop by my office on your way out. I want to know more about this gay prom."

# CHAPTER THIRTY-ONE

# Beckett

I stand in front of the full-length mirror in my bedroom admiring my handiwork and deem it worthy of the Beacon Hotel Grand Ballroom. Dad let me raid his closet, because he knows my love for all things vintage extends beyond television and movies, and he's kept just about everything he's ever worn since the fourth grade. My ensemble for the prom is sickening and highlighted by a baby blue polyester tux jacket with wide black lapels that Dad inherited from his father. It's hideously fabulous, especially combined with a Chippendales-esque black bow tie and a *like-new* pair of black crushed-velvet pants I scored at the thrift store. I cut them into shorts and rolled them up to an upper-thigh hem. I hold up the tail of the jacket, turn, and look over my shoulder into the mirror, confirming how good my ass looks in the shorts. And it does. Perky and perfectly rounded. I can't imagine who wouldn't want to motorboat that thing all night long. It really is a shame no one will get to see my new rainbow thong. Once again I wonder how the hell I ended up dateless for the first Rainbow Prom in the history of Florence.

I pick my phone up off the bed and check it. There's a text from Shelby saying they're on the way. I'm a little disappointed that there aren't any other messages, and curse myself internally for that. Jax finally stopped texting me, which I guess is a good thing. After the way he turned on me in the park, I shouldn't really care. His texts say I *have it all wrong* and that he *wants to explain, but in person*. Explain what, exactly? That you can't accept who you are and you use people as pawns in your sick little games? I despise myself for missing him all week, though. His kiss lingers on my lips like phantom pain, tingling every time I think about it, which has been like a gazillion times. And more than that, my heart just . . . hurts.

Before my eyes start to get all itchy with tears and ruin my guyliner, I check Bangr for DMs from Brock to get my mind off Jax. Nothing. I wonder if he'll actually show up tonight. I guess he's my *sort of* date. In his last DM he swore that he'd be there, but I'm still not 100 percent sure that he's not just a product of my imagination. Since he wouldn't be able to pick me out of a police lineup by the profile pic I posted, and I know what he looks like only from the neck to the waist and shirtless, I described the T-shirt I'll be wearing to him. I found it online with free two day shipping, and it's perfect for the Rainbow Prom. I turn back to the mirror, open my jacket, and once more admire the tee's simple message in large white block letters:

I DON'T MAKE MISTAKES—GOD

"Nice shirt." Dad, in his bathrobe, stands in my doorway. His smile worries me. Not nearly as bright the last few days as it has been lately. I'm pretty sure I'm responsible for that.

"You're not dressed yet," I say.

He comes in and stands beside me in front of the mirror, giving me a once-over. "I've just got to jump in the shower. Might be a little late. You look great, but are we maybe showing off a little too much thigh tonight?"

I ignore his lame attempt at *dadness*. Rose knows better than to lecture Dorothy. He shoots me another weak smile that breaks my heart. I can't help myself from prying, but I tread lightly.

"So are you picking Tracee up or is she meeting you there?" I hope they have air-conditioning in hell, at least in the VIP section.

Dad hangs his head and shakes it. "She came by the office the other day and told me that she couldn't see me anymore. She seemed really upset but wouldn't tell me what was bothering her."

A full confession would do wonders for the soul right about now. *Maybe it's because her adopted son was physically abused as a child, and I let her believe you knock me around too.* But I don't have the guts or the balls to say it.

"I wonder what that's about," I say, feigning surprise and concern as best as I can. It's official. I am a horrible, unredeemable piece of shit.

*Note to self: Spend summer doing charity work—taking meals to shut-ins, mentoring a gay teen with no fashion sense, reading erotic romance novels to illiterate prison inmates. Supposedly, it calms them.*

"Not sure," he says, glancing up at me. "I know she'll be

there tonight, though. She wouldn't miss it. I'm going to talk to her and see what's going on."

*Oh shit.*

"I wouldn't push her, Dad," I say. Better to let sleeping dogs lie.

A car horn sounds outside. I go over to the window and pull back the curtains. Parked on the street in front of the house is the longest black limo I've ever seen. The rear window slides down.

Shelby sticks her head out and yells at the top of her lungs, "Bitches be balling tonight! Get your gay ass down here, hooker."

"I'm sure the neighbors appreciated that," Dad says. He walks over and taps me on the shoulder. When I look back at him, he pulls me into a bear hug, kissing me on top of my head. "I just wish you had a real date tonight," he says. "No offense to Shelby and your friends, but the Rainbow Prom is all about being with someone special, no matter who they are."

I rest my head on his shoulder. "Actually, I think it's just about being comfortable in your own skin, which I am. Besides, I'm meeting someone there."

He pushes me back and holds me at arm's length, his smile turning undeniably genuine for the first time in a week. "That's great! Do I know him?"

"Um," I say. "I doubt it. I don't really know him myself."

Dad crinkles his forehead but withholds admonishment. This is where I usually get a *gay pass*. He's so stoked at the possibility of me having a real boy date that he's willing to overlook the likely dubious origins of said date.

"Just—"

"—don't forget my raincoats. I know, Dad." If he only knew I've never used even one. Never had the chance.

He smiles and kisses me on the forehead. "Have fun tonight, Dorothy."

"You too, Rose."

Just after he slips out of the room, my phone buzzes on the bed and I grab it. A DM from Brock flashes on the home screen.

*Save me a dance?*

Hmm. Maybe he'll show up after all. I reply with a winking face emoji and hit send. I go over to the window and wave to let Shelby know that I'm coming. She waves back with her boobs hanging out the window. It slowly begins to rise. I'd better get down there before the poor girl chops both her tits off.

When I get outside and approach the car, a driver wearing a black suit opens the back door for me without making eye contact, like I'm too famous to be looked upon by the help. *Baller.* Voices, laughter, and Ellie Goulding spill out of the car. Her music. Not the actual Ellie Goulding—that would be *beyond* baller. I slide in beside Shelby only to find that I'm the last one to join the party. Asa sits on Shelby's right and waves over at me, looking ridiculously adorable in a chic black tux. Like a real, grown-up tux. Boy went all out.

"Nice jacket, Beck," he says. When Asa smiles, his whole face gets in on the action. His pearly white teeth sparkle, his eyes look like mini smiles themselves, and his cheeks grow full and rosy. How have I not noticed how freaking cute this guy is? Still, my gaydar's on the fritz with him.

"Thanks," I say, waving back to him and then at the rest of our posse.

"*Bonjour, mon ami,*" Chevy says. He and Anya sit facing us, and Chevy looks *très* dapper in a white tux coat with black pants and bow tie. I'm beginning to feel a little underdressed.

"Beckett!" Anya says, and claps her hands a little. "You look so hot!" Her smile is ridiculously adorable like her twin brother's, and her sleek purple dress makes her honey-colored skin practically glow in the dim track lighting.

"Hey, guys," I say to them, and also to Jen and Lexi. I wasn't expecting those two at all, but I'm delighted to get the gay count up in the car—we are going to a *gay prom*, after all. And like me, they're dressed with more personality—Jen in mismatched suit pieces it looks like she stole from her dad's closet, and Lexi in black leather pants and spilling out of a matching bustier that shows off the smooth, dark skin of her arms and chest.

"Love the shirt, Beck," Jen says. She got her already short blond hair buzzed on one side. Lexi has a new nose ring and a freshly shaved head. They look pretty badass for high school lesbians.

"Thanks, Jen," I say. "You guys look amazing."

I look over at Shelby, and that's when I really take note of how fabulous she looks tonight. She managed to re-create a lot of the drag magic she learned from Amanda Rimmer. Her shiny copper hair cascades down onto her shoulders in wavy curls, her makeup is spot on, and the sparkly blue dress I picked out for her looks even better on her now than it did in the department store, accentuating her curves in all the right places.

All in all we make a pretty hot-looking group. But with Shelby and Asa chatting, Chevy teaching Anya French curse words, and the scissor sisters making out like we're not even here, I can't help feeling like a seventh wheel. I guess I could be sitting here with Carter Treadwell. I feel bad for never responding to his message asking me if I had a date tonight. Oh well. Maybe Brock is a normal, human boy without any priors who'll join our walking Benetton ad at the hotel and hold my hand all night long. If he's Latino, even better for the ad.

It just completely sucks balls that the only person whose hand I really want to be holding right now is Jax.

# CHAPTER THIRTY-TWO

# Jaxon

I keep telling myself that I decided to come to the Rainbow Prom because it's the right thing to do. Be that example everyone's been telling me I should be. I already came out to the team, so the news will spread through the student body like a bad virus anyway. Everybody either knows now or will know soon enough, so why not come? But even though I keep trying to convince myself that my motives are noble, I know the real reason I came tonight. It's not to see if our plan to break up Mom and Roger works. I came to see Beck. To talk to him. To apologize. To tell him how I really feel. But he's expecting someone else. Brock.

The first thing I notice when we pull up to the Beacon Hotel is the restless crowd gathering across the street, and acid churns in the pit of my stomach. A small mob of homely-looking women in long denim skirts and dentally challenged men with slicked back hair hold signs with all manner of hate scrawled on them. The protesters are not, however, the first thing that Mom notices. Ever the optimist, she focuses in on the grandeur of the elegant hotel and the specially decorated street entrance to the Grand Ballroom.

"Jaxon, look," she says, tugging on my shirtsleeve as I fight the urge to plow down the protesters on the sidewalk. "The red carpet. That was my idea."

She says it like it's the first time she's told me this, but I have to hand it to her, the red carpet is a nice touch. Lined with velvet rope and massive planters housing baby palmetto trees, the only things missing are a couple of those giant spotlights pointing up and shooting crisscrossing beams into the sky.

"Nice, Mom," I say, smiling at her and turning into the hotel parking lot. "It really looks great."

"Well, the mayor saved our butts by letting us have the prom here. I don't know who we have to thank for making that happen, but they deserve a big old kiss, that's for sure."

I have an idea who we have to thank for it. That would be one Mr. Beckett Gaines, and I wouldn't mind giving him that kiss, not one bit—if he'd ever speak to me again. He might not know that I broke it off with Tiffany and came out to the team yet. I hope he doesn't, because I want to tell him myself. I want him to be proud of me.

As I guide Mom's car into an empty parking space, she gathers her bags, anxious to get inside and add some finishing touches. "Thanks for driving me, hon, but don't you have a date tonight? Isn't Tiffany coming?"

I've been so focused on what I want to tell Beck that it didn't even occur to me to tell my moms anything about what's been going on in my life.

"I doubt it," I say, killing the engine. "Actually, we broke up this week."

Mom stops fussing around with the bags and shoots me a raised eyebrow. "Broke up? Is it because of the bisexual thing?"

I fight off an eye roll, reminding myself that Mom isn't being nosy. She's just concerned and supportive. Why should that be so annoying?

"Partly, I guess," I say, looking over at her. "Tiffany and I just aren't right for each other."

Mom's eyes grow cloudy and distant. She pulls the strap of her purse up over her shoulder and nods. "I know exactly what you mean."

There's my opening. I knew something was up with her the last few days. "Why didn't Roger pick you up tonight?"

Her face flashes a shade darker as she reaches for the door handle. "Turns out there may be more to Roger Gaines than meets the eye, and not in a good way. I think it's best to keep some distance there."

I don't know what to say, so I just nod. But it sounds like whatever seeds of doubt Beck planted in her have fully taken root. Hopefully, mine have done the same with Roger. Now, if the remaining pawns just show up tonight and play their parts, our plan just might work after all.

By the time we reach the red carpet, the group of protesters across the street has grown and gotten a little more organized. They hold their signs in front of them like shields and chant their signature mantra in unison—"Fags burn in hell. Fags burn in hell."

Honestly, they don't seem too enthusiastic about their

mission tonight. Maybe it's because their leader, Pastor Doug, hasn't arrived yet. Or maybe it's because their early targets are just a handful of timid teenagers hanging their heads as they hurry out of the spotlight and into the side entrance of the hotel to escape the unwanted attention. I want to march across the street and give those fundie fuckers a piece of my mind, but it appears someone has beaten me to it.

JoJo's hard to miss, standing there in front of the group with her hands shoved into her pockets like a human wall trying to shield the gay kids from the hate being hurled at them. Doris stands beside her, decked out in her police uniform and with her arms crossed over her chest.

She's engaged in a heated debate with a red-faced woman who looks like her head is about to explode. She has that look in her eye, like some of the vitriol she's spewing might be directed at the color of Doris's skin. Doris, on the other hand, is as cool as a cucumber. She and JoJo make a formidable pair. Maybe too much so.

Mom spots them soon after I do. "What is your mother doing over there? I swear to God, if she gets those crazies riled up, it's going to get ugly."

I shrug at her. "It's already ugly, and they haven't even gotten started yet."

It's like she didn't even hear me. Mom grabs me by the hand, dragging me over to the crosswalk like I'm six years old and can't be trusted to cross the street on my own.

JoJo glances over at us and holds her hand up to slow our approach. "Everything's fine here. You guys should head on into the hotel."

"Are you sure everything's okay, Ma?" I say, zeroing in on some familiar faces in the growing crowd of protesters. The two pricks I nearly laid out in front of the Crusty Cup stand shoulder to shoulder with Bobby Jenkins and his right-hand asshole, Billy Porter, but they don't notice me yet. Bobby and Billy push their way through the crowd to the curb, and Bobby sets a brown grocery bag on the ground beside him.

"I'm fine, sweetie," she says, nodding hello to Mom without smiling.

Doris takes a much deserved break from the verbal lashing she's receiving from the female Jesus zombie and comes over to say hello to us. Mom is speechless. She just stares at Doris, then back to JoJo, then back at Doris. I've never seen her face redden so quickly. *Bingo. God, I'm actually good at this meddling thing.*

"What's she doing here?" Mom finally asks with an unmistakable edge in her voice.

JoJo shrugs nonchalantly. "Doris volunteered to help keep an eye on things tonight."

Mom is rarely at a loss for words, so this is new territory for us all, but a special kind of crazy begins to solidify in her eyes. Best to cut this initial interaction short. Give Mom time to digest and stew on this development.

"Mom," I say, drawing her inspection away from Doris. "Shouldn't you get inside to make sure the lighting is set the way you want it?"

Mom looks at me, horrified. "You're right. Nobody knows how it should be but me. I'll see you in there." She kisses me on the cheek, glares at the protesters, and crosses the street without another glance at Doris or JoJo.

I look over at JoJo. "You coming inside?"

She cuts her eyes at Doris in a way that pings in my gut and then shakes her head. "I think I'll stay out here a while. Just in case Doris needs backup."

I don't feel great about leaving JoJo and Doris there by themselves. Not that either one of them would need my help laying one of these yahoos out. The two hicktards from the Crusty Cup still look leery of JoJo. Bobby finally spots me, and his face hardens. He raises his sign up high over his head and points it in my direction.

REPENT, COCKSUCKERS

Classy. But the sight of him standing there holding that sign doesn't enrage me as much as I thought it would—it's just sad. Bobby didn't come by his hatred honestly. Someone taught him how to hate—a father, mother, brother, or even his pastor. He's just regurgitating the example that's been set for him his whole life, which helps me fight the urge to go over and put my fist through his face. The way he scowls at me, he's probably dealing with the same urges.

Jimmy turns the corner with three cups in his hand. "Coffee?" Doris and JoJo each take a cup and offer their thanks.

"I'm afraid I'll just throw it in someone's face," I say, declining.

Jimmy chuckles and takes a sip from the remaining cup. "Oh, this is nothing. Just wait until *Pastor Doug* shows up. That's when the real fireworks will start. He likes to make an entrance."

We keep about twenty feet of neutral sidewalk between us and the protesters. Other than Doris's initial debate with

Jesus's ugly stepsister, they've pretty much ignored us. I guess when they encounter people who aren't the least bit intimidated by them, it sort of takes the wind out of their sails. But the traffic across the street at the hotel entrance is picking up, so they have plenty of new targets to focus on.

Some of the promgoers I recognize from school, but I couldn't say that I *know* them. Plenty of others I don't recognize at all, and I assume they're from other schools in the area. It's hard to tell who's gay, bisexual, trans, or straight, and I guess that's kind of the point. I'd be much happier standing here watching the whole thing from afar than actually going inside, but it dawns on me that's pretty much how I've lived my entire life. Maybe tonight I'll have the balls to actually participate in and enjoy my youth before it completely passes me by.

"I think you're on the wrong side of the street, Parker," a familiar voice behind me says.

I take a deep breath and turn to face Bobby. Billy stands at his side, sneering at me. I honestly didn't think Bobby would push his luck with a permanent suspension from the team, but I guess his hate is stronger than his love of football.

"Where's your little fag boyfriend?" Bobby says. "At City Park sucking random cock?"

Anger heats the back of my neck, but I do my best not to let it show. "Well, I guess I'm not surprised to see you here, Bobby. You must have plenty of time to participate in these pathetic demonstrations now that you've been suspended from the team." His face reddens and he steps up to me. I don't move a muscle.

"Is there a problem here, boys?" Doris walks over with JoJo in tow.

"Jax?" JoJo says. "Who's this?"

"You remember Bobby and Billy from the team, Ma," I say. "Well, Bobby *used* to be on the team. He was recently relieved of his duties due to massive assholery."

Bobby looks over at JoJo and Doris, not even trying to mask the hate etched on his face. Doris tugs on her utility belt, drawing Bobby's attention to her holstered gun.

"Why don't you boys take those clever little signs of yours and go rejoin your group?" she says to them.

Bobby inspects Doris's badge like he suspects it to be fake or something, but finally backs away. He and Billy return to their group, and JoJo gives me a what-the-fuck roll of her eyes.

Across the street, the party is in full swing, and the entrance to the hotel looks like a swanky island of misfit kids. Everyone's mingling, taking selfies, checking out one another's outfits, and introducing themselves to kids from other schools. I'm sure it's a dry party, which will be challenging for both the teens *and* the parents. Still, the mood is upbeat for the most part as they try to ignore the hate being spewed at them from our side of the street. It's like they're determined not to let the protesters dampen their spirits any longer. This is their moment, and they refuse to scurry back into the shadows. They take their time on the red carpet, mingling and rubbing all their gay joy in the protestors' faces with their heads held high. I spot Carter Treadwell walking down the red carpet, holding the hand of a surprisingly hot guy I've never seen before. *Go, Carter!*

A couple of local TV news crews have arrived and position themselves near the protesters to our right. I hate that they'll have any screen time at all. This should be about the Rainbow Prom, not the Florence Holiness Tabernacle shitting on it.

The reporters and camera techs spark to life when the mayor arrives. Everyone over there greets him like he's fucking JFK's ghost or something. He practically glides down the red carpet with a boss brunette on his arm, neither of them giving the protestors a second look. The girl seems a little young for him—probably the daughter Beck mentioned. Speaking of Beck, I've yet to spot him and wonder if he decided to blow the whole thing off.

With Jimmy there and backup on the way, I feel better about leaving Doris and JoJo. As I'm saying my good-byes, a black stretch limo pulls up to the hotel, drawing my gaze. A driver hops out, buttons his blazer, and casually strolls back to the passenger door. When he opens it, a familiar mop of chocolate brown hair pops up, and my heart thumps hard in my chest.

*Beckett.*

I can't see what he's wearing, but apparently, those milling around on the red carpet approve, because a small cheer rises in the air when he steps forward. He looks over the top of the limo in my direction, and like a lovesick loser I wave. *I actually wave.* How pathetic is that? He doesn't see me, thank God. His worried gaze is glued on the protesters.

A redhead pops out of the limo next. Shelby Timmons. Her hair is freshly washed and styled, which has to be a first for that girl. She really looks great. Some others pile out behind them—the Filipino twins, Chevy, and that lesbian couple. Beck struts down the red carpet like he's working the runway at New York Fashion Week. Phone cameras flash all around him. Now I'm able to see his outfit, and I get what all the fuss is about. I can't help but chuckle. He looks adorable, ridiculous, and hot all at the same time. In tight black shorts rolled up nearly to his crotch, his long, bare legs are toned and smooth. The blue vintage tux jacket is hideous, but again, Beck somehow makes it work. And that bow tie. My cheeks ache from smiling so hard just watching him. He looks so happy. So . . . Beckett.

Out of the corner of my eye, I catch a glimpse of movement and look to my right. Bobby and Billy have their hands deep inside the brown paper bag on the ground, and a pinch of anxiety twists in my stomach. What the hell are these pricks up to? My brain orders my feet to move, but they are slow to respond, trying to process what Bobby and Billy pull out of the bag. When my feet finally obey, it's too late.

They stand holding eggs, three in each hand. They swing their arms back and take aim across the street. Even breaking into a full sprint, I can't reach them before they launch the first round into the air.

# CHAPTER THIRTY-THREE

# Beckett

The whoosh buzzing my ear is nearly imperceptible, but the thump a second later whacks the side of my head like an open-handed slap. I stop cold in my tracks, stunned, and raise my fingers to the point of contact. Something wet is matted in my hair. Blood? I spin around, facing the street, and the second assault nails me in the center of the chest—two hits soaking my shirt with a cold, gooey substance. I look down, trying to compute what's happening. The sticky ooze of egg yolk runs down the front of my shirt and the side of my face.

Shelby screams somewhere behind me, and I turn on my heel. Her boobs were obviously the intended target, and whoever threw the eggs had great aim and two really big bull's-eyes. Two blots of splattered yolk and shell dot each of her tits and seep into the silk of her fabulous new dress. She looks down to inspect the damage, and her cheeks redden instantly, eyes brimming with tears.

Asa takes a direct hit in the back of the head and yelps.

Lexi gets nailed right in the cooch and doubles over. I train my gaze on the protesters across the street. A few of them stand stifling their laughter with their hands and looking away, good Christians that they are. Bobby and Billy stand in the center of the group on the edge of the curb, taking aim once again as Jax barrels toward them. They manage to get off another round before he can reach them, and one of the eggs flies straight at me.

I turn to run and plow right into Asa and Shelby. I grab on to them both to get my balance, but end up taking all three of us down. My head bounces off the sidewalk. Sharp pain pierces through my skull. Shelby lands right on top of me, cursing so loudly, I wonder for a moment if I'll ever regain full hearing in that ear. Asa seems to have landed on top of Shelby.

I don't know how long I'm under there. Urgent voices trickle down from somewhere above. They're muted, and I can't quite make out what my potential rescuers are saying. Finally, a familiar voice calls my name as Shelby and Asa roll off me. I take in a lungful of nonperfumed air, and the stars slowly dissipate from my mind's eye. Jax hovers over me, out of breath and his eyes wide with concern.

"Beck, are you okay?" he asks.

I have a hard time forming my response. I'd hit the sidewalk harder than I thought, and the back of my head is throbbing like a motherfucker. Everything is a little blurry. I must be hallucinating, because I think I see Carter Treadwell standing nearby, looking distraught in the arms of a hot Latino boy. *Brock?*

"Oh my God, Beckett," Carter screeches. He drops to his

knees with melodramatic flare like he's a character in a tele-novela. "Are you okay?" In my mind he says it in Spanish.

I reach around and touch the tender spot. A jolt of pain shoots through my skull. I look over to my left and find Shelby sprawled out flat on her back. Her dress is riding up, exposing her freshly waxed business for all of Florence County to see. In hindsight, I shouldn't have assumed she would take the initiative to add panties to her new ensemble unless I picked them out for her. My bad. Asa gallantly kneels beside her and pulls her dress down.

Shelby turns her head in my direction, a dazed look cloud-ing her eyes. "They shot me, hooker," she says breathlessly, "right in the tits. I always knew I would die young and beauti-ful, but not with my angry marshmallow on display."

I reach over and take Shelby's hand. "Don't worry, girl. You're not dying. Not today."

Asa and Chevy help her to her feet as Anya rushes over with tissues, wiping the egg goop off Shelby's tits. *Sure. Don't worry about me down here. Save the dress!*

Jax slips his arm under the crook of my shoulder and helps me sit up. With bruised and bloody knuckles he pro-ceeds to inspect my face and skull.

"What happened to you?" I ask with a groan and a wince when he touches the tender spot.

Jax nods across the street, directing my gaze. "Just a little herd thinning."

Both Bobby and Billy are facedown on the sidewalk. JoJo stands with her hands casually in her pockets and a foot on Billy's neck, like she's squashing a bug. A curvy, black lady cop has her knee planted squarely in the center of Bobby's back, holding his hands behind him. The protesters shout at the two women, shoving signs and fists in their faces.

"There's no blood," Jax says. "Just a small bump. You'll live."

His words barely register. A black SUV passes, claiming my attention. With tinted windows and a Jesus fish decal sticker in the lower right-hand corner of the back one, it looks suspiciously familiar. The vehicle pulls up to the curb in front of the protesters and stops. I know I've seen that SUV before, but the lingering fog in my brain prevents me from placing it. The TV news crews rush over and get into position just as a tall man in a dark suit hops out of the driver's side and circles the SUV. The passenger door opens and a blond man emerges. The driver I immediately recognize as Pastor Doug of the Florence Holiness Tabernacle. The other guy I can't place right off, but he looks familiar. He's attractive, quite a bit younger than Pastor Doug, and has wavy, bleached blond hair. The fog clouding my brain finally clears. I *have* seen that SUV before. Twice, actually.

"Help me up," I say to Jax.

With two of their own being subdued, the protesters are already good and riled up. But Pastor Doug's arrival has invigorated them even more. It's like he sprinkled a fresh batch of fairy hate dust all over them. I'm filled with so much rage, I'm afraid I'll explode right out of my tight-ass shorts.

I push away from Jax, moving toward the crosswalk. He reaches for me, grabs my arm, and pulls me back. It's a good thing too, or I might have been plowed down by the school bus that rumbles to a stop right in front of us like a bright blue and gold wall blocking out the protesters. EAST FLORENCE TIGERS is printed in bold black letters along the side of the bus. When the front door folds open with a loud scrape, we find none other than Coach Wayne sitting in the driver's seat, a determined look etched deep into his face.

"Coach?" Jax says, letting go of me and moving toward the door. "What the hell?"

Coach Wayne hops out of the driver's seat and heads down the steps, waving for his passengers to follow him. "I thought we might be of some assistance, Parker."

Terry Fox is the first one off the bus. He bumps shoulders with Jax and leads a parade of what seems like the entire varsity football team off the bus and down the sidewalk. They all wear jeans and their East Florence Tigers jerseys. Jax, as well as the rest of us, stare at them dumbfounded as they pass. Sai Patel, Jody Chambers, Alejandro Cardenas, and a bunch of others line up shoulder to shoulder along the edge of the red carpet, facing the protesters and clasping their hands behind them like they're posing for a team photo.

The entrance to the hotel and everyone arriving for the prom are completely shielded behind a barricade of broad, jersey clad backs and muscle. Shoulders squared and spines straight as boards, they face their opponents across the street with line of scrimmage focus and hell-bent determination. Nobody's getting through them. They even start singing the Tigers fight song at the top of their lungs, completely drowning out the hateful chants of the protestors.

The surprising overture of support from the team for

queer kids they themselves teased and bullied in the past causes the pesky itch in the corner of my eye. I glance over my shoulder at Shelby, Asa, Anya, Chevy, Jen, and Lexi. Their mouths hang open. Six sets of glassy eyes stare at the players. Carter Treadwell rests his head on the hot Latino boy's shoulder, and a tear trickles down his cheek. I look over at Jax. His eyes also well with tears that he doesn't bat away and doesn't seem ashamed of. I've never seen *The Great* Jaxon Parker's eyes leak before. It's both chilling and endearing.

The sheer emotion of the moment rattles me in a way that I normally don't allow. Feelings are messy things for us Dorothys. But perhaps it's that messiness that fortifies my resolve to take care of some unfinished business. I shed my tux coat, throw it over to Shelby, and push my way through the beefcake barricade. An oncoming car honks at me, slowing down as I cross the street. I don't even look over at it. I just give it the hand and keep walking.

"Beckett," Jax says, following me. "What the hell are you doing?"

I don't answer him. I make a left onto the sidewalk and march my black crush-velveted ass right over to the most hostile-looking group of *Christians* I've ever seen. Their numbers have grown to at least fifty now. Bobby and Billy kneel with their hands bound behind them and traces of Jax's handiwork marring their faces. TV cameras hover over them. Jimmy from the Crusty Cup stands in front of the protesters with his arms crossed over his chest, his pointed glare daring them to move any closer.

JoJo heads straight for us with her cop friend in tow.

"Come on," she says, trying to herd us back with outstretched arms. "Everything's under control. Why don't you guys head back over to the party, okay?"

"A backup unit is on the way," the lady cop who I assume is Doris says, as if that will calm me. I ignore them both. My sights are set on the slimy-looking motherfucker standing dead center of the mob—Pastor Doug. He watches me approach with a twinkle in his eye that could mean one of three things.

*Number One—I'm a lost little lamb that he needs to save for Jesus.*

*Number Two—He's so disgusted by the sight of me and my flaming gay ass that he wishes he had more than a sign in his hand with which to greet me.*

*Or, Number Three—He wants to bend me over the hood of that SUV of his and fuck Satan right out of me.*

I'm betting everything on number three.

# CHAPTER THIRTY-FOUR

Jaxon

I can barely keep up with Beck as he plows through the crowd and marches right up to Pastor Doug. The blond guy standing beside the pastor steps in front of Beck as if to block the crazy, diseased gay kid from getting too close to his master.

"I'm sorry. I didn't catch your name," Beck says to Blondie with a pointed glare.

Blondie squares his shoulders and looks down his prissy nose at Beck. "Jasper Brooks, music minister of Florence Holiness Tabernacle, and I'll ask you to back up right this minute, young man."

Pastor Doug nudges Blondie out of the way and steps forward. He's taller than I thought he would be and has an oily countenance about him. He looks down at Beck with a hateful sneer twisting his shiny red lips, taking his time reading Beck's egg soaked T-shirt before he speaks.

"That's right, son," he says. "God doesn't make mistakes. But you're not a mistake, you're an abomination. God had no part in the creation of your deviance. You did that all on your own. But there's always hope, *if* you turn away from your sexual depravity, repent, and come back to Jesus. Otherwise—I'm sorry, but like the signs say, 'Fags Burn in Hell.'"

"Are you getting this?" a reporter on my left whispers to her cameraman. He nods and adjusts the zoom of his lens.

Beck is silent for once, which is surprising, to say the least. I glance over at him and see why. A single tear slips out of the corner of his eye, triggering the instant boil of blood in my veins. I turn my attention back to Pastor Doug and jab my finger into the center of his chest. Blondie moves to step between us, but Pastor Doug holds him back with a raised hand. A light touch in the small of my back gives me pause. I know that touch—I've felt it many times before. Terry steps up and stands shoulder to shoulder with me, and he brought backup. Beck and I are flanked by four monster defensive ends, two cornerbacks, and a safety. They don't say anything. They don't need to. Their sheer height and girth say it all.

Taking a deep breath and plastering on my signature smartass smile, I return my attention to Pastor Doug. "If you and your Bible-thumping zombies are what Christianity is all about, then we want no part of it. And God help you if you ever talk to my friend that way again. He has more Christian love and compassion in his little finger than all of you hateful people combined."

Pastor Doug holds his sneer and his silence as well. Smart move, because I don't know how long I'd be able to keep my fist out of his face if he said anything else.

I glance over at Beck. "You okay?"

His eyes are drenched now, but his jaw is tightly set. He widens his stance and squares his shoulders. He's back.

"If all us fags are going to hell," Beck says, "then maybe we can hitch a ride with you in that big SUV of yours? Because I know that backseat has seen enough *sexual depravity* to get you a one-way ticket as well."

Audible gasps ripple through the crowd, and the TV news cameraman points his lens right in Pastor Doug's face. The man's whole body goes rigid. He purses his lips. A mixture of surprise and disdain hardens his gaze. Judging by the murmurs and raised eyebrows, the sudden change in Pastor Doug's demeanor doesn't go unnoticed by his flock, either. I just stand there with my dick in my hand, wondering what the hell Beck's talking about.

He looks over at Blondie and raises an eyebrow. "Has the good pastor here ever fucked you in the sanctuary, or do you prefer City Park?"

More gasps. Even louder this time. And I can tell by the steely look in Beck's eye that he's not bullshitting. A chortle slips out before I can stop it. I raise my hand to cover my mouth.

Jesus's ugly stepsister lunges forward and spits on the sidewalk in front of Beck. "How dare you, you blasphemous degenerate."

Beck's eyes are bone dry now. He crosses his arms over his chest and narrows his gaze on her. "It's true. I saw them there myself." He points to Blondie. "He drives a light blue minivan, right? And has a wife, two kids, a dog, and a cat, if I remember the sticker in the back window correctly."

The woman's eyes widen, and a rumble of shock snakes through the crowd. A second TV news camera swings in Beck's direction.

"They were both on their knees," Beck says, "but I'm pretty sure they weren't praying. Not unless you folks usually pray with your panties down around your ankles."

My stifled laughter sneaks out as a snort, which only further enrages the woman. Her face turns so red so fast, I wonder if her head is going to explode. Pastor Doug stands there with his fat mouth hanging open. It's probably the first time this asshole has been speechless in his entire life. I see in his eyes that he's working out his options here. Deny. Admit. Ignore. He chooses the latter. With no more than a sneer and a huff, he turns away from us, pushing his way through the crowd toward his SUV. Blondie scurries after him but finds the passenger side door locked as Pastor Doug hops in the driver's seat and starts the car. He stares straight ahead, even as Jasper frantically raps his knuckles on the window. Pastor Doug drives away, leaving his flock and his boy toy stranded in a state of complete shock and bewilderment.

"All right, folks," Doris says with no small measure of authority. "Looks like the party's over. Head on home now. I believe you all have church in the morning, and it seems you have a lot to pray about tonight."

The wind knocked out of their sails, the mindless mob complies and begins to disperse. Satisfied that the threat is over, my guys follow Terry over to the crosswalk and back to the hotel, with the reporters sticking cameras and microphones in their faces the whole way. With Pastor Doug and the protesters gone, their interests apparently have shifted to the story of the high school football team showing up to protect the queer kids at the town's first gay prom. Bobby and Billy remain on their knees with hands zip-tied behind their backs.

"Okay, boys, let's take a ride," Doris says, helping them up to their feet and into the backseat of a police cruiser that just pulled up. JoJo hugs me and kisses me on the cheek. She does the same to Beck before joining Doris. Jimmy slaps me on the back and heads around the corner to the Crusty Cup. So now it's just me and Beck standing there shoulder to shoulder, facing an empty sidewalk.

"Thank you," he says, staring straight ahead like he's in a trance.

"For what?" I say.

He turns to face me. "For the things you said. For sticking up for me."

"Yeah," I say, looking over at him. "*Finally*, right?"

He stares at me, and, judging by his flat tone and his blank face, I can't tell if he's just emotionally spent or if he's still pissed at me. With an almost imperceptible nod, he walks away, crosses the street, and heads toward the Beacon Hotel. He doesn't look back. Not once.

I guess now I know.

# CHAPTER THIRTY-FIVE

# Beckett

After retrieving my tux jacket from Shelby, I make a beeline for the hotel lobby bathroom. I wash my face and get most of the egg out of my hair, but the T-shirt is a gooey, smelly mess. It's ruined. Luckily, my crushed-velvet shorts and vintage tux jacket were spared. In a moment of sheer fashion inspiration, I take off the T-shirt, toss it in the trash, and put the black bow tie and jacket back on over my bare torso. I check myself out in the mirror and approve. I look *hot*. It's like a midshow costume change.

When I step into the Grand Ballroom of the Beacon Hotel, I stop dead in my tracks. The mayor was right. This room is *sickening*. I don't think I've ever been in a place this nice before. With its Grecian columns, marble floors, and tricked out chandeliers, you might think we were in some palace in the Mediterranean, not anywhere remotely close to South Carolina cotton fields.

In the center of the room, a large dance floor is packed

with writhing bodies. My limo mates are all out there dancing together. Chevy, Anya, Lexi, and Jen. Even Shelby has pulled herself back together and is shaking her business all over poor little Asa. Brent and Kenny are *sort of* dancing . . . with everyone . . . but they seem to be hearing a different song in their twice-baked heads. And I have to say, sleazy Justin Black is killing it in the deejay booth, spinning an EDM set fit for any club in New York or L.A. With no bouncers or bodyguards around, people freely mill around the deejay booth, taking selfies with him and watching him work. It actually seems like he's into it—posing for every picture and signing autographs. Maybe he remembers what it was like for him, growing up gay in Florence, South Carolina.

I scan the room, wondering if it'll be impossible for Brock to find me in the dense crowd and dim lighting. It doesn't help that I don't know what he looks like, and the shirt I told him I'd be wearing rests in the bottom of the trash in the bathroom. Maybe he already gave up trying to find me and left. I hope not. I really need the distraction. I want to forget about the protesters, Pastor Doug, and his boy toy. And Jax, for that matter. But damn if I can get *him* out of my head. I have to admit, he was amazing standing up to Pastor Doug. Where has *that* guy been the last few years? I tell myself it's too little, too late, though.

I focus my search on the dance floor, but the only way I would be able to recognize Brock is if he were dancing around shirtless. I walk over to an area with high top cocktail tables, a bar, and a small buffet. I spot Mayor Davenport standing near the bar, flashing that million-dollar smile to everyone who greets him. A girl not much older than me stands at his side. I assume it's his daughter. Apparently, hotness runs in the Davenport gene pool, because the girl is freaking gorgeous. The mayor is a little more casually dressed tonight, but he still fits in with the Grand Ballroom decor like he was born in this room. He's probably one of those guys who always looks perfectly put together for any occasion. *Total baller.*

Davenport whispers in his daughter's ear and steps over to the bar. I'm sure a full-sugar soda is about the most dangerous thing they have to offer tonight. I need to thank him not only for coming, but for letting us use this incredible space. I take a step in that direction but freeze when my mom steps up beside him at the bar. Her hair is wild and perfect as usual. She looks amazing in the sleeveless emerald dress we found, exposing the smooth skin of newly toned arms. She looks good. Healthy. The only thing marring her appearance are the lines of worry etched in her face.

When the mayor turns with two drinks in his hand and discovers her standing there, his ear-to-ear grin is instantaneous. Mom's return smile is minimal and forced. I know it well. The mayor puts his drinks down on the bar, and they hug—awkwardly. Mom looks uncomfortable, but there is hugging nonetheless. Just that innocent greeting of two old friends/lovers should be enough to get Dad's attention, but I don't even know if he's here yet. Someone knocks my arm, interrupting my surveillance, and I turn. Shelby stands there holding two plastic cups full of clear soda over ice. Asa stands just behind her with one of his own. Shelby has cleaned up her dress a little more from the egg assault, but there are still two dark water stains dotting her tits. She doesn't seem to care.

"Nice shirt, Beck," Asa says, pointing at my bare chest and giving me a little flirty wink. So confusing.

I look down at my chest and shrug. "Yeah. Had to improvise."

Shelby hands me a cup and leans in. "I spiked it." She kind of growls it out, like she's already had a couple herself.

"With what?" I take a sip. The alcohol content is generous and burns my throat going down.

Shelby slips her index finger and thumb down into her cleavage and pulls out a cordial-sized bottle of vodka. She quickly tucks it back down in its hiding place, before anyone looks our way. "There's more where that came from."

I'm sure there is. I bet she could hide a six-pack of beer down there.

"Did you find Bangr boy?" Shelby asks.

"Brock? No. I don't think he's going to show. With my luck he was probably some forty-year-old serial killer, anyway. Maybe I should go buy a ten-inch dildo and be done with it."

"Don't knock it. I've had some meaningful, long-term relationships with dildos and vibrators." She nods over her shoulder. "By the way. You have a stalker over there, staring at you like he can't decide if he wants to eat, fuck, or kill you."

I follow Shelby's gaze over to the right. Jax leans against the wall, staring at me, his electric blue eyes cutting through the artificial haze of manufactured smoke and colored lights like a laser pointer.

"The game is *marry*, fuck, or kill, hooker. Not *eat*. And no, he just can't decide if he wants dick or pussy, and I'm *not* playing that game," I say.

Asa raises his eyebrows and grins like he's not used to this kind of language, but he likes it.

"You weren't always so comfortable in your own skin either," Shelby says, taking a sip and arching an eyebrow at me.

It stings, but she's right. Am I being just as intolerant as the Tabernacle haters?

I purse my lips and push out a deep sigh. "We kissed that night at the park."

Shelby punches my shoulder so hard that spiked Sprite spills over the rim of my cup. "Shut the back door!"

"Front door, sweetie." I nod. "But when Tiffany showed up, he couldn't get out of there fast enough."

"So?" she says with her wide-eyed *spill the tea, bitch* face. "How was it?"

I glance back over at Jax, who hasn't looked away or moved an inch, and ponder Shelby's question. How was it? It was freaking amazing. It gave me chills on every square inch of my body. My lips still throb every time I think about him pushing his tongue inside me. I get weak in the knees remembering the way he looked at me, like I was the only person who existed in the world. And I'll certainly never look at a green apple Jolly Rancher the same way again. But how do I sum all that up?

I look back at Shelby. "It was everything. And then it was gone."

Shelby's face sags. I tip my cup at her and suck down the rest of my drink in one gulp. "I think I'm done with trying to get my cherry popped, though. I'll just get some cats and put a padlock on my ass for the next forty years. This is too much work." I glance over her right shoulder. Asa has wandered just far enough away that he can't hear us. I nod toward him. "So . . ."

Her cheeks flush red. "It turns out pretty boy has a thing for redheads." Her lips curl up.

"OMG!" I say, the vodka really warming me from the inside out. I am so happy for her I want to kiss her full on the lips. I lower my voice and lean in to her. "Asa? I love it!"

"Okay, calm down, hooker," she says, rolling her eyes at me.

Fully riding the vodka buzz train now, I glance over to the bar. My mom and the mayor are still talking, though it looks more serious than flirty, which was *not* part of the plan. "I need to go find my dad," I say, handing her my cup. "Can you be a good little hooker and refill this for me? Maybe a little less Sprite this time?"

Shelby takes my cup and nods toward the back wall. "Roger was over there in the corner eye-fucking your mom until Mayor Hotness showed up."

As Shelby and Asa head back to the bar, I scan the room for my dad, finally spotting him by the wall—alone. And he's not staring at Mom, he's staring at the back of Tracee's head as she sits alone at a table a few yards away. A dark cloud of tension hangs in the air between them, and the look on Dad's face destroys me. It's that defeated, blank stare I saw every single day for a solid year after mom left. But ever since he met Tracee, he's had a pep in his step and a goofy-ass grin plastered on his face twenty-four/seven. Now that's all gone.

Thanks to me. But I was just looking out for him, trying to spare him another broken heart after the mess that Mom made of him. Maybe my motives weren't entirely selfless, though. Dad and I have grown really close since Mom left. I helped him come back to life. He needs me, for God's sake. At least he did before he met Tracee.

Shelby and Asa return with the drinks and they're even stronger this time.

"Oh hell," Shelby says, nodding over my shoulder. "It's showtime."

I turn on my heel and sip flawlessly without spilling a drop. "What?"

The mayor and my mom walk side by side in Dad's direction, but he doesn't notice them yet. He stands behind Tracee, talking to the back of her head. I down the rest of my drink in two big gulps, stripping all the lining right out of my throat. The room shifts a little under my feet.

Asa grabs me by the arm and steadies me. "You okay, Beck?"

Shelby leans over and mumbles in my ear. "Incoming."

When I look back up, Jax stands in front of me. *Shit.*

"I need to talk to you," he says.

I push my cup into his chest, forcing him to grab it. "Not a good time," I say. It came out a lot more slurred than I'd intended. "I have to go save Dad and Tracee's relationship."

Jax cocks his head at me. "*Save* it?"

I don't have time to explain. I turn and make a beeline across the room.

The quickest way to them is to cross the dance floor. I

push through a sea of people, parents and students all dancing together, laughing together, happy together.

Someone grabs my arm and spins me around. I almost bite it.

"Hey, Beckett," Carter sings in a lovely three note melody. The vodka makes his voice sound better to my ears.

"I'm glad you're okay," he says. "Hey, I wanted you to meet my date. This is Ryan. He's the president of the GSA at Darlington High."

But my eyes are peeled on my parents and the mayor.

"Beckett?" Carter says. "Are you okay?"

I look back at them and, *holy Bruno Mars on a cracker*, his date is *hot*. I shake the guy's hand, but my tongue is not currently working at full capacity so nothing comes out of my open mouth. I think I'm a little jealous that Carter did so well without me.

"I'm sorry," I finally say. "It's nice to meet you, Bruno." I think that's what Carter said. All I heard was *not Brock*. "I have to go."

They both look at me like I have three heads, which is appropriate, because that's exactly how I feel right now. The whole room is moving with me as I plow forward. Like I'm on one of those moving walkways at the airport. When I emerge on the other side of the dance floor, Dad stands just ten feet away, facing Mom and the mayor. Tracee stands a couple of feet behind Dad, like she's listening, but also trying not to intrude. None of them have noticed me yet. I can just hear them over the music.

"I can't believe you invited him here," Dad says, shaking his head at her.

"Roger," Davenport says with a conciliatory tone, "I can appreciate how you feel, but please don't blame Lana. She didn't invite me. That's what I came over to tell you."

If my brain wasn't operating in a vodka haze, I might have had the sense to eavesdrop a little longer so I could figure out what the hell was going on. Instead, I walk right up to them and clear my throat to get their attention.

"I invited him, Dad," I slur. "He's the mayor. What's the big deal?"

Dad just gapes at me. All of them do, actually. But it's the look in Dad's eyes that's instantly sobering. All the hurt of the last two years is back, clouding his eyes, and I finally get it now. I was so stupid not to see it before. So stupid not to listen to Dad. Now I get why he reacted the way he did when I first mentioned the mayor. Davenport came back to Florence two years ago. Mom left two years ago. I don't know if they had an affair or what, but their three faces staring at me right now tell enough of the story. Tom Davenport played a key role in my dad's heartbreak. And here I am, rubbing his nose in it. I can't hold Dad's gaze. Not while he looks like this. I glance over and find Tracee hovering nearby. Her face is a caked-on canvas of uneasiness. I need to clear something up. Right now.

"By the way, Tracee," I say. "My Dad has *never* hit me. Ever. Not once. Not even a spanking when I was bratty, sassy kid."

Tracee's eyes grow wide but she remains silent. Dad's countenance, however, has changed on a dime. His face reddens, his nostrils flare, and I wouldn't be surprised if steam drifted out of his ears at any moment.

"You told her that I *hit* you?" he says with an almost

imperceptible growl that I've never heard come out of him.

I shake my head. "No. But I let her think it, which I know is just as bad. I'm *so* sorry, Tracee."

Tears well in her eyes. I *really* hurt her. But God bless her, she gives me a slight nod of forgiveness, which is way more than I deserve.

"Dad," I say, looking back at him, my voice cracking with guilt. "I'm sorry."

Dad doesn't say anything. He just stares at me like he doesn't know me. I want to curl up and die.

The mayor squirms and pivots. He graciously takes the heated attention off me. "Roger, I'm sorry to have ruined your evening. I'll find my daughter and we'll leave."

There's an awkward silence as Dad stares at him. For the first time in my life, I don't know *what* he's thinking.

Luckily, the mayor's daughter steps up to the group with a huge smile and touches his arm, disrupting the thickening tension.

"Dad, I got to meet Justin Black! I got a selfie. Look."

She holds her phone in front of him, but Davenport is visibly distracted. His face is muddled with conflicting emotions, and he tries to pull it together into one forced smile.

"That's great, honey," he says. He clears his throat and looks at all of us. "This is my daughter, Sloane."

Mom smiles and nods at her. "Nice to meet you, Sloane. I'm Lana," Mom says, then waves me closer. "This is my son, Beckett."

Sloane gives me a bright, sparkly smile and one of those this-is-awkward-but-we're-in-it-together kind of hello chuckle/waves. I like her instantly. If for no other reason than she's gorgeous and her little black dress is fierce. And I'm a little tipsy. *Short and stout.*

"Hi, Tom," Tracee says, gallantly recovering from the hurt of my betrayal and extending her hand to the mayor. "You might not remember me from high school. We didn't exactly travel in the same circles. I'm Tracee Parker. But I was Tracee Brock back then."

At first, the name whizzes by me. In one ear, out the other.

Davenport takes her hand, and it's obvious from his squinty-eyed smile that he doesn't remember her at all. "Oh yes, Tracee Brock, of course."

On its second pass, the name gives me pause and settles a little deeper into my alcohol-soaked consciousness. Did she say "Brock"?

No. Fucking. Way. And right on cue, he touches my arm. I turn, my face on fire.

"Beck, I really need to talk to you," Jax says without a glance at his mom or anyone else standing near us. Except Sloane, that is. She gets a quick up and down. *Of course.*

I cross my arms over my chest and take a step closer to him. We stand nearly nose to nose with only my folded arms separating our bodies.

"I need to talk to you, too . . . *Brock.*"

# CHAPTER THIRTY-SIX

# Jaxon

The driving thump of music dies down right on cue, and the first slow song of the night begins. It's the new one by the gay kid from England everyone's obsessed with. Justin was reluctant to bring the party down with a ballad. It took more flirting than I'd hoped to convince him to help me out. *Perv.*

But his timing is spot on. If Beck hadn't figured out that I was Brock before I had a chance to tell him myself, it would have been perfect. I go with it anyway, because it's the only plan I have. Taking Beck by the arm, I guide him out onto the dance floor. More than a few eyebrows raise in our direction. Beck—they would expect to see dancing with another guy. Me—not so much. We're nearly to the center of the dance floor when he pulls back, stopping me in my tracks. I turn to face him, and slide my hand down his arm, lacing our fingers together in a ball. He looks down at our hands like he doesn't recognize them.

"Just dance with me, Beck. Please," I say over the music.

He stares at me. Those normally vibrant, puppy dog eyes of his are weary and drooping. Lifeless. I'm afraid that I'm the reason for that.

"Look, it'll be easier to hear each other if we're dancing," I say. "Please, just give me the length of this song to explain, and then I'll never bother you again."

After a few long seconds eating into my self-imposed deadline, Beck relents with one of his signature eye rolls. He steps closer to me and slides his free hand around my waist. The moment the front of our bodies touch, a shiver runs the length of my spine. That's never happened with Tiffany. *Never.* I place a hand on his hip and the other on the small of his back.

He leans into my ear. "So who exactly am I dancing with? Jax or Brock?"

Not an easy answer, actually, so I stall by pulling him a little closer to me. I slide my hand under the back of his hideous tux jacket. His bare skin is so soft against my fingertips. I think he shivers a little bit. Or maybe that was me. There's no way in hell he doesn't feel Jax Junior pressing into him through my jeans. I take a deep, calming breath into my lungs. I need to focus. And Jax Junior needs to chill. For now.

"Well?" he says, impatience adding a distinctive edge to his tone.

"I'm sorry," I say. "But you wouldn't take my calls or respond to my texts. You would only talk to Brock."

Beck's lips spread into a thin line across his face, and his eyes narrow on me. "Jax, you lied. You *catfished* me, for fuck sake. You don't play with someone's emotions like that. *Ever.*

Hell, I thought I was going to lose my virginity tonight to someone who doesn't even exist."

I nod and look away, ashamed. "I know. It was a dick move." I look him in the eye. "Here and now, I promise I will never lie to you again. And to prove it to you, I'll start by saying that you smell like an omelet."

He stares back at me, visibly struggling to keep his lips from curling up. I know he doesn't want to give me the satisfaction of making him smile. He wants me to suffer. I don't mind. I'm not going anywhere. He finally gives up with a chuckle and a shake of his head.

"One song," he says, and rests his head on my shoulder.

We hold each other, swaying to the music, and for a brief moment everything between us feels perfect. Couples close in around us, holding each other close like we are. Guys with guys. Girls with girls. Guys with girls. Parents with their kids. It really is one of the most beautiful sights I've ever seen. Shelby and Asa are dancing near us, and for once Shelby isn't looking at me suspiciously. Her focus is 100 percent on Asa. When Beck looks over and sees them, his face lights up. Asa leans in and kisses Shelby. And I mean *kisses* her. That boy is hungry for Momma. Beck stares at them with his mouth hanging open and his eyes wide.

My teammates have huddled around the perimeter of the dance floor, with Terry front and center. I have to admit, their blank stares as they watch me dancing with Beck make me uncomfortable. Maybe the overwhelming support they gave me in the locker room was all they had to offer. Watching their bisexual quarterback slow dance with an openly gay guy—*in public*—might push them to their limits of acceptance and tolerance. In the end they're still public high school students in a small Southern town.

"Can I ask you something?" I say, suddenly aware that my time is running out.

Beck nods, but he's still watching Shelby and Asa and grinning at them like a kid on Christmas morning.

"Why would you want to lose your virginity to some stranger you met on a hookup app?"

Beck looks back at me and his eyes glaze over. "Do you have any idea what it's like for someone like me?" He motions to the people dancing around us. "For *us* to find someone in a town like this? Someone we're attracted to, who's also attracted to us? Someone who won't beat the shit out of us if we act on mixed signals and get it wrong? I'm seventeen years old and, other than my dad, I've never even been *held* by another guy. Never been wrapped up in a guy's arms and felt loved, wanted, and safe. I'd gladly trade my virginity for just five minutes of that."

He has my undivided attention now, and even though my heart aches for him, I don't have a freaking clue as to what to say to the guy. I've only ever known how to comfort people with my body—not my words.

Beck looks down. "And after a lifetime of rejection, some faceless, nameless guy on a fuck app is about the surest thing I'm going to get around here."

If he doesn't stop talking, I'm not going to be able to hold my shit together, and nearly every player on my team stands less than twenty feet away, watching us. I lift his chin with the crook of my index finger.

"Look. I know you still have doubts about me, and God knows I've earned them. But just know that with you, *I'm* a sure thing. And you don't have to give up your virginity if you're not ready, just to be held."

Beck stops moving and stares at me. The song vamps its way toward the end, and people around us begin to release one another from their embraces. But I don't let go of Beck. I can't. Not yet.

"I'm sorry about what happened in the park," I say. "But I think you misunderstood."

"What was there to misunderstand?" Beck says, the edge returning to his voice. "*You* kissed *me*, and when your girlfriend showed up, you freaked out and started yelling that it 'wasn't what it looked like.'" He uses air quotes.

I sigh and lean into his ear so he can hear me clearly. "Tiffany thought you were making unwanted advances toward me. I went after her to set her straight about that. And then I broke it off with her."

Beck pulls back, his eyes widening. "You broke up with Tiffany?"

I nod and give him a pointed gaze. "Tiffany's not who I want to be with, Beck. It's you. And I'm not afraid anymore."

He searches my eyes like he's hunting for any kernel of doubt. He won't find any, so search away. After a few seconds Beck nods over to my teammates. "And what about them?"

"I told them," I say, glancing over at the guys with a nod. "They're cool with it. Well, most of them, anyway." When I look back at Beck, his face is still unreadable, and I feel like he's on the verge of pulling away again.

"I'm glad for you, Jax," he says, finally. "I really am. But you say you want me *now*. What happens next week when you start craving vagina again?"

I pull him into my arms. He fits perfectly there, like we're the two final pieces of a puzzle snapping into place. There's no way he doesn't feel Jax Junior pushing into him. But by the look in his eyes, I know he's more interested in my words than my dick right now—something else I'm completely unfamiliar with. But I like it.

"You're right," I say, matter-of-fact. "I'll always be attracted to girls. All I know is that the only *person* I want to be with, is you. And I've never been more sure about anything in my life."

I close my eyes and lean in, my heart thumping hard against my chest. I know everyone is watching, but I really don't give a shit anymore. I touch my lips to his. His whole body stiffens at first, like he's fighting not only me but himself, too. I wonder if maybe I should pull back. Maybe he doesn't want me to kiss him. But his muscles finally relax, and he melts into my arms. Our lips seal together perfectly, and I'm so nervous it's like I suddenly forget how to breathe through my nose. But our tongues greet each other with an urgent hunger. Beck's shaking in my arms, sliding his hands down to my hips, pulling our bodies closer together. In that moment, it's like we're the only two people in the world. But as the song fades away, a raucous chorus of cheers, whistles, and applause erupts around us. Slowly, Beck pulls away from me, and I open my eyes with no small amount of trepidation. Terry, Jody, Sai, Alex, and the rest of team surround us in a huge circle in the middle of the dance floor. Their smiles are genuine and warm. I sold them short.

"Get a room," Alex shouts.

The cheers and whistles only grow louder. You'd think Beck and I just cured cancer by sucking face. Beck stares at them with an adorable, shy smile curling his lips. I guess he doesn't quite know what to think of the broad show of support from a group of guys he always classified as *them*, and with good reason. Terry walks up and slaps me on the ass. He doesn't forget about Beck, either, who actually jumps a little with the unexpected whack. Shelby follows right behind Terry and repeats the gesture, but I think I got a little squeeze, too. She pops Beck's ass so hard he yelps.

A driving EDM beat cracks like thunder through the speakers. My guys raise their hands in the air and spread out on the dance floor—each pairing up with the closest parent or queer kid. Jody and Sai find themselves without a partner, so they just start dancing with each other. The mayor's daughter stands on the sidelines watching until Brent and Kenny lure her out into the madness. The dance floor is packed, and everyone is so . . . real. And happy.

"Wow," Beck shouts in my ear. His grin has taken over his entire face. "Can you believe this shit?"

I look over my shoulder in the direction of our cluster-fucked group of parents. Roger and my mom are huddled off to themselves, talking with slightly softened faces. Beck's mom and the mayor are locked in some intense conversation by the bar. JoJo stands by the door with Doris back at her side—smiles and laughter flowing freely between them.

I look back at Beck and lean in so he can hear me. "Apparently, we suck at destroying relationships."

Beck scans the romantic carnage left in our wake, throws his head back, and laughs. "I think you're right." He grabs my hand. "Come on. We've done enough damage. They'll figure it out."

He drags me through the dense crowd of oddly paired, gyrating bodies, and out the front door. I barely have a chance to wave good-bye to JoJo.

"Where're we going?" I shout as we spill out onto a deserted, red-carpeted sidewalk.

He looks back at me. "You'll see."

At the end of the block sits the black stretch limo that he arrived in. The driver appears as if on cue, circles the car, and has the back door open before we reach it.

"I like the way you roll, Beckett Gaines," I say, sticking my head inside to take a peek.

Beck gives me a push on the ass, and I tumble onto the long leather seat. He scoots in beside me, and the driver closes the door. Beck looks at me with a mix of fear and excitement brimming in his eyes, and it's contagious. He takes my hand, folds his fingers over mine, and leans over to kiss me.

The driver gets in up front and clears his throat through the open partition window. "Where to, gentlemen?"

Beck pulls back. His lip curls up on one side and he calls back to the driver, "The duck pond at City Park. And do you mind raising that window?"

"Not at all," the driver says, clearly relieved as the tinted window rises quickly to the top.

The car rolls forward and we roll with it—down to the floor, with me on my back and Beck straddling me. Well, straddling the tent pole in my pants. He doesn't move off, though. He looks down at me like he's trying to decide something.

"What is it?" I ask.

Beck taps his chin with the tip of his index finger. "Just trying to decide which of my inner Golden Girls will win out tonight."

"Well, I wouldn't know a Golden Girl from a Gossip Girl, so I can't help you."

He leans down and rests his head on my chest. "For now, just hold me."

My breath catches in my throat, and I swear I hear my heart thump in my chest. I wrap my arms around him so tight that I worry I might break him, but he doesn't seems to mind.

And I hold him.

# CHAPTER THIRTY-SEVEN

Beckett

I crack open the bathroom door and peek down the hall. All clear. Dad must still be asleep. Slipping out, I hurry buck naked toward my bedroom door. I nearly have my hand on the knob when his voice stops me in my tracks.

"Well, good morning, sunshine," Dad says behind me. I can practically hear the smirk curling his words. "I didn't hear you come in last night."

I cover my candy with my hands and turn to face him. "Morning, Dad. Yeah. Got in pretty late. Went straight to bed. Great party though, right?"

Standing there in his robe, holding a coffee mug in one hand and an envelope in the other, he gives me that condescending grin that says, *I know you're lying to me, son, and it's just adorable that you think I'm that stupid.* He walks over and offers me his coffee.

I glance down. "Kind of got my hands full at the moment, but thanks."

Dad raises his eyebrows. "Modest all of a sudden, huh?" He narrows his eyes on me. "Interesting. Especially considering the way Jaxon Parker was dry-humping you on the dance floor last night."

"Ew, Dad. Please don't say the words 'dry' or 'humping' ever again," I say, leaning against the wall, trying to look cool and casual. "We were just dancing."

"You're right. My bad. It was more of a tonsillectomy kind of procedure."

I roll my eyes at him. It's way to early for him to be getting all up in my Kool-Aid. "Okay, Dad, I get it. You're going to bust my balls about this for the foreseeable future. Hilarious."

He chuckles into a sip of coffee, and I realize that I have somehow already been forgiven for my betrayal with Tracee. I still feel like a total shit about it, though.

I readjust my hands. "Dad, I'm really sorry for messing things up with you and Tracee."

He waves me off and leans against the wall—the *thin* wall that separates us from my bedroom.

"I know you are," he says. "And I know why you did it."

"You do?"

He nods and stares right through me. "Sure. You wanted your mom and me back together. You have this fantasy that it can all go back to the way it was." He lets his head fall in my direction. "But it can't, Beck. I'm sorry."

"Maybe that was part of it," I say. "But mostly, I just didn't want to see you get hurt again. It was bad after Mom left, for a long time. I can't lose you like that again."

"You'll never lose me like that again, son." His eyes mist

over. He swallows hard, nods, and looks down. He takes a few seconds to collect himself and clear his throat. I need those seconds as much as he does. "And, in any case, Tracee actually left the dance with JoJo. She said they needed to talk. So it looks like you don't have to worry about that anymore."

"But, you seem . . . okay," I say cautiously.

He smiles back at me. "I'm fine, son. Rose is made of tougher stuff than you'd think." He pushes off the wall and taps my chest with the envelope. "Your mom asked me to give you this before she left."

I take the envelope, so I'm down to just one hand covering my candy. "Left?"

Dad crinkles his brow. "Sorry, son, but that's what she does."

I look down at the letter. "She had an affair with him, didn't she? The mayor. That's why she left two years ago." I glance back up.

His lips are a straight, thin line. "Read the letter. Then we can talk later."

I nod slowly. "Dad, I was just—"

"—looking out for me," he says. "I know you were. But sometimes the past is best left in the past, and I am perfectly capable of taking care of myself."

"Got it," I say, breaking the unnerving eye contact. I readjust my hands in front of me and cover my candy with the envelope. "I should probably get some clothes on."

Dad steps back, looks down at my crotch, and cups his cheek in his open palm. "Oh my God, you're naked! My son is naked and he has a penis! My eyes! My eyes!"

I try but can't contain a chuckle. He's so goofy.

"You looked great on the morning news, by the way," he says with a wink. "Both channels. They got it all. Your whole speech to Pastor Doug and his scurrying away in shame. Should shut those people up. For a while anyway."

"Wow," I say. I'd nearly forgotten all about *that* part of the evening, which is kind of cool. I give Dad a cocky smile and shrug. "I touch lives."

Laughing, he squeezes my shoulder and moves past me down the hall. "Read your letter and then get dressed. I'm taking you guys out for breakfast." He raps on my bedroom door with his knuckles as he passes it.

"Good morning, Jaxon," he calls out.

"Morning, Mr. Gaines," Jax's muted voice sounds from behind the door.

Busted.

Dad looks back me with raised eyebrows before he slips into his room. "Raincoats."

"Always, Dad," I say with a groan and open my bedroom door.

Jax sits up in the bed, the top sheet falling low on his waist. Golden pubes peek out at me, and my gaze travels up his rippled stomach, over the hills and valleys of his buff chest, and land on those ocean blue eyes. Just looking at him, my body aches in all the right places, remembering how he worked it over all night long. My legs are like butter and my muscles twitch with aftershocks of the intense pleasure he gave me. But not just pleasure. I slept more peacefully wrapped up in Jax's bulky arms than I have since before Mom left.

"Everything okay with your Dad?" Jax asks with one eyebrow raised. "I guess we're not as sneaky as we think we are."

"Oddly enough, he's fine," I say, walking over to the bed. Jax looks me up and down, and a fresh flicker of desire flashes in his eyes. I plop down on the side of the bed and stare at the front of the envelope. Mom's handwriting. My name. "Dad said Tracee left the prom with JoJo."

"What?" Jax says, falling back on the bed. "Maybe we don't totally suck at this after all." He rests his hand on my hip and squeezes. His touch on my bare skin still gives me chills. "What about your mom?"

I flip the envelope over in my hand. The seal hasn't been broken. Dad didn't peek. I know that was hard for him. "She's gone. Again. Left me this."

Jax sits up and straddles me from behind. Slipping his corded arms around my chest, he pulls me into him. Holding me. I love the way he holds me. I feel safe in his arms.

"I'm sorry, Beck," he whispers in my ear, lightly kissing the lobe.

I rest my head in the crook of his neck. "Thanks." We sit like that in silence as Jax marks a teasing trail with his fingertips, down my chest, over my stomach, and continuing south.

"Okay, okay," I say, covering his hand with mine. "You keep that up and we're never going to leave this room."

"Sounds good to me," he says with a mischievous chuckle. "It's Sunday anyway."

I sit up and look over my shoulder at him. "Dad wants to take us to breakfast, so get dressed."

He rests his forehead on my shoulder and groans in defeat.

Finally, he slides back across the bed and stumbles around the room, collecting his clothes like he's on a scavenger hunt. He grabs my rainbow thong off the floor and launches it at me like a slingshot. Even clowning around he looks annoyingly hot, and I can't help but smile at him. I stare down at the letter, trying to decide if I even want to open it. What can she possibly say that she hasn't already said a thousand times?

*I love you? I'm sorry? It's not your fault?* Or, *I fucked the mayor?* That would be a new addition to her canon.

It's all bullshit, and I can't believe that I screwed up Dad's relationship with Tracee in hopes of Mom coming home. If she'd hurt him again, which obviously she would have, I don't know if he could survive that.

Jax slips on his jeans. "Bathroom?"

"Yeah, sure," I say. "Down the hall on the right."

He winks and slips out the door. I stare down at the letter for another few minutes and then drop it on the bed beside me. I grab my phone off the nightstand and text Shelby.

*Hey, hooker. Sorry I bailed. Hope the limo got back to you guys in time. So?? Asa??*

Her reply comes quick.

*Let's just say that I have acquired a taste for egg rolls.*

I type, *Ok . . . that's straight up racist, girl. Call me later to spill the tea. I want the deets.*

I drop my phone on the bed and pick up the envelope. Still, I hesitate to open it, though I'm not totally sure why. Maybe I'm just tired of disappointment. After a good five minutes of debate in my head, I pull open the drawer of the nightstand, slip the envelope in, and close it. I don't want to be disappointed. Not now. Everything is too perfect.

The door opens and Jax strolls in, holding a towel around his waist, his jeans slung over his shoulder, and a goofy grin plastered on his face. His hair is damp, and water beads glisten on his smooth chest. "I took a quick shower. Hope you don't mind."

I shake my head. He dries off. I stare. I have no shame.

"Your dad and I just had the oddest conversation out in the hall," he says.

"It's his signature move," I say, leaning back on my elbows. "Catch you when you're naked and vulnerable, and then interrogate you."

Jax ties the towel around his waist. "Well, it's extremely effective, and our last interaction was not so pleasant. Anyway, you're not dressed and he's raring to go. I think he's either really hungry or he wants to hear all about our evening together, which could get creepy fast."

"I need to shower too," I say, jumping up.

Jax catches my arm before I slip out. "Hey."

I stare back into those ridiculous eyes of his, and I wonder if they will ever not make my heart skip a beat.

"What?"

Jax furrows his brow at me. "I've gotta make an honest man out of you before we have morning-after breakfast with your dad."

I cock my head at him, wondering what the hell he's talking about.

A timid smile forms on his lips. "Will you be my boyfriend, Beckett Gaines?"

Ugh. Why does he have to be so damn charming all the time? It's not fair how he can melt me with just a wink and a smile. I think hating him was way easier than this is going to be. But for five more minutes wrapped up in his arms, I think I can deal with almost anything. I lean in and give him my answer by pressing my lips to his. He slips his arms around my waist and pulls me into him. His towels drops to the floor, just like in the movies. *Fade to black.*

I don't know how long we stay attached like that. Minutes? Hours? Days? Rose could be skin and bones down there waiting for us to go to breakfast, for all I know. But there's one thing I'm absolutely sure about. Jax wants me. And I want him. I think I always have.

*Note to self: Delete Bangr profile, submit to a complete psychiatric evaluation, and bedazzle the hell out of a straitjacket. Because, God help me, I love* The Great *Jaxon Parker.*

## ACKNOWLEDGMENTS

I didn't do this alone, so—

THANK YOU:

Brianne Johnson (B-Jo!)—my dream agent and literary fairy godmother. For diligently combing through your slush pile and finding me, for taking a chance on me, for "getting me," for your encouragement, guidance, and consistently on-point editorial direction, and for only using your magical powers for good.

David Gale—my editor (and publishing rock star). How in the world did I get so lucky?! For also taking the aforementioned chance on me, for your patience with a newbie, and for giving my naughty little manuscript a pathway to the world. Thank God you had jury duty the week you got it!

Justin Chanda and the entire Simon & Schuster Books for Young Readers team, especially to Amanda Ramirez for the hand holding, Laurent Linn for the baller cover design, and the unsung heroes of sales and marketing for making this dream a reality. I hope to meet and thank every blasted one of you in person someday. (*slow claps*)

Becky Albertalli, Jeff Zentner, Kathleen Grissom, Tim Federle, Douglas Clegg, and Simon Curtis. For accepting my random friend requests, answering my mildly stalkery emails and DMs, and being so incredibly gracious with your time, experience, and guidance. It may not have seemed like much to you, but I am forever grateful and I promise to pay it forward. (Kathleen Grissom just called me right up on the phone, ya'll!)

Melissa Chambers—my writing wife, for giving me the

butt-kick I needed to start writing again. This book wouldn't exist if not for you.

Hal Cato, Michelle Thomas-Bush, and Tom Amirante— my "Shelbys." For unwavering support, thirty years of friendship, and a lifetime's worth of laughter. I love you guys to the moon and back.

A big shout-out to my high school and college English teachers: Don King, Bonnie Lundblad, Rich Gray, Paul Skoko, Claire Beck, Teri Hatcher, and librarian Mary Davidson. Whether you realized it or not, you all stoked a fire and a dream in me.

To all my friends back in Florence, South Carolina, for (hopefully) having a good sense of humor.

To the members of Holy Trinity Community Church in Nashville, Tennessee, for being the exact opposite of the fictional "Florence Holiness Tabernacle," and providing a safe and affirming place for *everyone* to explore their faith.

Susan Harris, Paul Junger Witt, Tony Thomas, Bea, Rue, Betty, and Estelle—for your timeless and endearing gift to the world, *The Golden Girls*.

Molly, Toby, and Riley—my beautiful, sweet fur babies and 4 AM writing buddies. No, they can't read this, but it gives me an excuse to say, *please adopt a pet and support the ASPCA*.

Steve Sipe—my husband, my cheerleader, and the best person I know. Through this writing journey you always said the right thing, at the right time, and for the right reason. I am so proud of you for following your own dream. I hope I gave you everything you gave me. I love you.

And finally, to the editor at Dial Books who rejected my

very first manuscript (masterfully illustrated by my buddy Michael Lee): I forgive you. You made me stronger. You prepared me for all the rejections I've since received from agents and editors. And you were so kind to send me that personalized letter inviting me to submit to you again in the future. I get it now. I was only nine years old and plagiarized the whole thing from a TV movie of the week. Lesson learned.

# ORGANIZATIONS SUPPORTING LGBTQ+ YOUTH

**PFLAG (www.pflag.org)**

Founded in 1972 with the simple act of a mother publicly supporting her gay son, PFLAG is the nation's largest family and ally organization. Uniting people who are lesbian, gay, bisexual, transgender, and queer (LGBTQ) with families, friends, and allies, PFLAG is committed to advancing equality through its mission of support, education, and advocacy.

**TYLER CLEMENTI FOUNDATION (www.tylerclementi.org)**

The Tyler Clementi Foundation's mission is to end online and offline bullying in schools, workplaces, and faith communities. Founded in 2011 by the Clementi family in memory of Tyler—a son, brother, and friend—the foundation's flagship bullying-prevention program is #Day1. Other programs include the Upstander Pledge, Upstander Speaker Series, Tyler's Suite, Workplace Training, and True Faith Doesn't Bully, a public education campaign that fights religious bullying. The Tyler Clementi Higher Education Act, introduced in Congress in 2016, would require colleges and universities receiving federal funding to prohibit harassment based on actual or perceived race, color, national origin, sex, disability, sexual orientation, gender identity, or religion.

**IT GETS BETTER (www.itgetsbetter.org)**

Founded in 2010 by gay activist, author, media pundit, and jounalist Dan Savage and his husband Terry Miller, the Internet-based nonprofit It Gets Better exists to uplift, empower, and connect LGBTQ+ youth around the globe.